I0761712

Celestial Banquet

Celestial Banquet

ROSELLE LIM

SWEET JULY BOOKS
A zando IMPRINT
NEW YORK

The characters and events in this book are fictitious. Any similarity to real persons, living or dead, is coincidental and not intended by the author.

Sweet July Books is an imprint of Zando.
zandoprojects.com

First Edition: June 2025

Design by Neuwirth & Associates, Inc.
Cover design by Karina Granda
Cover illustration by Sija Hong

Library of Congress Control Number: 2024950169

978-1-63893-126-3 (Hardcover)
978-1-63893-127-0 (ebook)

10 9 8 7 6 5 4 3 2 1
Manufactured in the United States of America

TO MIKE LASAGNA

And for those with an insatiable craving

for magic and mayhem

GUDLIN MOUNTAINS
BASRA
TEMPERANCE'S TEMPLE
INDULGENCE'S TEMPLE
PILGRIM'S VILLAGE
LUCK'S TEMPLE
DEATH'S CHASM
XIANLING
XI DESERT

The World of Celestial Banquet
THE CROSSROADS
CELESTIAL PONDS
LUPONG
MUTYAN ISLANDS

CELESTIAL BANQUET TEAMS

Team			
 KAMA	Cai	Seon	Tala
 PUBU	Songwon	Yoshihiro	Hideo
 GUOLIN	Zi Rui	Jeong-ho	Zolzaya
 XI	Chan-yeol	Muyang	Han
 SENLIN	Daichi	Akinori	Tohya

When the major gods banished Death and his demons into a great chasm, they built a new heavenly world free from the shroud of darkness. Mortals can still die, but they do so from natural causes, accidents, regretfully, murder—no longer at Death's whims and moods. To commemorate this great victory, they vowed to return to the mortal world for a decennial feast called the Celestial Banquet. Teams from each province of the mortal empire assemble—a sponsor, a noble, a guardian, and a candidate—to compete to win the gods' favor at the banquet table. If chosen, they are each rewarded with a gift: a peach of immortality.

If they fail, they face the wrath of the gods.

—*ORIGINS*, SECOND SCROLL,
GREAT LIBRARY OF XIANLING

ONE

Inside the auction house, the air vibrated like a locust swarm. Kama, our local minor god, held court at the edge of the crowd, pushing off the followers trying to shower him with pricey culinary tributes. His magnetic, pupil-less eyes sparked with their own energy. It was the draw of legendary ingredients that brought him here—otherwise it was rare to see him up at this time.

The murmuring mass moved toward the podium for the day's prize. My boss, Tondo the Tall, watched on the balcony reserved for restauranteurs along with his rival, Lao Sung.

I elbowed my way to the front of the crowd. A giant golden singing carp glistened in the dim dawn light, transforming the balcony gallery where the heavy purses of our city of Lupong's restauranteurs waited—fingers itching to spend and snap up the best haul from the incoming Mutyan ships, into a prismatic rainbow. Truth be told, it was mostly held by their assistants—the rich couldn't be bothered to rise before the scorching sun hung high in the sky.

For the rest of us in the Peninsula, coin wasn't going to earn itself if you didn't get up early. Someone would always be hungrier, ready to snatch opportunity from your hands. And the only way you could taste the faraway ocean was through the jewels

Mutyan fishermen harvested from its depths. Every shell cracked and fish gutted yielded the briny perfume of endless water.

I raised my eyes to catch the signal my boss made. He tugged on his left earlobe to confirm the plan to acquire the carp. A female carp yielded a small number of eggs, and this particular rare species created a buttery, nutty roe that was prized by the nobility.

The buzz swept under my skin. I might get to taste this miraculous fish for myself. If I won the auction today, it'd be served up over a steaming bowl of seven treasure congee at Tondo the Tall's flagship restaurant, the Majestic Isle—a glorious two-story building serving as a tribute to his maternal Mutyan Island heritage. Tondo the Tall thumbed his nose at the elite, poked prejudice in the eye, and won by succeeding as one of the three Mutyan businesses on the mainland. He would demand an exorbitant price from the nobles for this dish. Of everyone I worked for, he was the only one who earned my respect. It also helped that he was once best friends with my baba.

Workers moved to clear a tank of spiky purple eels to make way for the fabled carp, which was placed on a box of ice at the center of the room.

All the prized goods in the auction house came with the adage "Buyers beware." Everything was presented "as is." The onus was on runners like me to inspect the goods before purchase. With quick jabs of my pointy elbows, I jostled to dislodge two interlopers flanking me. Everyone wanted a closer look, but nothing was going to stop me from my examination.

The carp's scales shimmered, and its vacant eyes were glossy—indicating it was at the peak of health during capture. All eyes were on its distended belly and its promises of a cache. The last golden singing carp had sold three months ago, and it was male. It had commanded a steep price of seven hundred gold pieces. A female could fetch even more.

I leaned closer but was yanked back by my collar.

"Don't even think about it, Cai."

I recognized that jerk's voice.

Junfeng was Lao Sung's runner on the floor. He was seven years older than me and had the temerity only a firstborn noble could possess. While many considered him handsome, I would beg to differ. I'd rather clean the public outhouses for a year than give him the time of day.

"Keep your hands to yourself!" I smacked his arm away. "Don't you have a doorway to darken or older noblewoman to woo?"

"Are you jealous?" He made a hasty confirmation signal to his employer above. "I'm winning the carp for Lao Sung. Don't get any ideas."

I snorted, craned over his shoulder to get a better view of the carp's tail, and caught sight of the vent. There was something about it . . . Before I could examine it any further, Junfeng subtly tugged his ear, signaling that he had confirmed the carp's sex as female.

Given Junfeng's determination, the resulting price would be far too astronomical to risk, especially since it wasn't my coin to spend. My boss had taught me that value was universal, while price was driven by emotion. I caught Tondo's eye and scratched my left eyebrow. We'd bow out. His subsequent nod was almost imperceptible.

Bidding began at a cautious eighty pieces.

"One hundred gold pieces," Junfeng cried. Then hissed in my ear, "A dirty Mutyan like Tondo will never win against Lao Sung."

That did it. No one was allowed to talk garbage about my employer and get away with it. Junfeng and his elitist employer would pay.

I raised my hand with three fingers to increase the bidding to three hundred. I kept my eyes firmly on the auctioneer and prayed

Tondo the Tall trusted me. This would only work if it seemed real. If not, I was gambling with someone else's coffers—and my job.

Junfeng shadowed my movements. I kept raising the price until it climbed to one thousand pieces. It was between him and me—disproving his insult earlier about Tondo the Tall's financial capacity.

"Fifteen hundred gold pieces," Junfeng declared to a silent room. His face was flushed with triumph.

I shook my head and made an exaggerated gesture of defeat by stomping my feet.

The auctioneer pointed to Junfeng and declared him the winner. The rat pumped his fist and danced around with glee. Above him, Lao Sung scoffed at Tondo the Tall and readied to head down to the floor to examine his trophy. I ignored the corners of my lips that itched to smile.

"Cai!"

I turned my head and found Bo, my best friend, waiting nearby. He stood a head taller than everyone else and was still half a head shorter than my employer. He used his broad shoulders and size to weave his way through the crowd to my side. Bo came from a family of farmers living outside of Lupong. The scent of sunshine, sweet grass, and pine trees clung to his skin. His ink-dark hair was tied in a topknot, and his rugged features drew looks from the girls nearby.

"Wow. Is that a female carp? No wonder . . ." His words trailed off when he noticed my smirk.

I cupped my hand over his ear. "Somebody overpaid."

Bo let out a low whistle and stared at the fish being handled by Lao Sung. "Did you do what I think you did?"

I winked.

After many bags of coin had exchanged hands, Lao Sung hoisted the big fish above his head to the roar of the crowd. Patience was a virtue that I never had much of, but today, I stretched out what little I possessed. They all waited to see the cache of precious roe. Too bad they'd be disappointed.

Tondo the Tall came down to the floor to join us where we watched the scene from a few feet away. His steps were light despite his size. He wore traditional Mutyan robes in woven gold and bronze batik, which contrasted against the silk robes of his peers. Fluid tattoos of water and waves covered his muscular brown forearms. He wore Mutya well and with pride.

"It's a male, isn't it?" Tondo the Tall turned to me with his lips tipped upward. "And that cocky bastard paid twice as much. This is a delicious development."

Lao Sung pulled up his silk sleeves. His long moustache twitched as he withdrew an ornate knife from his belt. He made a careful incision in the fish, hoping to showcase his prize for all to see . . . then cursed when he saw the belly, impressively thick and marbled with fat but empty of roe, not worth anywhere near the price he paid.

Tondo the Tall's baritone laughter echoed in the large space and was soon followed by a chorus of jeers.

Bo clapped me on the shoulder. "How did you know?"

"The vent looked too clean and wide." I gave him a smug grin. "I suspect it was cut by a paring knife. When something looks too good to be true, it usually is."

The crowd dispersed when Lao Sung yanked Junfeng away, threatening to boil his bits in a soup.

"Be sure to boil the ones he'll miss most," Bo called out with a cackle.

I giggled.

A nobleman, one I didn't recognize, tapped Tondo the Tall on the shoulder. The embroidery on his sleeves and the quality of his scarlet and onyx robes implied he was from Xianling, the capital of the Continent. He whispered something unintelligible to my employer.

"Looks like I'll see you tomorrow morning, Cai. There's business afoot." Tondo the Tall handed me a tiny wrapped packet. "Well done today. You deserve this."

The two walked away and joined a cluster of restauranteurs waiting nearby.

"What do you think that's about?" I asked Bo as I checked to see what I was given.

As if on cue, two young men in uniform hoisted a gold and scarlet banner across the highest beams of the room, prompting a collective roar that sounded like a monsoon, and my voice was among them, hoarse from emptying my lungs. In gilded script, it announced the opening of the Celestial Banquet. Oh my gods, it was finally here. Every day of this decennial year, I had been anticipating this moment, yet I still felt completely awestruck. Bo and I grabbed each other in a hug.

Today, of all days, I would be chosen to cook for the gods.

I had to be.

Folks could claim they served their dishes to dignitaries, kings, and empresses, but few had the impact of cooking for immortals. And it wasn't only the honor that drew people to the banquet, it was its life-changing prize. The winners of the Celestial Banquet would each receive a priceless gift: a peach of immortality.

Three vertical banners in shades of jeweled green bearing the names of the major gods unfurled next—Luck, Temperance, and Indulgence. Everyone on the Continent worshipped the gods. They presided over our world but only came down every ten years for the competition—a legendary celebration of the vanquishing of Death. They were the arbiters of taste. Not only did they shape the culinary landscape, but their choice of whom to award the peaches had a far-reaching impact—the valuable prize provided the winning team the bargaining power to dominate or to defend. For me, it would mean making my dreams a reality and honoring my father's dying wish.

All year, the upcoming cooking competition had been the chatter of the city. Gossip leapt from magistrate to merchant, from fishmonger to farmhand. Greed and the pure, naked hope for fame and fortune—rose from rich and poor alike. If the team from the Peninsula won, it would change everything.

But our minor god, Kama, had already declared he wouldn't be hosting a team. For some reason, even with the promise of a peach that would fuel his immortal power for the next decade and beyond, Kama refused to participate. He called the competition a "waste" and "childish." I was determined to change his mind.

I wanted to compete, to win. I *needed* to win. And without him, my long-cherished dream was impossible. Each team needed an immortal sponsor—the minor god of their region—to formally represent the team in the competition. He didn't realize how much was at stake, how much I wanted this. His behavior was akin to snatching a meal from a starving person.

Bo and I had it all planned out. If we were to win, we'd sell our peaches to the highest bidder—likely a minor god from one of the wealthier regions—and buy our own restaurant and farm in Lupong. I'd run the restaurant and Bo would work the farm, providing only the freshest spices and ingredients to our community. I wanted to honor my baba's memory. After all, he was the best chef I'd ever known. To eat his food was a transcendent experience. I wanted to give that to everyone.

"Continent folk keep winning that damned competition," Bo said, rubbing the short stubble on his square jaw. Ever since he'd started growing facial hair, he preened because it made him feel older.

"Agreed. But we can change that." I distractedly picked at the sachet from Tondo the Tall to reveal a batch of tiny two-toned red-and-blue peppers shaped like daggers the size of my fingernails. I let out a quiet gasp.

Bo leaned in and admired the peppers. "What did Tondo give you? I haven't seen those before."

"They're icy spicy peppers from the north," I replied, trying to contain my excitement. If we were impressed by these, I could only imagine what we'd have access to at the Celestial Banquet. "They're super rare." I rewrapped the package and tucked it into one of the many hidden pockets of my robes.

"They're supposed to be extremely spicy but have an immediate cooling effect. Can you imagine putting this into something unexpected, like a savory mochi?"

Bo snorted. "Would it be as unexpected as the time you put dirt in my congee because you thought it smelled 'mushroomy'?"

"That was *one* time when we were *five*." I jabbed him in the ribs even as my cheeks flushed. The crowd around us had started to disperse. It was time to begin the day. Plus, I had better get cooking if I didn't want to miss my chance to woo Kama. I tore my eyes from the banner.

"Shut up and just walk me to my stall."

After their victory over Death, the gods venerated five mortals into godhood, thus anointing the minor gods Xi, Guolin, Senlin, Pubu, and Kama. There may have been others but they are now all forgotten. The five are tasked with watching over the mortal realm in the major gods' absence. Each minor god has the opportunity to bring a team to the Celestial Banquet, earning them great honor in addition to their prize.

—*ORIGINS*, FOURTH SCROLL,
GREAT LIBRARY OF XIANLING

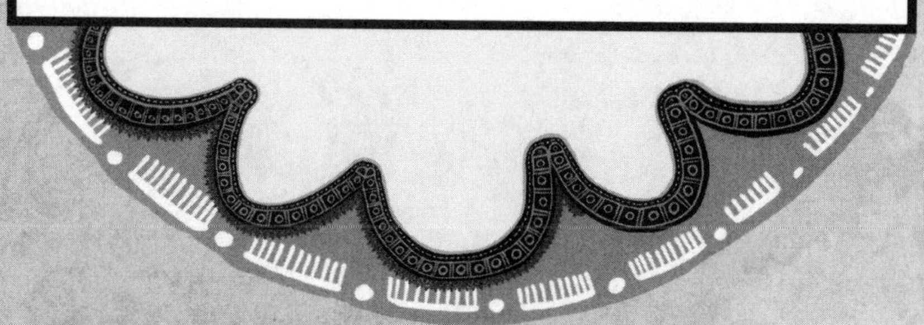

TWO

Box-shaped bronze streetlamps and vibrant rectangular paper lanterns strung across windowsills illuminated the main thoroughfare of Lupong as the amber-pink sunrise blazed across the horizon. Two-story oiled-wood and rough-stone buildings with slanted dark clay-tile roofs leaned over the road. Bright, poppy-red lacquered signs advertised a variety of businesses—dressmakers and jewelers, herbalists and acupuncturists, bakers and butchers, fortune-tellers and alchemists, and, my favorites, candy and tea shops with rooftop gardens. I took in Lupong's charm; it was the center of the Peninsula for a reason.

Just beyond those shops, Bo and I rounded the corner, where the cacophony of the market greeted us. Old Se Eng's grilled smelt, Ashitaka's mochi cakes, and Poleng's banana leaf–wrapped sticky rice were all tasty delights, but my noodles were the main attraction. Some even declared they were the best in the city. Bo liked to say anyone who disagreed was either a fool or a liar.

Bo escorted me to my stall, wishing me luck with the task ahead, then headed to his family's stand at the farmer's market on the other end of the space.

Once I unlocked my stall and pulled the stools from the narrow galley to the other side of the counter, it was time to cook. I began with a pale arc of flour, eggs, and water flowing between my fingertips, combining into a single strand before separating into two, then four, doubling with every twist of my wrist until there were hundreds of threads. The steady slap of wet noodles against the wooden block sounded like a drum announcing the start of a feast. I made the white, ribboned noodles dance to the rhythm thrumming under my skin.

I stirred the simmering broth as tender pieces of brisket rose to the golden surface like koi fish eager for pellets. Grabbing a clump of fragrant spring onions from a nearby basket, I minced the stalks into ringlets on the butcher block, preparing them as a garnish for the soup.

Kama was due to make his appearance soon and I knew he'd be hungry. I was hoping to use that to my advantage.

He often dropped by for a bowl of noodles after a hard night of drinking ale and potent plum wine. Today, I knew he'd be extra hungry after viewing the tantalizing foods at the auction house. For a god, he wasn't what you'd describe as the respectable kind. The others, like Guolin and Xi, lived in elaborate palaces. They were known to have a regular council with the Empress of Wan, who ruled all of the Continent. Kama reeked of stale beer, sweat, and whatever unpleasantness you could find staining the tavern floor. He lived on the fringe like us Peninsula dwellers. No one on the Continent thought we were respectable or civilized—just like our lord. Beside the errant jolt of electricity, I often forgot Kama was immortal at all.

Like clockwork, Kama approached a few minutes later, waving his hand in a vague gesture before ruffling his salt-and-pepper hair. Tiny sparks of blue lightning escaped with each head shake. "Tell the sun to stop doing that thing . . ."

"What? Shining?"

"Too bright." Kama covered his eyes, hissed at the sun, and handed over a silver piece. "Need noodles."

I thanked him for the payment and readied his bowl. "Tondo the Tall rewarded me with something interesting at the auction house this morning."

Kama grunted. I hadn't noticed it from afar, but he seemed worse for wear this morning. The bags under his bloodshot, glowing white eyes carried the burden of his immortal years. Eternal life looked tiresome. Whatever he was doing wasn't meditation and clean living.

When I didn't respond to his guttural outburst, curiosity eventually got the best of him. "Oh?"

My lips tugged into a small, triumphant smile. "Icy spicy peppers. Would you like some with your noodles?"

Kama brightened as a surge of energy lifted his shoulders. He touched his fingertips together, and the ensuing zap turned his limp, greasy hair into quills. "Yes! They're delightful. I haven't had them in a very long while. Last time, I ate them with stir-fried beef and bamboo shoots."

"How much should I add?" I asked as I laid out one lone pepper on the butcher block.

The minor god squinted at the spice. "You have to cut that in half for it to work properly. Separate the blue from the red. Otherwise, the results will be unpredictable. Each half provides a different effect. In my case, I want both."

This was why Kama fascinated me. His culinary knowledge was boundless. Everyone tended to dismiss him because of his appearance, but he had something to offer. Not to mention, he was actually kind beneath all the bluster. He was a good egg through and through.

I did as he instructed and dropped both halves of the tiny pepper into his broth.

From the corner of my eye, I spotted my favorite customer heading toward me. I tried to keep the flush from flaring in my cheeks.

I wiped my hands on my green tunic and brushed the stray strands of dark hair from my forehead as he approached. Seon was one of the wealthy students at a nearby academy, and his presence at my stall always made my insides fizz like a fiery pear sparkler from the rooftop tea shop. All my nerves were exposed to the air while my mind wandered in heart-shaped patterns.

We first met when I delivered a meal to his family compound a year ago. A week later, he'd wandered past my stall to pay their compliments, and we wound up talking for an hour about our favorite foods and stalls. He lived and breathed food as much as I did, as much as Kama did—I seemed to bring in a certain type of customer. He loved it so much that he spent a few years in Xianling, pursuing culinary studies, something I could only dream of. And he'd been a regular ever since. Nowadays, I considered Seon more a friend than a customer.

"How is the prettiest noodle maker in the city?"

Okay, a very flirty friend.

I sighed. "Just working hard as always." This was a helpful segue, as I had been waiting for Kama to get nice and fed before I made my ask.

Seon's playful smile almost made me swoon. "The Celestial Banquet has been announced, but we still don't have a team representing the Peninsula." He looked from me to Kama expectantly.

To his credit, Kama didn't even glance up from his bowl. He emitted a loud slurp as he sucked a noodle into his puckered mouth, splashing bits of broth into his scruffy beard.

Seon's high cheekbones and light-brown eyes were paired with a full mouth known for stealing kisses—though none from me yet, despite my daydreaming. He usually swept up his hair in a topknot, but it had been sliced off in last week's sword lesson. His hair now fell just past his ears, highlighting his perfect bone structure. Handsome, intelligent, and a member of the nobility: heartbreak wrapped up in the prettiest of packages.

Seon accepted his bowl of noodles from me, tipping his head toward Kama and slipping me a wink. "Must be intimidating, not having won all these centuries. I wouldn't want to go against the fearsome Guolin, the charming Senlin, and the slithery Xi. You'd be a long shot like Pubu."

Ah, *that* tactic. I went along with it. "The competition might be too hard on him. He is getting on in years. He might not even make it out of the city gates without help. I don't know how he manages to—"

Kama cleared his throat angrily and handed me his empty bowl and chopsticks. "Manages to what?"

This was my moment—I just hoped I could seal the deal.

"You young folk tend to run your mouths, thinking you know everything. Well, you don't." Kama crossed his arms and scrunched his thick brows. "Tell me why you think a prized peach is worth the risk of your near-certain death—and thus my near-certain dishonor."

Kama had a valid point. The Celestial Banquet might be a feast, but the stakes were life and death. Many who entered the palatial arena never returned. Some people even suspected that looking into the eyes of a major god was enough to turn your brain into scrambled eggs. There was no guarantee I'd even survive the competition, let alone win. I had only heard rumors about the experience, given that the Peninsula had never participated during my lifetime. Who knew what was actually true.

I swallowed and squared my shoulders. "I'm not risking my life. I'm risking a half-life." I looked to Seon for support and he nodded, so I continued. "It takes three jobs just to keep a roof over my head and enough food in my belly. Every day I scrape to tuck away a silver coin to fund my dream of having my very own restaurant. It was my baba's dream, and now it's mine. I'd name it after him, and his name would be on everyone's lips in Lupong. I want nothing more than for his memory to live on—for his afterlife to be far richer than the one he left behind. I care nothing for immortality."

Kama scoffed and rolled his eyes. "Ah yes, the classic reason: naked ambition. Let me do you a favor and tell you a little secret. It's not worth it."

He was wrong, but it was time to try another approach. As a minor god, he would be revitalized. It was clear he needed that. "And you, you'll regain that youthful glow. Peaches restore your glory. All those pesky wrinkles and gray hairs will disappear, and you'll be more powerful than you are—perhaps even strong enough to zap the rest of the minor gods and get away with it. Winning has made them cocky. Not to mention the food you'd get to try . . ."

Kama perked up a little, but still didn't look sold.

Seon added, "It's not only for personal gain. What about the lives of everyone in the Peninsula? Are they worth it to you then? The skirmishes with the Empress's army are increasing by the day. With more power and money, we might actually keep them out."

Kama tapped his fingers on the counter, considering. If our ambitions weren't enough to persuade him, perhaps the love for his home would be.

I leaned my elbows on the counter and nodded vigorously. "We can't let the Continent take anything else from us. They know we're weakening. That's why the Wan Empire is breathing down our necks. We are the last independent nation standing on the Continent, and our freedom means everything."

The Empire destroyed my father. I'd do anything to keep the peaches—and our homeland—away from that decrepit, greedy Empress.

"We can't have war in the Peninsula. We'd never survive it," Seon added.

I clenched my jaw. "And I can win, Kama. I know I can."

It didn't matter that I was sixteen—I could cook with the best of them.

Seon stood from his stool. "And my mother finally agreed to let us use the sigil of her noble house! I have enough funds to pay the required tithe. We have a real chance to win for the first time in a generation."

Kama met my gaze, and for a moment, we were all silent.

"Those peaches sound mighty tasty right about now." Kama scratched his beard and widened his stance. The tension snapping his shoulders released, allowing him to assume his usual slouch. "It's been so long since I've had a bite. Perhaps it is time to see Xianling again after all."

Was this it? Perhaps the god Luck had been watching us closely.

Seon and I locked eyes. His dark brows arched, mirroring mine.

"Are you sure, children?" Kama furrowed his brow. He turned to me and I nodded solemnly. Something in his expression changed and he sighed, seeming almost resigned. "Be at the tavern by sunset."

The peaches of immortality change the lives of mortals and immortals alike. For mortals, eating them will extend a life for twenty-five years, not to mention the bounty that can be collected from selling them. For immortals, the peaches provide even greater power—and prestige. Feuds between the minor gods can last centuries, for some petty grudges know no end.

—*ORIGINS*, FIFTH SCROLL, GREAT LIBRARY OF XIANLING

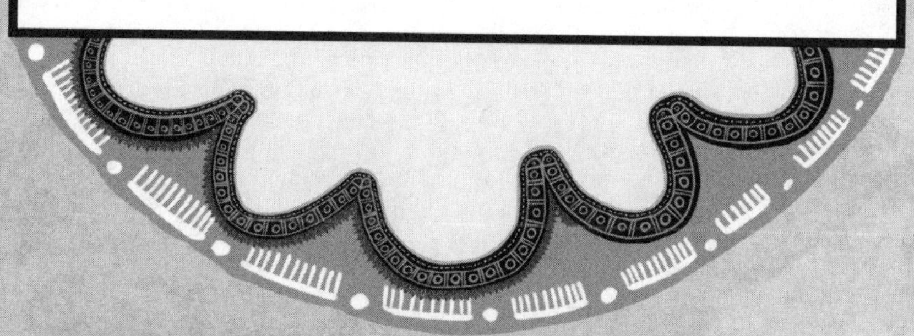

THREE

This was real—this was happening. Kama was going to the capital, and I would be going with him. I could taste the possibility of winning the Celestial Banquet as much as the meager rice porridge I had for breakfast this morning. For the first time, maybe ever, anything felt possible.

Right before sunset, I finished tidying up the stall; I'd need to be thorough as, for once, I wouldn't be back the next morning. I had already sent word to the Golden Lotus that I'd be taking a short leave of two weeks—which is about the duration of the competition including travel time to and from Xianling. I knew Tondo the Tall, of all people, would understand. Then Bo—whom I'd hastily filled in during an outhouse visit earlier—joined me to head toward our destiny.

The Three Cranes Tavern, where we'd be meeting Kama, was a rickety two-story building splashed by soured rice wine, damaged by drunken brawls, and ready to ignite with the smallest spark. Its sole claim was that—unlike any other drinking establishment—it was frequently patronized by a minor god: the aforementioned Kama.

On the walk over, I caught up Bo on Kama's change of heart, what this meant for us. I'd expected him to be as ecstatic as I was, but he became increasingly quiet as we neared the tavern. By the time we arrived, he was barely giving me monosyllabic answers. It was as if he was taking the competition more seriously.

"Cai!" Seon called out from the entrance. He waved as he threaded through the growing crowd. "It's crammed in there. You'd better get in quick."

Bo stopped beside me. He stiffened and lowered his voice. "What's he doing here?"

"He's the noble for our team, silly," I said. "Seon helped me convince Kama to go. Didn't I mention it?"

Bo's stony expression hardened. He'd never liked Seon. He hated all nobility on principle and rightly so. Most acted as if they were better than others, lording their wealth and privilege over the working class.

But not Seon. He'd been nothing but kind and supportive to me this past year. I'd tried to say as much to Bo, but it never seemed to make much of a difference.

Seon wore his familial robes in scarlet and black, marking his noble status. He wasn't the only one. Several other nobles loitered outside, and I imagined there were more inside, vying for a space on the team. Word traveled fast in our small city. Little did they know that the team was already decided.

"It hasn't started yet, has it?" I asked him.

Kama was a drama queen and no doubt he had something outlandish planned. The sooner he announced that I was his candidate, the sooner the celebratory drinking started. After that, we'd take off for the jeweled city.

"Not yet, but soon." Seon nodded his head in Bo's direction as a subtle greeting.

Bo grunted in response.

I tsked. *Be nice*, I mouthed to him.

A shower of sparks accompanying the crowd's roar erupted above the glittering red clay roof tiles. I held my breath and slipped inside the tavern.

Kama was holding court in the back by a massive stone hearth. A crownless king among the company of laborers, indentured servants, and the inebriated. He held a tankard in the air—toasted himself—and then slammed the empty cup down on the mantel, chipping the ceramic rim. He was finishing the end of a Mutyan sailor song about two brother fishermen falling in love with the same mermaid.

Seon, Bo, and I found a table near the back. I counted seven nobles in the crowd paired with the most famous cooks of Lupong. Something was afoot, but I wasn't ready to go down without a fight.

Kama rose from his makeshift stool throne and raised both his hands. Electricity crackled back and forth between his fingertips. The room hushed. "I suppose you are all here for my big announcement. One comes here eager to prove her worthiness to compete in the Celestial Banquet. But is she? Tonight we will find out!"

His proclamation was received with raucous applause. He promised *me* this, and now he wanted me to prove myself? My fingers trembled as outrage bubbled inside my chest. I could call him out as a liar or I could get over myself and prove that I was the right choice. Maturity won out as I readied myself to defend what was mine.

The crowd buzzed, a sea of eager faces all leaning forward to ensure they didn't miss a word.

"Tonight is one to remember. We are making history in this place." The minor god clapped and sent chains of thunderbolts scorching the rafters. The oiled wood blackened but didn't ignite. The pleasant smoky scent of charred timber filled the tavern.

Kama stroked his beard. "A good cook needs to trust their tongue. Cai, why don't you come up here and prove that you should come with me to Xianling." He crooked his finger and waved me forward.

I jumped up from my seat and joined him before the hearth. Bo cupped his hands around his mouth and shouted his support to drown the questioning murmurs from the crowd. Though he wasn't as eager as I was, I could always count on his loyalty. Seon pumped his fist in the air, hollering. I beamed.

The minor god waved his hand. "There are many of you who doubt my choice."

A rousing vocal agreement rang out in the tavern that didn't surprise me—I expected as much. Their objections ranged from my gender to my age to my class. It didn't matter that those with better pedigree had never brought home the peaches of immortality.

"But I promise you, we will select the best of Lupong tonight!" He wagged his finger, producing a sizzling bolt encircling it. "Only the premier team will walk with me to Xianling. Cai, consider this your first trial. I have brought forth two excellent chefs who would like to challenge you for the spot."

The experience among the crowd ranged from line cooks to head chefs at the most prestigious establishments. Some cooked from their hearts, others from habit or duty. I admired the ones who had been working at their craft for decades—these uncles and aunties, grandmas and grandpas toiled all their lives to perfect one dish. They had forsaken all others to focus on a single bowl of soup or sticky rice cakes.

"Well, I suppose it's time to announce the challengers." Kama clapped his hands. "First: Arhan. Owner of the Spicy Wok and the Spicy Bowl restaurants and senior member of the Restaurant Association. Perhaps tonight, he can prove his mettle once more."

Arhan joined me and stood to my left. He was a reedy, gaunt man with a sparse moustache. He wore an earthy bronze round-necked silk robe reminiscent of crushed cinnamon over a vanilla tunic. An hour in the kitchen would destroy that garment, which undoubtedly cost ten times what he paid his cooks.

"And Mao! So strong. Such a presence." Kama imitated a wrestler's pose with his paltry build. "Owner of three grill stalls and a surefire bet if you ever frequent the boxing matches."

Mao came up and stood to my right. He loomed above three heads taller than me and was five times as wide. Dark stains and char marks covered his taupe long-sleeved cotton tunic with its wide black sash. Burns and fading cuts marred his powerful arms. Most came from the kitchen; the rest from his hobby of night brawling.

The giant leaned over and winked at me. "Nice to see you here, Little Brawler."

I claimed the nickname with pride years ago. Imported exploding star anise arrived every few weeks, depending on the surplus crop, and I was already a runner back then. The restauranteurs and their managers sent their apprentices rather than risk their own skin. Broken bones were common. After one savage fight, I had left with a swollen left eye, a pouch of peppers, and a reputation.

"And this little lady is Cai," Kama announced with great flourish. "Our local noodle chef and an impressive young talent to watch."

The compliment prompted a flush to spread across my cheeks. I'd never been comfortable with praise. It felt thick, going down my throat like raw honey.

"Will she, just a girl, be seasoned enough to defeat her rivals?" Kama asked the tavern.

Ah, that was something I'd heard too many times before from other cooks—too young to know enough and too little experience in the kitchen. My father encouraged me to pursue cooking from a young age, and I did so. I shouldn't be punished because I received my education at the auction house, markets, and Golden Lotus instead of the fancy culinary institutes in Xianling. All of this, on top of the fact that society's expectations were confined to how I could suit the men around me, which I had no intention of doing.

Several people hooted in affirmation or derision; I couldn't tell.

"The challenge will be one that will break at least one or all of you." Kama pushed up his ratty sleeves. A murmur spread through the crowd—rumbles mimicking a distant, approaching thunderstorm. A crease formed between Bo's dark brows while Seon steepled his fingers against his lips.

"Tonight's challenge will be to make noodles . . ."

I nearly whooped with joy until Kama finished his sentence.

"Without eggs." The minor god cracked his knuckles, sending more sparks into the already blackened rafters. "Prove to me that you're worthy of entering the Celestial Banquet!"

My stomach knotted, and I covered my face with my hands. The swelling groan from my chest was drowned by the roars of outrage from my two competitors.

I'd always made my noodles with eggs at the stall. My proficiency had gotten to a point that I could make them blindfolded. In addition to adding flavor, eggs gave the noodles their elasticity—without them, the mixture would crumble in my hands. Kama had asked me to do the impossible.

Maybe that was his point.

Servants set up three cauldrons full of water at the hearth for us, each with a prep table to the side. Arhan and Mao mirrored my defeated expression. Kama had fooled us all. It wouldn't be the first time. Kama was a scoundrel with a long string of debts in Lupong that dogged his shadow—ranging from the butcher for his love of cured sausages, the sweets shop for their specialty ba bao fan (beautiful eight treasure rice pudding cakes dotted with various fruits and nuts), and this very tavern, where Kama had promised his firstborn child to the tavern owner, Shuyi. At this rate, he owed at least a dozen children as promissory notes. The minor god had lethal charm and sugared words when he needed them—might be the reason why he escaped his debt collectors with ease every time.

Bo cupped his hands over his mouth and shouted, "You can do it!"

I snapped out of my brief reverie and gave Bo a small smile. I could do it—I *had* to do it. Our future depended on it. If Kama wanted magically eggless noodles, I'd find a way.

I moved to the last empty table. Only a small mountain of flour and a bowl of tepid water were provided. I blew out my lips and got ready to work. With kneading, I was making batches of doughy failure. Too much water meant the mixture stuck to my skin like honey, and with too little, it flaked off in pieces, shedding as I worked to keep it together. The elasticity was missing—the way dough moved to the rhythm thrumming under my skin with a good stretch, how it could multiply a hundredfold with the slice of my cleaver.

To my right, Mao turned the air blue with his colorful curses as he pounded the table. Some I'd used myself, and others I tucked away for future use. Arhan had enlisted one of the cooks from his restaurants to do the work while he supervised—scrutinizing and snapping at the poor sod. Kama hadn't kicked him out yet, so I assumed it was allowed.

I racked my brain. Clearly I was not going to succeed in making these noodles with what I had on the table. My eyes searched the room, landing on a large earthenware vase of forsythia beside the hearth. Baba once heard that the ashes of certain plants could be used to make noodles. We spent an entire weekend covered in gray soot to see if it worked. We hadn't figured out the right combination or the right plant. I focused on the yellow stalks. They weren't poisonous. It could work . . .

What other choice did I have?

I stole a handful of forsythia and stuck the tips into the tavern's roaring fire. The makeshift bonfire cracked in my hand. To anyone else, I appeared to have lost my mind and was on the verge of burning everything down. Only the former applied.

I dumped the bowl of water onto the floor and placed the smoldering bundle over the empty vessel. The fire devoured the vibrant gold, transforming it into charcoal and ashes. I gathered the precious specks of gray and added them to a new batch of dough.

May Luck turn their bright eyes on me.

I thanked a helpful servant who brought me another bowl before incorporating a sprinkle of water into the mix. The dough warmed in my hands. I squeezed and tugged. It was binding!

With a hearty laugh, I stretched, gathered, pulled—performing to the crowd in triumph. The dough bowed to my will between my fingertips, multiplying from one to a hundred with every twist of my wrist. The pale threads draped across my hands as I manipulated them in a glorious arc.

Bo raised his fists and whooped. He chanted my name, and soon, the entire tavern joined in. I made those noodles twirl to the crowd, showcasing their glory.

The steaming bubbles in the cauldron popped and hissed as I stirred the noodles beneath the surface with my chopsticks. Mao and Arhan hunched beside me with their own batches going somehow.

A servant brought a clean bowl to each table while another waited to scoop broth into it. The three of us readied to transfer our noodles. I twirled mine around my chopsticks in an effort to gauge their stability. Mao treated his batch like precious newborns—moving them one at a time while muttering a prayer under his breath. In contrast, Arhan moved his chopsticks in a blur as if he were handling volatile fire dragon eggs.

We all took our places to the right of our bowls while Kama sat down and brandished his chopsticks. Mao was up first.

The minor god plucked a single noodle from the bowl, and it tore in half midair. Kama repeated the gesture, and the noodle fell apart in three pieces this time. "Ahh, Mao. If only your noodles had your strength."

Mao lowered his chin, sniffed, and crossed his arms over his chest. I reached over and gave him a firm tap of solidarity with my fist. He acknowledged the gesture by ruffling my shoulder-length hair.

Kama waved Arhan forward, and the restauranteur presented his entry. His confident and smarmy smirk prompted a loud boo from Bo, which turned into a chorus from the crowd. I snorted to keep myself from cackling. Arhan's wealth made him bold. If he had only two pieces of copper to rub together, he wouldn't get away with a fraction of his donkey dung. Half the people in Lupong hated him, with good reason, and the other half hadn't met him yet.

The minor god wound his chopsticks around the noodles, and they held their integrity. Kama sucked the noodles into his mouth and started chewing, and chewing, and chewing. The dramatic faces he was making elicited a round of laughter from the crowd.

Arhan stomped his foot and declared, "You're exaggerating."

"Oh, am I?" Kama pushed the bowl forward. "Taste it yourself."

The effort Arhan made to keep a natural straight face when chewing would impress the actors at the city's only opera house. He opted to swallow instead of prolonging his torture and almost choked as he beat his chest with his fist. "It was very acceptable," he managed in between coughs. "Great elasticity."

"I don't like lies." With a flick of Kama's fingers, Arhan was zapped. The hair on his head stood up in a massive cluster of frizz, the scent of singed hair wafting in the air.

This side of our local god was refreshing. I could get used to it.

The tavern shook with laughter.

It was my turn. I delivered my bowl to Kama and waited. It all came down to taste. It was too late to cram a handful of forsythia in my mouth to see how it would influence the noodles. Or was it? I plucked a few blossoms left on my table and sneaked them between my teeth. My jaw tensed as the bitterness spread across my tongue. The first rule of cooking was to taste everything first, and I violated that. Of all the stupid . . .

I held my breath as Kama tasted a noodle. Then, he spun his chopsticks and gathered the pale strands into a makeshift tornado before devouring it with what appeared to be relish. My eyes widened, and I blurted out, "It doesn't taste bad?"

"It has a subtle, interesting bitter note," he replied in between bites. "Quite pleasant."

I sighed in relief. My noodles weren't terrible.

My hands trembled. I might have done it. My palms itched as I curled my fingers in, hoping to dissipate the anxiety building under my skin.

The minor god finished his bowl and rose to his feet. "This"—Kama hoisted my left arm in the air—"is my winner."

Then, the pain came without warning. The skin on the inside of my forearm stung from the song of a hundred invisible needles, like tiny cuts drenched with red wine vinegar.

Next came a gray-bluish glow, as sharp crackles of Kama's lightning bathed my arm. His mark—a dark raven with glossy midnight feathers and a long, pointed beak opened in silent mid-caw, surrounded by a frame of clouds—materialized on my arm. The elaborate design ended with Kama's name emblazoned in liquid gold.

I dragged my fingernails across my skin, and tiny pops of light trailed behind them. The feathered harbinger of death watched me, the heavy gray clouds merging and parting as if it were alive and not superimposed on my skin.

Two tears escaped the corners of my eyes as I shoved my fist into my mouth to stifle the scream of excitement and joy building inside of me. Baba's and my impossible dream had come true.

I was going to the Celestial Banquet.

While the major gods are all powerful and can manipulate reality, minor gods have the ability to transform only their defining element. Pubu can command and change the shape of the water and its properties. Senlin can manipulate plants and nurture growth. Xi commands the desert, and the shifting sands move according to his whim. Guolin has dominion over the earth, creating quakes, chasms, and hills. Kama has been known to bend lightning to his will.

—*ORIGINS*, SEVENTH SCROLL,
GREAT LIBRARY OF XIANLING

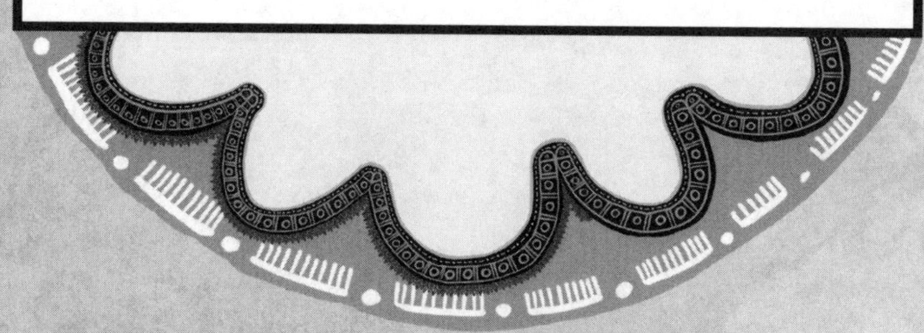

FOUR

I'd barely had time to process my victory when Bo's strong arms gripped my waist and he spun me in the air before gathering me into a tight hug. I blushed at the intense show of affection and was surprised to see him doing the same.

Bo let go of me and cleared his throat. "I'm so proud of you, that's all." With an awkward cough and furrowed brow, he remarked, "We still have to get you through the competition itself, though. We need to make sure Kama knows that I'm your guardian." The guardian on a Celestial Banquet team was key in protecting the candidate/chef, and the rest of the team. We didn't know how a cooking competition could be so dangerous, but legend had it that the gods never made anything easy and a solid guardian was almost as important as the candidate.

My team had room for two members aside from myself: a guardian and a noble. Seon made his way through the crowd to be by my side. My noble. Nobles were needed to gain financial entry into the competition, and to provide the scholarly advice that only the most moneyed citizens had access to. It also helped that Seon was a trained swordsman. With the three of us, we had a full team. A team that could actually win this thing.

Seon started talking, as if reading my mind. "Cai, no one else can bring the peaches of immortality to Lupong. The city will immortalize your name." He reached toward my arm, hands trembling. With a voice filled with awe, he asked, "May I?"

I nodded.

With gentle reverence, he traced the raven's head, its wings, the clouds, and, finally, the characters of Kama's name. His actions were clinical, almost academic, yet I shivered at his touch, my skin tingling with goose bumps.

"I can't believe it. We're going to the Celestial Banquet." When Seon realized he was absently stroking my tattoo, he pulled away and kept his hands behind his back. "We should leave tomorrow morning. It will take us a day to get there, and then we'll at least have one night to rest before the banquet begins—"

"Slow down," Bo interrupted with annoyance, coating his deep voice. "You're not the one in charge here—Cai is."

"He's just trying to help," I pointed out.

Kama waltzed into our impromptu huddle. He draped his arms around Bo and Seon's shoulders. "Interesting." He wagged his shaggy eyebrows. "A pretty girl with not one, but two boys. I'd watch just for the drama alone."

I choked, cheeks aflame, and wished the floorboards would give way so I could slip into the ten levels of hell to escape this scrutiny. I dared not check how Bo and Seon reacted to the unwanted commentary.

"Which one is the noble?" Kama asked, even though he clearly already knew. "I'll need to give him my mark."

Seon pushed up his sleeve and offered his left forearm. The god placed his two index fingers on his skin. Bolts of blazing light snaked along, gathering in coils, as the image of a solitary disembodied raven's wing and Kama's name appeared in silver. It was half as large as mine.

Bo offered his arm. "My turn."

The minor god narrowed his eyes at the offering. "I cannot."

"Why not?" I asked. "We still need a guardian."

"Because I've already chosen one." Kama moved aside to reveal his selection. "We must have the best in order to have any chance of winning this."

A stunning girl emerged from the crowd to stand before us, dressed in a patchwork of multicolored furs. She was nothing like the high-society noblewomen of Lupong—she was sharp where they were soft. Her high cheekbones highlighted a round face dominated by dark-lined eyes. Bright cherry-red tattoos decorated her hairline. Glinting weapons hung along a star-anise-brown leather belt. On her hip, a jagged hook was attached to a coil of silk rope. She cradled a large black bird with a long neck in her arms like a baby.

She was a Nomad.

Nomads weren't allowed to compete as a team, but because of their fierce skills, they often participated as hired guardians. They belonged to a secretive matriarchal society in the cold north. Incredible women warriors who seldom left their homeland unless it was for the Celestial Banquet. Having one on any team was a clear advantage.

"Tala is well-qualified to be your guardian, I assure you. Far more than a farm boy, I'm afraid." The minor god tapped his beard. "You'll need to say goodbye to your friend. He can't come with us."

"No." I shook my head in disbelief and turned to Kama. "When did you make this decision? You never told me, I don't—"

"I chose you, Cai. Don't make me regret my decision." The firmness in his voice gave me pause. "The fate of the Peninsula is in my hands and yours. I don't need to remind you what is at stake."

Kama's joviality vanished. For the first time, he was serious, and I couldn't help but admire his determination. Despite his lackadaisical nature, he cared about our city and the Peninsula. He wanted a peach as much as all of us.

Betraying Bo wasn't what I wanted to do when I was setting out for my adventure. But as much as I yearned for him to come with me, to fulfill our dream of doing this together, jeopardizing my position as Kama's candidate was out of the question.

I turned to Bo. "I promise I won't be gone for long. Before you know it, I'll be back with a peach. Besides, your sisters would've killed you if they'd found out you'd left them. At most, it's two weeks—that's two market days. You won't even miss me."

Rationalizing my guilt for leaving him was far easier than acknowledging my selfishness in doing so.

His lips pressed into a hard line before reaching out to brush a lock of hair away from my eyes. "Are you sure you want to do this, Cai? It's not too late to back out."

"This is too important to me, to us. How else are we supposed to have a real life here? I'll be safe, I promise."

Bo cupped my face and pressed his forehead against mine. "I don't want you to die. Please stay in Lupong, where I can protect you."

"I'll be fine. I'll come back victorious. Don't worry, I'll be home soon."

Nothing I could say would take away the wound I glimpsed in his dark eyes. I wondered if his concern for my safety was purely out of brotherly protection or something more, but quickly shoved that thought aside.

Before I had a chance to reassure him further, he pulled away and disappeared into the crowd.

After agreeing on the details of our journey to Xianling the next day, I headed for home.

My small room at the Wide Roads Boardinghouse was tucked on the third floor with a window overlooking the florist's private rooftop garden. My father had bargained well to switch us from a dark room on the ground floor. I was especially grateful when the soft perfume of peonies hung in the moist air after it rained.

Even though Baba died years ago, traces of him lingered in this tiny space. His beloved wok lay in the corner, while a faded illustration of the Celestial Banquet was pinned above the narrow bed. He was the one who told me about it—spinning outrageous tall tales of what might have happened in past competitions and how winning it would mean being one of the greatest chefs in a century. He was the only parent I ever really had—as my mother had tragically passed away during my birth. She lived in my heart but it was Baba who really motivated me.

I wished he was here to see his daughter participate. Though he'd never had the chance to compete—Kama had refused to participate for the last five decades—he would have been my biggest supporter. I lit a sandalwood incense stick and sat on the floor cross-legged. I sped through the short formal prayers to Luck, asking for guidance, Temperance for gaiety, and Indulgence for gallantry, before turning my attention to my deceased father.

Communing with our dead ancestors was a common practice. If I had more coin, I'd be burning gilded joss paper during the Lunar New Year to ensure Baba had enough for the afterlife. Instead, I spoke to him at least once a month through incense and prayers.

After pouring out tonight's events in graphic detail, I gathered my doubts for him to hear.

I ended our conversation the same way I always did. "Baba, I hope your belly is full and you're happy where you are."

I withdrew the worn yet sturdy rucksack from under the bed and began packing. I didn't have much. When you worked so many hours a day just to survive, it was hard to accumulate, or justify, any excess material possessions.

Other than the wok, I had my journal, two jars of current culinary experiments, various cooking utensils, and a cache of spices. My father loved to dabble in strange concoctions that should have been tasty but ended up being far from it. He never feared mistakes as much as I—he embraced them. Baba always said, "You learn more from failure than success."

I leafed through the pages of the thick notebook, full of illustrations of every ingredient I'd tried and its corresponding attributes transcribed through symbols. I'd never learned how to read or write—been too busy trying to survive.

Finally, I pulled out a worn painting. It must have resembled something at one point, but age faded all the lines, and its colors blended into one another, forming a dreamlike puddle. I folded it into fourths and added it to the pile. All my worldly belongings fit into the rucksack.

I adjusted the straps and leaned forward, pressing my forehead against the bare wall. "Baba, I'll make you proud. I promise."

Tomorrow at dawn, my new life would begin.

Xianling is located south of the major gods' temples. Receiving the waters of the Yang River, it was first a trading post. Mutyan ships made their way from the Singing Sea into the river with their valuable and rare ingredients—to feed the city and its glorious guilds. Considered the capital of the Continent, its residents number half a million. Folks of different origins end up making their lives there—ranging from beautiful courtesans to clever smugglers to drunken monks.

—*FOUNDATION*, THIRD SCROLL,
MASTER ARCHIVES OF ALCHEMY GUILD

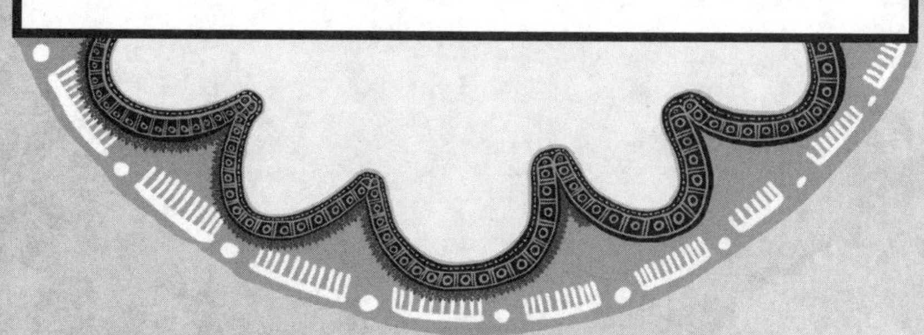

FIVE

I stood before Xianling's open gates. The city looked like a jeweled cake, sprawling as far as the eye could see.

Lupong was a tiny nibble compared to the feast of this famed city. Baked rooftop tiles sparkled in vibrant colors of peacock, paprika, pumpkin, pineapple, and pear. Gold was reserved for the four towering temples anchoring each cardinal direction. The cobblestone streets formed concentric circles and cutting diagonals to mimic interconnected pie slices. All this opulence was set against a background of the endless sea of sand dunes of the Xi Desert to the south of the city's doorstep.

Unlike the wealthier teams who no doubt had the luxury of horses and wagons, we'd had to make the long, hard journey on foot. We were at the mercy of the main road and its dangers. We had one close contact with bandits that Tala dispatched with ease. Kama's complaining was on constant repeat. He had us carry him around in a makeshift palanquin, and when he did have to walk, he dragged his feet. We were all tired, yet our sponsor insisted that he was far more so due to age—and not the lack of exercise.

The more time Seon and I spent together, talking over miles and miles instead of just for a few minutes a day, the more I realized that we had far more than food in common. On the other hand, Tala barely uttered a word, and when she did, it was to her cormorant friend, Ulan.

"Does it live up to your expectations?" Seon asked me now, gesturing toward the city.

Anyone who wanted to be a renowned cook dreamed of making a pilgrimage here. I was no different. The motto of the city echoed in my mind. "For every craving, Xianling will satisfy." I couldn't wait to explore it. But it was strange being here, too, standing next to a different boy. Bo and I were supposed to have this adventure together. Without him, the city already looked different from how I imagined it. Instead of saying this, however, I rubbed my hands together.

"Can't tell yet. I need to taste it first." I looked over to Seon and grinned. "I wonder how many restaurants and stalls we can visit before the competition starts."

Suddenly, the ground shook, dust rising like someone blew across a flour-dusted table. We all turned around to see a giant elephant, draped in tassels and dyed silks, lumbering across the main thoroughfare. Its twin-domed head and long-lashed eyes were massive. It arched its long trunk and trumpeted. Bo would be gawking if he were here. He loved legendary beasts of any shape and form—especially dragons. I couldn't let regret over my friend ruin this for me, though. A literal elephant had just walked right by me. I needed to savor every moment.

A firm tap on my shoulder drew my attention. Tala cradled Ulan under her left arm like a large kitten. "I have business in the city. I'll return to you when the ceremonies start."

Before I could respond, the huntress vanished into one of the nearby streets, leaving the three of us behind.

"She'll be back for the presentation to the Empress." Kama's tone carried no hint of worry. "We should make our way to the ceremonial hall to pay the tithe."

I asked, "Can we also talk to past winners? I was hoping we could gather more information."

"That's not possible. The major gods ensure that those who return have impaired memories," Seon replied, opening his book to a page he indicated had a list of past winners.

He kept notes of his research on the Celestial Banquet and other important tidbits. His writing was meticulous, and he even offered to read parts of it to me sometime.

"You're telling me no one remembers what they cooked?" I asked him.

"Their memories are simple. At best, they remember some of the new creatures or plants they encountered. Obviously, the ones who perished can't be counted on for any information. I suppose it's a way for the major gods to keep the competition fresh." Seon closed his book. "Even the winners don't remember what happened."

Kama nodded. "The manipulation of memories is disturbing . . . they do this to minor gods as well."

An even more ominous reason hit me. "Maybe if folks actually knew what happens at the banquet, they wouldn't be willing to enter it." I took a wobbly drink from the water gourd Seon offered me. I needed to shake it off. "After the tithe, we can go exploring, yes?" I asked.

Already, my senses were swimming with the influx of delicious aromas from every direction. I counted four stalls and five restaurants within steps of where we stood. It took all my willpower not to run off to take a closer look.

"Yes. I can't wait to show you the city in all its glory." Seon extended his hand to me, his eyes gleaming with hope.

I reached out with trembling fingers but changed my mind at the final moment. It wasn't that I didn't want to take his hand. It felt like betraying Bo somehow, and I wasn't sure why.

At my hesitation, Seon flushed and lowered his arm.

The ceremonial hall for the Celestial Banquet was an ostentatious pagoda decorated with long golden silk banners. The glimmering salmon-pink roof tiles contrasted against the hammered brass pots of joss sticks that left wispy serpentine trails in the air. Resting at the south edge of the busy mercantile district, the grand building was surrounded by a small lush garden complete with koi ponds. The bits of greenery muffled the hustle and bustle, giving an oasis of quiet respite.

Inside, the mosaic floor depicted Luck, Temperance, and Indulgence, the three major gods, and their mystical animal familiars dancing against the cloudy sky. I sucked in a breath. I couldn't believe I'd be cooking a meal for each of them.

In the middle of the grand space was a thin-mustachioed official sitting at a wide onyx desk flanked by two assistants in matching robes.

Seon took the lead and approached the dais. He withdrew a golden medallion necklace from his pocket and placed it on the table. With a voice full of authority, he declared, "I'm here to pay the tithe for our team for the Celestial Banquet."

The mousy bureaucrat donned his spectacles and examined the crest. "I haven't seen this symbol in a long time. This noble house was impoverished decades ago, no? How interesting . . ." I was confused by his words—in Lupong, Seon's family was one of the elite. What was this talk of impoverishment?

The man continued, "This is irregular, but acceptable. Time will tell if you can lift the disgrace associated with the family name." He finally glanced up to see Seon. "And who is your sponsor god?"

I gave my sponsor a little jab in the ribs until he finally stepped forward and waved. Kama even sent out a little ball of spark toward the man's nose. It popped, sending the thin hairs of his moustache standing on end. "Present."

"Noted." Nonchalance coated the administrator's reedy voice. "Now that that's settled—tithe, please." The official made a beckoning gesture with his palm.

Seon lowered his rucksack and fished out five full bags of gold coins. An assistant immediately pounced on the task of counting. Once the total had been tallied, an ornate scroll was stamped with a gold seal.

"Good luck to you and your team. You'll need it. If you have any other business, state it; if not, be gone."

Seon retrieved his pack and made a farewell gesture. We followed suit and exited the building.

The amount of gold exchanging hands on that table was far greater than what I'd made in all the years I'd worked. But if things went our way, it would be well worth it. Kama would get to eat his peach. Seon would elevate his name—guess it made sense that he also had his own personal motivation. And Tala . . . I didn't know yet what she wanted to do, but for her to be here, she must have some goal.

We were greeted by a host of palace guards when we stepped out of the ceremonial hall. Their black-and-scarlet uniforms bore the phoenix crest of the Empress. The leader of the group bowed before our sponsor. "Lord Kama, we are here to escort you to the palace. The Empress summons you and the rest of the minor gods."

Kama stopped in his tracks and scratched his temple. "Now? Isn't it a bit early? Will I at least be fed?"

"Your attendance is required." The guard's serious expression broke for a moment, and he lowered his voice. "I do believe there will be a lavish dinner involved."

At that, Kama grinned. "See you later, children!" He waved at us before trotting off with his palatial entourage.

My stomach rumbled. It had been a while since we'd all eaten.

I squeaked. "Lunch?"

Seon beamed. "I know just the place."

He escorted me to a tiny restaurant east of the ceremonial hall. Inside were four square tables and we occupied the one closest to the windows. A steaming bowl of conpoy and mustard-green congee revived my senses. Pungent cilantro leaves and golden-fried minced garlic accented the surface of the rice porridge. I dipped my wide ceramic spoon into it and tested the consistency. The rice grains had popped enough to form a silky, creamy texture. The hint of white pepper created a perfectly balanced song on my tongue. A contented murmur vibrated from my lips.

Seon lowered his head in acknowledgment. "It has always been my comfort food growing up. My mother makes her own special batch with vegetables from her garden. She uses chicken broth as a base and salted egg yolks."

"That sounds so lovely. Baba had a similar signature dish." I took a sip of the tea. "Lady Yoona must be very proud of you. Her son is competing in the Celestial Banquet."

Seon nodded. "As you probably picked up, my mother is from here. When I was young, she would regale me with stories about the competition. She told me all about the magic, the splendor, and the prestige. When I went to the academy here in Xianling, I sent her weekly letters sharing everything I'd learned in the Grand Library. It gave her quite a bit of joy since my father is difficult to live with."

Seon rarely spoke of his father, and I never pried. I'd only been to his family compound once, that first time we'd met. His mother was the most beautiful woman I'd ever seen, and she radiated kindness. She floated when she walked, and her perfume of peonies and jasmine reminded me of the rooftop garden near my window. Seon's father couldn't be more different. Where his mother was all softness, his father was hard edges. And he had a reputation around Lupong for his short temper, his inclination to cause a fuss if things weren't to his liking. People warned others to watch his fist above the table and assume the other hand held a knife. I couldn't imagine what he might be like behind closed doors.

"I can't wait to see what your mother says when you come home with a peach." I placed my hand over his fist. "Maybe this will convince your father to move closer to the capital for her health." That was the other thing. Everyone knew Lady Yoona was sick, and it was here, of course, where the best care could be acquired.

A shadow crossed his face. "And that's why we must win." Seon's perfect smile returned in full force. "It only takes one to buy the equivalent of a kingdom. Those peaches will change our lives."

Blood rushed to my cheeks as I lowered my eyes. The weight of everyone counting on me felt heavier than a wagon full of rice sacks.

"Will you take me to see the three guilds?" I sidestepped and returned to safer topics. I had always dreamed of visiting the guilds, the holy grail of high culinary society. I wouldn't waste a moment of my free time in Xianling.

"For you, anything. Finish your congee first."

The peaches of immortality from the first banquet helped create the legendary culinary guilds of Xianling: Alchemy, Blade, and Palate. At the guilds, chefs and culinary enthusiasts have access to the premier training and ingredients on the Continent. Thus, they draw many members, especially those eager to win the Celestial Banquet.

—*HISTORY*, FOURTH SCROLL,
MASTER ARCHIVES OF THE ALCHEMY GUILD

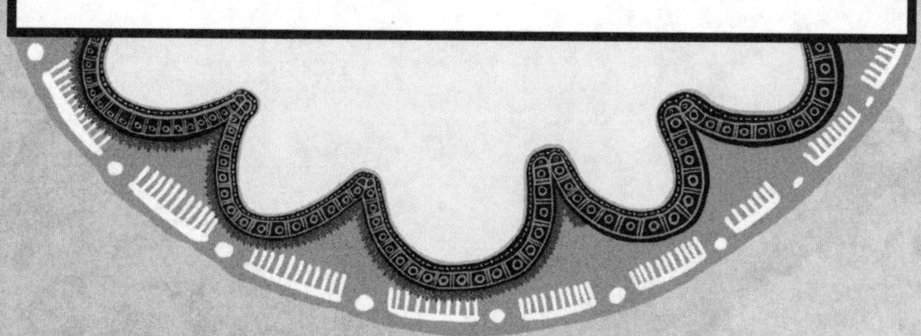

SIX

"Why does everything formal have to be so damned itchy?" I tugged at the collar of my new robes.

The gray fabric, upon which Kama's name and raven had been embroidered, was clearly low-grade, even for me. Was this some sort of punishment for my sponsor's infinite losing streak?

It was now evening, and all the Celestial Banquet teams were gathered in an open room resembling a courtyard with a roof, waiting for the ceremonial first meeting with the Empress of Wan. To her credit, Tala did indeed make it back in time for this. It was clear she was the type to honor commitments. She donned the same robes, and whether they bothered her, she never gave any indication.

Seon tried his best not to scratch, but his fingers trembled at his sides. Out of all of us—including Kama, who already had various stains on his garments—he appeared the most regal and dignified. His smooth jaw and hooded brow bore the mark of nobility no matter what he wore. I swallowed hard and looked away. I had bigger things to focus on.

"Watch what you say to the old raisin." Kama lowered his voice to a whisper. "She can have your head chopped off with a twitch of her painted eyebrows. In our meeting earlier, I'd have died a hundred times over if I weren't immortal. Since she'd advocated for and then won the ability to have a mortal ruler present ages ago, she lords her position at the table over everyone."

Seon added, "Best not to speak unless spoken to."

What Seon and Kama didn't know was that I hated this woman with every fiber of my being. She was responsible for Baba's death. When the skirmishes with the Wan Empire began at the border five years ago, deliverymen were needed to bring food to the front. My father was one of them. He was too old to fight as a soldier, but felt a strong duty to protect his nation. Baba was hit with a poisoned arrow. He spent two years confined to his bed before dying. I could never forgive the Empress for what she had done. The only reason she hadn't managed to fully invade was the narrow pass of land that connected the Peninsula to the Continent. She made her intentions known that she would come for our land. My only hope of resistance was getting enough coins to help fund the army when they arrive at our city gates. But if I could murder the old crone with chopsticks to the neck, I would.

I craned my head toward the presentation hall to get a better view of the other minor gods, who were all mingling together with their protégés. There was something about them that seemed wholly different from Kama. They seemed more lively, for one, but there was something else . . . Then I realized they were actually *glowing.*

"Umm, Kama?" I said, unsure of how to be diplomatic. "Don't you feel left out? Shouldn't you be hanging out over there?"

"The rest of my cohort are insufferable pests." Kama rolled his eyes before squinting at the iridescent group. "Bragging about how many peaches they've already eaten . . ."

Clearly this was a sensitive topic for Kama, but my curiosity got the better of me. "Can you glow like that?"

"Oh, I lost that ability centuries ago. Believe me, I don't miss looking like a firefly at all." Kama lowered himself into a comfortable squat. "I'm not like *them*. All they care about is riches. They don't give a damn about the people they're supposedly watching over."

I appreciated Kama's integrity. I believed he meant it too. Still, I couldn't help but wonder whether he'd be glowing along with them after we won this thing.

As I surveyed the room, Seon filled me in on the other candidates who were mingling nearby. Through his high-society connections, he'd picked up a dossier while we were out and about in Xianling. He pointed out the strongest team first. "See that minor god with the umber glow? That's Guolin, known for his ferocity."

Guolin's candidate, Zi Rui, resembled his bear minor god and was a member of the Blade and Palate Guilds. He had a barrel chest, a small balding head with an unruly beard, and large fists to ensure no one made any unflattering observations. He leeched the room of all light and joy with his presence. He wasn't the eldest chef, yet he commanded the most respect.

"The next one to watch out for is Xi's, the desert minor god. They've formed an alliance with Guolin's." Seon tipped his head toward the golden lit figure and his team.

Chan-yeol, Xi's candidate, was less formidable. He resembled a nervous otter—narrow-bodied and twitchy right down to his pointed whiskers. While I didn't doubt that Chan-yeol was worthy of his culinary skills (he was a member of the Alchemy Guild), I'd still bet I could beat him in a fistfight. He couldn't intimidate a newborn squirrel. He was younger than Zi Rui and trailed after him like a shadow.

"And the last team we should worry about is Senlin's, the forest god lit up in green." Seon crossed his arms over his chest. "It helps that I've been keeping up with the gossip. Senlin would have been allied with Pubu had their love not gone sour. It's said that Senlin promised something quite valuable to join that powerful coalition with Guolin and Xi—something along the lines of sending his most beautiful devotees to both gods."

I rolled my eyes at the horrible idea of using mortal women as promised cattle.

Daichi, Senlin's candidate, was a member of the Blade Guild. He resembled a jolly uncle who'd had too much to drink. His perpetually flushed skin traveled all the way up to his bald pate. Flasks of strong spirits dangled from his waist. Of the three mortals, he was the most senior. Scraggly white hairs decorated the area around his ears, complementing the dark tufts in them.

Zi Rui, Chan-yeol, and Daichi had now gathered together in conference, erasing any question of whether the top three were allied.

"Any rumors you've heard about that trio are true," Seon added. "Plus all the other candidates aside from you and Pubu's candidate, Songwon, have membership in at least one guild. It has also been mentioned that Songwon has a diminished sense of taste."

Seon and I had visited the historic, secretive buildings just before this. The culinary guilds were temples to food in its preparation, history, and art. Being a member was a badge of pride and a lifetime goal of many passionate cooks. They offered discoveries and special teaching seminars to the public—all at a steep price. Culinary scholarship was expensive, as were the rare ingredients involved. Hence my lack of membership.

The three guilds were Alchemy, Blade, and Palate. Alchemy members were experts in ingredients, spices, and lore. It was the most erudite and elite of the three. Those in the Blade Guild were the masters of the knife and preparation. I'd seen a Blade member butcher a full stone-heart bison carcass in under an hour. They had the best smiths and forges who created superior instruments of our trade. The last and most covert guild was Palate. Of the trio, this was the one I yearned to join and shake the secrets out of.

Seon went on to point out the final team, Pubu's, which, while strong, was far less threatening than the allied trio. Just as he finished explaining, my eye caught on a magnificent woman. It was clear she was another Nomad huntress. She stood at least a head taller than any man in the vicinity and at least one and a half heads taller than Tala. The same crimson tattoos marked her forehead, framing beautiful angular features and golden-brown eyes. A battle axe and longbow were strapped to her back while sharp daggers dangled around her waist. Her furs matched Tala's. The three of us were the only women present.

"Who is that?"

"Zolzaya. She was the winner of the games that Nomads hold to determine who is worthy to attend the Celestial Banquet. She was hired by Guolin's team."

"She looks like she can kill me with her thumb."

Seon laughed. "Probably. And me too."

The imposing huntress caught Tala's eye, and they exchanged a slight nod of respect accompanied by a mysterious hand gesture.

I craned my neck to get a peek at the rest of the guardians—who were almost completely blocked by Zolzaya's imposing figure—when I spotted a familiar face. My heart hammered. No, it couldn't be. There was no possible way for him to be here. It would take a miracle for . . .

Before I had a chance to process what was happening, Bo turned and met my gaze. His face split into a wide grin and in a few short strides, he swept me off my feet.

Relief flooded through me, overwhelming all other thoughts. He smelled like home, of fresh-cut grass and open air. As his strong arms enveloped me, my thoughts scattered as if they were spilled mung beans on the kitchen floor.

"But how?" I reached up to touch the stubble on his cheeks. "I don't understand how you're here."

Bo let out a deep, throaty laugh and released me from the hug.

"Cai, I joined Pubu's team," he said, gesturing at his silky uniform, clearly of finer material than my own.

My eyes widened as I took him in. His seafoam uniform fit him well, stretching across his wide shoulders and muscled chest. This was the boy I'd known for almost all my life. A tiny scar emerged from his hairline at his left temple from when he fell off the family's horse while goofing around last summer. This was my best friend. And now, my rival? My excitement quickly dissipated.

"What have you done?" I asked, my voice barely a whisper. My best friend pushed up his sleeve to reveal Pubu's mark—a beautiful fantail goldfish in reds and bronzes swimming in a circle, blowing bubbles with the character of her name above it. The confusion in my stomach twisted and became something more like dread. None of this made any sense.

"Cai, this is a good thing. I can help you now," Bo said. Then he turned to Kama, who had materialized behind us, and clapped him on the back. "He made an alliance with Pubu, ensuring my spot on her team."

I stared at Kama in confusion. My sponsor god shrugged and raised his palms. "I did what was needed to help us win. Pubu needed a new guardian since their previous, Hideo, was poisoned."

"Poisoned?!" I pressed my palm against my chest.

Seon asked, "When did this all happen, Lord Kama?"

Kama placed a finger on his lips. "For me to know and you to figure out."

I looked from Kama to Bo, incredulous. "You can't be serious."

But they were. Just then Pubu, the waterfall goddess, called Bo back with a flick of her wrist just in time for everyone to be ushered into the throne room. Each team donned the color of their minor god. We all stood in five columns of charcoal gray, seafoam, gold, umber, and emerald.

The Imperial Hall was open air with no walls, flanked by massive scarlet columns with gilded caps. Jasmine flowers and clementine trees arranged in great painted vases surrounded the ornate gold-and-jade throne with its carved dragon-head armrests. The high elevation gave a breathtaking view of the city from the south and the turbulent Xi Desert with its intermittent swirling sandstorms to the north. The map of the known world formed the mosaic floor, and under my feet, fittingly, was the jut of the Peninsula. All the teams stood in order of candidate, sponsor god, noble, and guardian.

The Empress of Wan was a diminutive woman swallowed by the puff of silk cushions. Her face was branded into my memory from posters and scrolls from Xianling. Her heavy jeweled headdress teetered on the back of her head. The thick coat of powder only accentuated the wrinkles of age around her eyes and painted mouth. I knew that under that frailty was potent vinegar, simmering and waiting to explode.

Eight young handmaidens sat at her feet dressed in layers of blushing pink and gold embroidered silks. Six more stood to the left and right of the throne. Seon's whisper traveled to my ears. "Those pretty faces are trained to defend and kill at the Empress's command. They are her personal guards."

Impressive.

The Empress opened her mouth to speak. Her unwavering voice was a formidable weapon unsheathed. "The Celestial Banquet has put five teams in competition decennially for the last thousand years. Or, more often, four teams." She shot a cutting look at our group. "It's an honorable tradition we follow and respect." The corners of her lips upturned. "The bloodier the better to teach you all to be grateful. To the gods. To me. I look forward to the team eliminations."

She made a dismissive gesture with a flick of her wrist. "Need I remind you that you reside in Xianling and on the Continent? Your fealty to me is binding. The power of this throne is absolute, and those who won't accept that will pay a steep price."

This horrible woman just threatened the Peninsula without even blinking an eye. I didn't need to look over to see Bo's look of disgust. We'd suspected this, but to hear it directly from the royal hag's mouth . . .

We *had* to win those peaches and tip the balance of power.

She wasn't my empress, and she sure as hell won't be welcomed on our land.

"Beginning tomorrow, you shall have the chance to prove your standing as noble houses. You are dismissed." She held up a finger as one of her attendants leaned in and whispered something in her ear. The Empress let out a long, suffering sigh. "May you honor Luck, Temperance, and Indulgence with your cooking. The Celestial Banquet has officially begun."

The great doors opened, and the competitors were herded into the imperial dining hall, lined with massive, bejeweled columns, for the pre-competition welcome dinner.

Four round tables with the Empress's phoenix crest emblazoned in the lacquered wood filled the large empty space. The outright opulence extended to the embroidered silk tablecloths and filigreed plates.

Having grown up in poverty, I bristled at the gaudy display.

Bo would feel the same way, for his humble origins at the farm were nothing like this.

I turned to Seon for reassurance but was interrupted by a servant guiding me toward the table for candidates. I glanced back to see Kama stomping the whole way to his own table with the other minor gods. He sat, crossed his arms, and scowled at his companions.

At our table of five, I was seated between Daichi, Senlin's candidate, and Songwon, Pubu's candidate, so my supposed ally. Zi Rui commanded the conversation with Daichi and Chan-yeol bobbing their chins. When I tried to smile at Songwon, he kept his gaze on his plate and his lips shut. He was about a decade older than me with soft, friendly eyes and a narrow face. His minor god may have agreed to an alliance, but it seemed he had a mind of his own. I'd need to win him over to make our partnership solid.

"I know everyone at this table except for you." The hulking Zi Rui squinted at me while steepling his hands. "Kama's loser candidates are always so unlearned. Tell me, what is your pedigree? Do you run someone else's restaurant?"

"Perhaps you wash the dishes?" Chan-yeol asked with a snicker. His chin whiskers bristled with nervous energy. "Or clean the tables?"

"I run my own noodle stall." I couldn't keep the sharp knives out of my voice. "And work in the kitchen at the Golden Lotus."

The elder, flush-cheeked Daichi stared me down. "They'd let the likes of you cook at a proper restaurant? That must be a lie!"

"I'll give her the benefit of the doubt," Zi Rui cut in, though his dubious facial expression said otherwise. "Who is your father?"

Beside me, Daichi cackled. "Probably some day laborer. It's clear she lacks the polish of nobility.

I took a deep breath, and the retort unwound from my lips faster than I could process.

"He was the head chef of the Golden Lotus and is distinguished in Lupong. If he were still alive, I have no doubt he'd be in my place. He was going to apply for membership at the guilds before he was killed."

I challenged my fellow candidates with a sharp look as my left hand clutched my chopsticks. Under the table, my right hand trembled. I shouldn't care about these candidates and their opinions, yet I couldn't help but try to prove myself, to fit in where I was so overtly out of place.

Thankfully, the parade of sumptuous dishes came just then, ushering in a mutual silence. Platters of royal honeyed jellyfish, cold slices of peppery night hens, roasted sugar pork belly, and glory songbird nest soup. Even the richest nobles in Lupong would be impressed by this opening course. The jellyfish alone cost more than half my yearly earnings. I locked eyes with Bo across the room at the guardians' table. He was unreadable as he looked away. I yearned to speak with him and commiserate.

Loud laughter exploded at the nobles' table. Seon's hands moved as he told a story to entertain his peers. His infectious charm even reached me across the room. He caught my eye, winked, and grinned. My heart squeezed, and my breath caught a short hiccup.

When the Empress of Wan was a young maiden, she was already a widow. Her beauty and charm caught the attention of the major gods. With honeyed words, she gained a seat at the table and created the official ceremony of ushering in the Celestial Banquet. All teams must have an audience with her as her wisdom guides them, and more often than not, she predicts the winner.

—*THE EMPRESS: A BIOGRAPHY*, SIXTH SCROLL, PRIVATE LIBRARY OF XIANLING PALACE

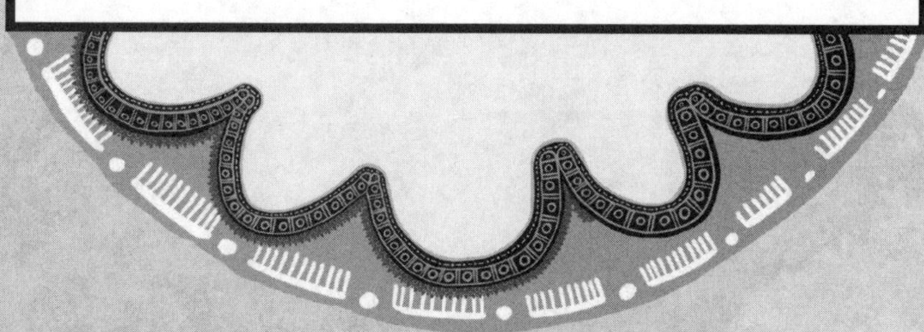

SEVEN

I was able to retreat into myself for the rest of the meal. Afterward, stomachs crammed full of delicious food, we were all herded out of the palace by the guards and directed toward a cluster of buildings near the northern city gate facing the desert. These were our temporary lodgings for the duration of the competition. The teams were promptly separated, leaving me no opportunity to steal off with Bo. I'd been feeling guilty for my reaction to him earlier, knowing he only meant the best, but I guessed my apologies would have to wait.

Our "room" was on the rooftop near the pigeon lofts, only accessed by a rickety rope ladder. We barely had three walls and a burlap roof. At least there wasn't a hint of rain in the air tonight. Such was the fate for the team who never showed up, let alone won.

Kama, Seon, Tala, and I took stock of our inventory and began to strategize. Ulan, the cormorant, found amusement in annoying the pigeons in their cages by honking. I was growing fond of her gleaming black feathers, her funny little antics.

It was weird to see Kama and Seon in this setting—at home, they were among the richest of Lupong. But here, we were all lumped together, nothing more than interchangeable citizens of the least favored district.

"These are all the teams." Seon took out a piece of chalk and drew on the rough clay floor.

He used symbols to represent each team and their guild affiliation—a knife for Blade, tongue for Palate, and a star for Alchemy. He must have remembered I couldn't read. He also added the marks of each noble's house. I knew that Seon's father's insignia was the falcon, but he had presented the nightingale.

"Why use your mother's name?" I asked.

"Because I want nothing from my father." Seon's voice then softened. "My mother was the last in her direct family line. Her father, under coercion, arranged the marriage to wipe out her family's debt. Her side of the family has only a handful of distant cousins. I'm certain you'll hear all this from the other teams soon enough."

The way he held my gaze assured me that my question didn't offend. Still, I suspected I had sliced open concealed and long-healed wounds. "You're implying there will be a lot of sabotage coming our way."

"It wouldn't be the Celestial Banquet without it. As we speak, they're already plotting."

I asked, "So, it's pretty obvious why we are the underdogs. But why is Pubu's team?"

"Their noble, Yoshihiro, is the least powerful of all the noble houses, and Pubu is considered one of the weakest minor gods. After the last competition, Senlin's team poisoned Pubu's potential picks—a testament of immortal grudges because the forest god had suspected that she had cheated on him. The fear has stuck, even a decade later." Seon pointed to Pubu's symbol, which resembled a waterfall. "No one wanted to be on her team in Xianling, except Bo."

Kama interjected, "Taking advantage of her misfortune was in my best interest."

"Wait." I gritted my teeth. "Does this mean Bo is in danger?"

"I doubt it. Killing another candidate is forbidden during the competition, and there are grave consequences when that happens. With that said, there are of course no such rules for the gods—and deaths that occur simply as a consequence of the competition's demands, those are also deemed fine," Seon replied sardonically.

Tala reached out and circled Guolin's team. "They came north to the clans and paid a steep price for Zolzaya's services." It was the first time she had talked that night.

I remembered the tall, muscular woman with the intimidating Zhenniao perched on her shoulder. She seemed to have a kinship with Tala. Perhaps there was a chance these two could help each other.

"Is it still possible to forge more future alliances?" I asked our sponsor.

Kama stood up. "You can throw that idea into the dung heap. Pubu's alliance was a gamble that paid off only because the others shunned her. My other three *colleagues* hate me for consorting with a mortal woman. I'll always be seen as lesser than."

Everyone knew the rumors. Major and minor gods both were meant to avoid relations with mortals, and Kama had gone ahead and fallen in love with one. He prided himself on belonging to his people and we loved him for it. Unapologetic, blasphemous, genuine, and *ours*. He was a defiant dark shadow where the pale sand met the starry night sky.

"Children, you need your sleep. I'll rouse you before sunrise to watch the major gods at work." Kama's voice took on an unfamiliar tone of parental solemnity. "The first day is tomorrow, and you must get as much rest as possible."

We readied our bedrolls. Tala chose a spot away from us near the sloped opening of the rope ladder while Seon laid his only a few paces away from mine. Kama chose to settle near the edge of the rooftop overlooking the desert.

"Good night," I said awkwardly, sitting down on my bedroll.

"Sweet dreams," Seon said. He stared at me intently, like he meant to say more. But instead, he lay down, turned over, and settled into sleep. I kept my gaze upward. Questions and fears floated through my head, but two thoughts kept returning time and time again. My best friend and I were opponents now. How would we both come out of this alive?

Something tickled my nose. I raised my hand to swat it away, then someone grabbed my wrist. I opened my eyes to see the dawn's soft light illuminating a familiar face. "Bo?"

He pressed his finger to his lips and tipped his head toward the ladder.

I pushed myself up without making a sound. I tiptoed past Kama mumbling in his sleep. He turned his head from side to side. "Ly . . . No. Ly. Ly." Seemed like quite the nightmare, but he'd be awake from it soon enough.

When I joined him, Bo was perched at the edge of the roof, his feet dangling over the side.

"This view is far more spectacular than from the tea house," he whispered. "But I still miss home."

Even at this hour, folks walked the streets of Xianling. Carts of produce and live animals headed toward the market at the edge of town. This big city was a marvel. The number of people coming and going was at least four times more than what I was used to.

"What do you think of Xianling?" I reached out and tucked a stray strand of hair over his eye behind his ear.

"Big. So much bigger than I imagined." He pointed to the destination of the carts. "I went exploring and found the farmer's market yesterday. I can't wait to tell my parents all about it. Of course, Mei is the only sister who would be interested. What about you? Does it live up to expectations?"

"And more. It's going to take a while to satisfy my appetite." I exaggeratedly rubbed my belly. "So much food, Bo! Can you believe it?"

He chuckled. "Of course, but how much can you cram in that belly of yours?"

I took his hand in mine, grinning. "More than you know. I can't believe we made it. Both of us. It's like we planned, somewhat. I'm just so happy you're here."

"Me too." A soft blush came across his cheeks.

My first kiss was with Bo. Two years ago when we were fourteen, he was the one I trusted the most, and when I asked, he obliged as soon as I finished the question. It was awkward but not unpleasant. We never talked about it afterward. We didn't want to ruin the bond we already had. The change from a deep friendship to something else was terrifying, considering what we could lose.

"Promise me that you won't do anything stupid." I gave him a playful punch on the arm. "I don't want to explain to your family . . ."

"I will do my best to stay alive. You need to make sure you win."

"Of course! I'm going to—"

He covered my mouth with his hand, shushed me, and pointed down toward my sleeping companions. "I better get back to my team."

I hugged him before he descended the ladder and snuck away.

Bo's presence gave me the comfort and confidence I needed for today. The gods needed to be fed, and it was my task to show them a meal worthy of a champion.

Luck is the first of the major gods that participants of the Celestial Banquet will encounter. The two versions of Luck represent the dual nature of the god's embodiment and have opposing personalities—from kind to cruel.

Luck is the most junior of the major gods and tends to defer to their elder siblings for any action or major decision.

—*ORIGINS*, SECOND SCROLL,
GREAT LIBRARY OF XIANLING

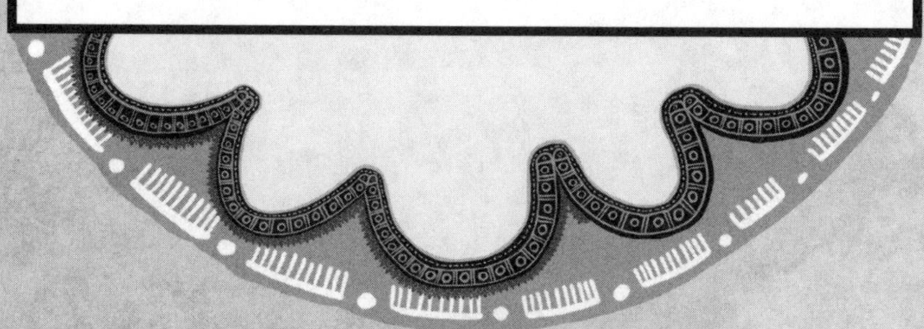

EIGHT

True to his word, our sponsor roused us before the sun had peeked over the horizon. I had managed to get another hour in after Bo's visit, and we were all rubbing the sleep from our eyes as Kama herded us toward the edge of the roof to look out at the golden desert sands.

"This is one of the only miracles I missed at this damned competition. Gods should be creating more wonders instead of manipulating and scheming." Kama yawned and stretched. "Let's see what you children think, shall we?"

Each Celestial Banquet, the gods constructed a new space to house the competition. Baba had described the lore of it to me once, but you had to see it with your own eyes to believe it. I watched in shock as the golden disk of the sun stirred the inert dunes into motion. Grains of sand floated upward, forming clusters, building shapes—coalescing into outer walls, towers, turrets, courtyards, and even the makings of a lake in the middle. Invisible hands sculpted a grand palatial compound from sand and sunbursts, all to a rousing song, played by dueling erhus, that filled the air.

"That is the prettiest sandcastle I've ever seen," I remarked, breathless.

Seon added, "Building something at this scale normally takes a hundred years. Xianling's palace took two and a half centuries to complete. The palace of the Celestial Banquet will only take moments."

Nothing seemed impossible for the major gods.

I drank in the spectacle. The rooftop accommodations might not be ideal, but they gave us a great vantage point.

At the crescendo of the song, the sand vanished, revealing an elaborate, fully built structure underneath. Greenery, stone, mortar, fabric, and a host of servants. A gorgeous lake, as predicted, sparkled just south of the structure. Before I could count the people or take in all the details of the buildings, the sound of a gong assaulted our ears.

The sensation of a thousand bees buzzed under my skin. Competition stoked the fire in my blood. It was time for the games to begin.

Tala stroked Ulan's back. "The elders warned us that danger lurks under these beautiful illusions. Do not trust the gods of the Continent."

Even Baba warned that Luck, Temperance, and Indulgence only cared about eating a fantastic meal and little else.

"I never realized how beautiful the process was." Seon stretched out a stubborn wrinkle at the hem of his tunic. "Scrolls tell you what to expect. This experience is far superior."

"It's like a recipe," I added. "It'll tell you everything but how it tastes."

He tapped his lips and his dark brows arched. "Or more like a kiss. You can dream about it all you like but the reality is even better."

He was staring at my lips. I felt myself starting to swoon, but then snapped out of it. Seon was a flagrant flirt. It was just who he was. I laughed it off and looked away.

We made our way out to the desert and soon stood in the palace's main courtyard. The smooth tiled floor beneath our feet comprised slates of polished obsidian with veins of gold. A canopy of wisteria blossoms in lavender and rose protected us from the hot sun. The overpowering, musky, sweet scent of the flowers was tempered by the copper pots of sandalwood joss sticks nearby. The sunshine-dappled cerulean waters of the lake in the distance reminded me of dancing fireflies.

The competition hadn't even started, and there was already posturing and chest puffery as each group clustered near the center of the courtyard. Guolin and Xi did their best to stare down the rest of us. Zolzaya's fierce, enormous eagle did most of the work for them. Its wingspan cast a threatening shadow. The warrior herself appeared detached, almost bored by it all.

Tala caught me staring and explained, "All this southern political behavior is not appealing to the clans. We participate because of the coin, not because we care about what happens here."

"Kama, do you think I should reach out to Pubu to introduce myself?"

"Do what you want. You're the candidate."

I absorbed his words, his emphasis on the last sentence. When I signed up, all I wanted was to cook. I didn't realize I'd have to become a politician too. Looking around at the other candidates, each exuding a cockiness cultivated from years of honing their skills in their fancy culinary guilds, I was intimidated. I'd be a fool, or worse, if I didn't acknowledge that. The desire of wanting to quit nagged at me, and I shushed it away. My team had earned the right to be here as much as theirs, I repeated to myself as I approached our allies. But I was here for myself, for my home. It was time to muster up the swagger that had allowed me to win the best stall in the night market for the last three years. Pubu needed to know that we were a strong team.

"It's a good idea to try and solidify the partnership." Seon nodded toward Pubu. "I'll come with you if you like."

"I appreciate that." I pushed up my sleeves and we headed in the direction of the minor goddess with the seafoam glow.

Pubu embodied femininity—a perfect powdered face, poppy-red lips, painted brows, and a pleasing form doused in patchouli and amber. Jingling jade and gold bracelets encircled slender white wrists. A pink lotus flower opened and reopened at the crown of her ink-black upswept hair. Mist and waterfall spray covered her low-cut pale blue silk gown while enchanting golden, white, and red goldfish swam along the fabric, bobbing in constant motion.

I bowed before her. "Lady Pubu, we wish to—"

"No." She held her pale hand in front of my face.

"Surely our alliance is—" I argued.

She flicked me on the forehead. "Stop talking. Go away."

"Giapxiao!" I attempted to slap her hand away, but Seon held my wrist, and his hand over my mouth muffled the more colorful parts of my vocabulary. Cementing this alliance was crucial to winning the competition and having all of us survive. This terrible excuse of a minor goddess wouldn't even hear me out. I stopped cussing when we were halfway to rejoining our group. Seon managed to catch the best bits of the insults and chuckled.

"She probably wants the alliance kept secret." He patted my arm. "I'm confident she'll honor her pact with Kama. I still believe in our chances."

"I get the feeling she just doesn't like me." Resentment and doubt slipped from my lips like the filling of an overstuffed dumpling.

"It doesn't matter if she doesn't. You have the talent and skills to win this," Seon repeated. "You need to see yourself as I see you."

"And how do you see me?"

It wasn't an invitation for compliments, but I was genuinely curious. He might be an incorrigible flatterer but he was also a culinary scholar.

Seon's dark brow creased, and a solemnity fell over his face. "You want a better future for Lupong. Not to mention that I've never had a better bowl of beef noodle soup. I don't think you're even close to your potential yet, and I can't wait to see it when it happens."

I opened my mouth to question or protest.

"Sometimes you have to accept praise with grace." Seon winked and walked ahead to rejoin the group.

A series of gongs rang out and I returned to stand with my team. This must mean the arrival of the first of the three gods we'd be cooking for. I couldn't wait to see whose palate I had to please.

I noticed flecks of gold gathering on Tala's inky braids. Then, more came down from the sky.

I laughed as I plucked one off my cheek. "Collect enough of this, and we can go home without even competing."

"Welcome, welcome!" A booming voice from nowhere and everywhere greeted us.

A spindly, heavenly being, with both masculine and feminine features, wearing flowing robes made of golden strands and emeralds, appeared in two places—hovering above us and reclining atop one of the tall columns. It was the major god, Luck, known for their fickleness and spontaneity. The presence of major gods sent my blood coursing, humming as if I were a struck gong. Raw power radiated from their presence.

I glanced across the room to share my excitement with Bo, but his attention was fixated on a one-horned, mythical beast with scales that was coming out of the trees. It had to be a Qilin, one of those strange creatures combining a horse with a dragon. This must be Luck's companion. Baba mentioned this in my fairy-tale bedtime stories. Each god had an animal familiar, one that never left their side, and at the Celestial Banquet it was required to cook for both god and beast.

"I am Luck. Am I as magnificent as you expected?" the major god asked us from atop the column.

"Much more!" the incarnation above us yelled. "Therefore, you must cook your best!"

The one on the column declared, "Something worth singing about! Lest you face death."

"A painful death at my hands," Luck from above announced. "The ingredient you must work with is found in the nearby lake and it has hard scales. Once you've managed to slice it open, it has the juiciest meat. Oh, but take care that you're still alive when you serve it."

I racked my brain for all the lake water fish that had been auctioned. Could it be a stony carp or brute perch or something else? While these were uncommon ingredients to me, the other cooks had probably worked with them already. Unless . . .

"Let's see who can fetch me the delicious and deadly *iron sea serpent*." Luck waved their arms. A hush came over the courtyard. Iron sea serpents were the most lethal sea creatures on the Continent, known for killing sailors with just a flick of their tail. Forget figuring out how to integrate one into a dish, we first had to catch it?

Luck seemed to bask in their stunned silence. "You have one hour."

Kama called us back. "Quick, children, gather round. The iron sea serpent's spikes are poisonous. It is imperative not to cut yourself on their sharp edges, as the consequences could be deadly. Know this before we go into the water."

Tala let out a battle cry as she peered over my shoulder and saw the other teams racing ahead.

"Go, go," Kama relented. "I'll be right behind you."

Our team ran toward the shore, while Ulan flew overhead as a scout. We were the last to arrive on the beach. Each team had been given a small wooden rowboat filled with nets and harpoons. Everyone else was already in the process of pushing theirs off. We made our way to the remaining boat, only to discover a gaping hole in the bottom of it.

"They destroyed it," Seon said exasperatedly, wasting no time to take off his rucksack and shrug out of his tunic. "We'll have to swim."

I puffed out my cheeks. "They wanted us out of the way early, those bastards."

If they were really our secret allies, Pubu's team should have helped guard our boat or even shared theirs. So we were truly on our own. "Wait, did you say swim?"

Tala strapped a belt with daggers around her waist. "How else are we going to get the sea serpent?"

The placid blue water was deep enough to drown in. I felt the blood drain from my face. "I can't swim." How would I? It's not like I had time to lounge at the coastal shores in the midst of my multiple jobs.

"You—what?" Seon took my hand. "Your participation is required, Cai. Otherwise, we'll be knocked out." He paused, deep in thought. "Maybe there is time to teach you."

"There's no time." Tala's voice cut through Seon's gentle tone, brusque as ever. "We're behind already. Unless you were a fish in a past life, we're going to need to learn to breathe underwater."

I tried to swim once in the bathhouses, and I almost drowned. If it weren't for a passing auntie, I'd be dead. I never forgot the sensation of water burning my nostrils nor the feeling of sinking, heart in my throat with lungs burning.

Seon turned to our sponsor. "Kama, can you do something?"

Our benefactor shrugged helplessly. "Lightning and water will not be a good mix . . ."

"Okay, I can swim with her on my back," Seon suggested.

"You two would sink to the bottom," Tala retorted. She kneeled and rummaged through her pack. "There might be a way, but it'll be risky. There's a Mutyan spice used for shipwrecks, and it's blessed by Dagat, one of their gods. Sprinkling it on submerged objects makes them float. I've never heard of it being used on a person before, but I don't see another choice."

I gulped. Ten minutes into the competition for the peaches, and I was already contemplating imminent drowning or some magical spice that could kill me instantly. Kama hadn't been joking about the stakes. I took a deep breath, steeling my resolve.

Well, one death was better than two. Besides, I couldn't live with myself if I was responsible for anyone else's demise. "Give me the Mutyan spice."

Each meal of the Celestial Banquet features a special ingredient—one teams must work together to procure. New creatures, plants, and materials are often brought into existence by the major gods themselves for the competition. The quest for these ingredients is so deadly that teams have been eliminated before they even had a chance to cook.

—*THE CELESTIAL BANQUET*, SIXTH SCROLL, GREAT LIBRARY OF XIANLING

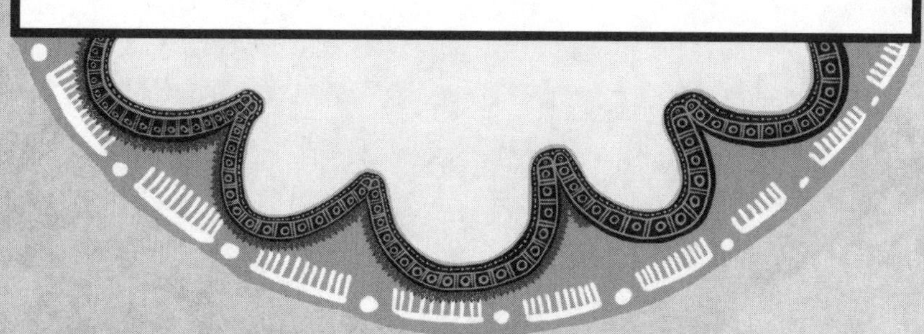

NINE

The fouler a medicine was, the better it worked.

I told myself this as I tried not to vomit the makeshift spice paste I just ate. Whatever Dagat, the Mutyan god, was responsible for, it wasn't taste.

Foul without any redeeming qualities—other than it not killing me. Yet.

After one dry heave, I squeaked out, "I do not recommend."

"We *have* to hurry," Tala urged, pointing out at the busy lake.

My eyes widened to see Pubu's candidate, Songwon, and her noble, old Yoshihiro, swimming fast in water with special shoes that looked like fins, a cluster of waves of the goddess's making pushing them from behind; this challenge was exactly Pubu, the goddess of water's, domain. I hoped Kama would get a similar favor later in the competition, but I wasn't going to hold my breath. I spotted Bo in the back of the group, in a boat with his sponsor goddess, chest bared, flexing his powerful arms as he paddled them forward. I gawked at his new-to-me muscles. How did I miss that?

Beside me, Seon stripped down and tied two daggers at his waist. His physique wasn't as large as Bo's. He was all lean muscles, but just as fit from his swordsmanship lessons. Tala nudged me, rolling her eyes. "Now, Cai."

I removed my shoes and took a few tentative steps toward the water. Ahead of me was a flurry of action, but it didn't seem that anyone had caught a serpent yet. We were still in this.

Seon and Tala were already in the water, waving me over. Even Kama had wandered in, bobbing like a wayward apple.

I closed my eyes and kept walking forward, waiting for the inevitable flood into my mouth and nose. Nothing. I opened one wary eye and stared down. My toes were soaked, but my feet weren't sinking into the shallow depths.

"You're walking on water!" Seon pumped his fist. "And look who also has the same powers."

The Qilin was walking on the water alongside me. The majestic red-and-green creature reared his front legs, its brilliant scales gleaming in the sunlight, and took off in a speedy gallop for the other side.

I spat in Fear's eye and sprinted, legs kicking, until I reached the middle of the lake.

Now that I was in it, the water was surprisingly transparent, making it easier for me to spot the wriggling shadows. I could see the serpents! Guolin's and Xi's teams paddled in their boats, casting nets while Senlin's team lagged behind all of us, their team members embroiled in a heated argument.

The sea serpents were quick. They wriggled and darted, slipping away as soon as anyone drew near. Whenever I spotted one and pointed it out to Tala and Seon, the little beast had fled by the time they reached it. Kama floated nearby in an invisible basket, watching our efforts with the same frustration.

"How can we make them stay?" I asked him. "Every time they seem to sense that someone is close, they scatter."

Kama scratched his head. "I'm trying to remember my conversation with a fishmonger in Xianling centuries ago. She mentioned something about what they eat and how to catch them."

"We're grateful for anything you might remember." I peered into the empty waters. "Sooner rather than later, of course."

A triumphant shout from one of the teams interrupted our conversation. Bo held the tail while two of his teammates hoisted the rest of a long, silvery iron serpent out of the water. In the stories, these creatures gnashed their jaws, flailed their muscular bodies, but this one seemed almost docile. Pubu's musical laughter accompanied her smug expression. Maybe it wasn't just the water she could control, but its creatures.

The rest of us had no such luck. Guolin's, Xi's, and Senlin's teams keep pulling in empty nets.

Seon tapped our sponsor's shoulder as he treaded water. "Lord Kama, have you remembered yet?"

"Eels!" Our scruffy minor god cried out with glee.

Tala, Seon, and I sported the same confused expression.

"They behave like eels. Watch this." Kama dipped his fingers below the water's surface and wriggled them. "Come to Uncle, you tasty, tasty snack."

Tiny sparks flew from his fingertips, creating vibrations, and Seon and Tala, submerged in the water, reacted immediately with a shiver. The wriggling shadows emerged from the depths, heading to the surface near Kama's position.

"It's working." I lowered myself to my knees and pointed, tracing the movements of the nearest iron sea serpent. "I see two coming our way. Keep the sparks going."

Tala went under, then Seon. I pushed against the surface harder so that my left forearm was submerged. I did my best to guide their hunt to the particular one I wanted. The ability to find the best quality ingredients was important to any cook. The education the auction house had given me was invaluable. There were three serpents swimming under me and one of them was far more lively, its scales brighter than the rest.

"Get that one!" I yelled, pointing and gesticulating under the water.

Tala moved faster and more adeptly—she managed to grab the tail first. The serpent thrashed itself out of her grip. Seon tried to catch it afterward but failed when it, too, slipped out of his grasp. They both resurfaced to regroup.

"It's stronger than I expected." Tala brushed a damp lock of dark hair away from her eyes. "Seon, you'll need to hold on to the middle when I get the tail. This way, I can move to the head and kill it; if I can't, I'll muzzle it."

"Its scales really are impenetrable." Seon shook his head. "My daggers did nothing."

I suggested, "Why don't you try the forehead? It might be a vulnerable spot."

"Good idea!" Kama pointed to a spot in the middle of his brow and accidentally zapped himself.

Tala nodded and prepared for the next dive.

Seon disappeared soon after.

They approached the serpent from two sides. Seon was directly in front as a distraction while she sneaked behind to grab the tail. Once she did, he moved to clamp down both hands in the middle. Tala used her dagger to try and stab the head, but the blade kept slipping. She tucked it back into her belt and withdrew a strong rope to wrap the jaws shut, adding an extra leash-like loop she used to drag the serpent.

I pumped my fist and jumped to my feet.

Kama clapped his hands. "And that's how it's done. Cai, do me a favor and push me in the right direction."

I obliged and shoved him toward the shore. We all returned to land far behind the other remaining teams. Seon and I wrestled the serpent while Tala pulled the poisonous spikes off. She then shoved the ornery beast into a woven basket with a lid before making a clicking noise with her tongue. Ulan went to her side, her long neck lolling and her big webbed feet flapping. The cormorant jumped onto her master's shoulder.

Kama clapped his hands. "Well done, children! All of us have to head over to the banquet hall and wait for the next set of instructions."

We survived our first trial. Barely.

I should have drowned, yet I didn't.

How many more times would I need to cheat Death?

The iron sea serpent appeared in one of the banquets in the first century. The major gods introduced this species into the Singing Sea after the competition. These dreaded sea creatures carry a potent poison in their spikes and in their blood. At best, the surviving contestants remembered some of the new creatures or plants they encountered. This invaluable information is treasured and saved by scholars. Of all the beasts that the major gods have created, this one is among the most feared.

—*BESTIARY VOLUMES*, FOURTH SCROLL,
GREAT LIBRARY OF XIANLING

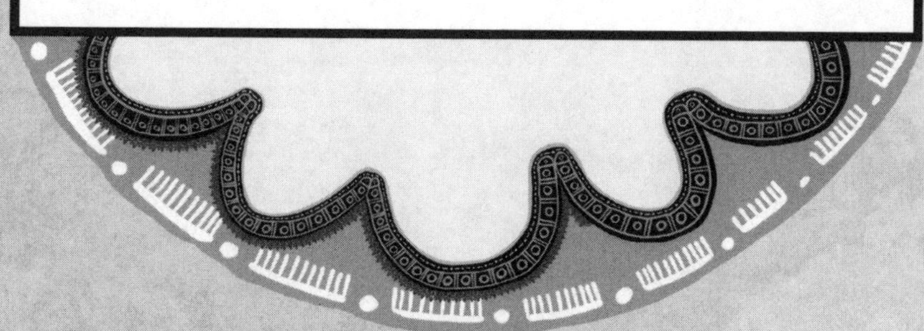

TEN

All the teams managed to secure their ingredient and had gathered at a series of tables on the beach, yet I noticed one person missing from Senlin's team. I gasped. Beside them was a shrouded body, ready for its funerary rites. A reminder of how close we came to Death's grasp.

A tremble shook my hands. Baba's dead body had also been covered with a sheet before he was cremated. There was an ugliness to death that had to be hidden. Seon's arm wrapped around my shoulders. I uttered prayers for this poor soul's family. The heartbreak from Baba's loss continued to haunt me even to this day.

I nudged Seon, fighting back tears. "What do you think happened?"

The answer came from an unexpected source—Bo, who joined our group. "Poison from the iron serpent. He got too close and grazed the spikes. I'm glad that your team made it."

Seon's tone was hostile. "Barely, our boat was sabotaged. Might be nice if our allies acted as allies."

"I'm sure Bo wasn't responsible for the boat." I stepped in between both of them. "He's on our side."

"Our boat was damaged as well. If it weren't for Pubu's powers, it wouldn't have floated. I'd never do anything to harm Cai." Bo stood beside me and placed his arm around my waist, effectively pulling me from under Seon's arm.

Physical intimacy wasn't new. We often linked arms while strolling in Lupong. Now, it felt different. The heat of his hand burned through the fabric of my tunic into my skin, combined with the weight of too many curious eyes, making me uneasy. I straightened my spine and shifted my feet, dislodging his grip.

"Whose side are you on? It's certainly not ours." Seon continued his interrogation. "You want to win so she'll see you as a hero when you give her your peach."

I stepped between both of them. "Seon, back down . . ." Then Kama, of all people, came to the rescue.

"Calm yourselves, boys. The beautiful maiden will decide her suitor when it's all settled and not before." Kama wagged his finger at both Seon and Bo, while I blushed furiously. "In the meantime, we need our wits about us."

Kama didn't understand that this tension with Seon and Bo wasn't even about me. They had never gotten along. Seon found Bo to be far too stubborn and narrow-minded. He once mentioned he thought my friendship with Bo held me back. On the other hand, Bo found Seon pretentious, not to mention that he once caught him flirting with his sister. Baba told me once that sometimes people just hate each other on sight, no matter what the excuse.

Seon shook his head and stalked off toward Tala, who was sharpening her arsenal of daggers. Kama followed, spouting off unwanted love advice in his direction.

I turned to Bo and exhaled, rolling my eyes. "Sorry about that. You holding up okay?"

"Fine so far. Pubu's team is—"

I noticed a tear in his pants near his left knee. "You didn't touch the spines, did you?"

"Thank goodness, no. I got it from kicking our broken boat." He looked sheepish. I moved to take a closer look, but he waved me back. "You're worrying too much. It's just a scratch. I'm supposed to be the anxious one, remember?"

"Fine." I brushed the concern away. "So, what did your family say? About all this?"

He flushed and looked away. "I . . . uh. I told them I had to follow you before you got yourself into trouble."

"Your sisters will have my hide if anything happens to you!" I wagged my finger. "They already think I've gotten you into too much chaos as is."

His parents and three very protective sisters were the most wonderful people I could ever imagine living under one roof. Their house was a noisy whirlwind of laughter and love—a maelstrom that I imagined I'd have for my own if Baba and Mama were alive. Even if they were worried, I knew Bo's family would believe in him, support his cause.

"They'll see it was worth it when we both get back. Besides, it won't change how they see you. They adore you and would sooner take your side than mine."

"Fine." I shooed him away when I heard the invisible gong. My team rejoined me.

Luck appeared as two identical selves before the doors. Their robes were in contrasting colors of gold and emerald with Qilin-patterned embroidery. The real Qilin rested behind them, napping with soft snores, puffs of smoke creating levitating rings in the air.

The left declared, "The first task is done. The next is even more tricky and potentially deadly."

I wondered, ruefully, how something could be *more* deadly than the trial we'd just overcome.

"Yes, much, much more," said the one on the right. "You didn't expect us to eat that creature whole, did you? Now you must butcher the sea serpent. You must do so by sunset unless you want to miss my feast." The right pointed up, and a spark darted from the tip of their finger to explode into a series of mesmerizing fireworks in the sky.

Butchering was part and parcel of the process of cooking. I learned how to carve many kinds of meats and even prepare some magical ingredients. But this was different. The iron sea serpent hadn't been seen in centuries—one wrong move and I could end up dead.

My team and I spent the next hour banging our heads against the wall, trying to figure out next steps.

"The only thing we know is that it's poisonous. We've taken care of the spines, but that venom has to come from somewhere within," Seon hypothesized. "It's how it protects itself."

"And the scales are hard," Tala added. "My daggers and Seon's katana didn't even make a mark."

Kama yawned and stretched. "I'm sure you children can figure this out. You have the innate ability to break things you're not supposed to."

"It'd be easier if you could remember anything else about this creature." I tried my best to keep the irritation out of my voice. I kept racking my brain. Kama had said they were like eels, right? At the market, I often picked up the foaming tide eel that was Tondo the Tall's favorite. It was a hideous creature and its secret was that the only edible part was a small fatty deposit near its tail.

"Kama, have you ever had sea foam eel? I think we need to figure out what part of the serpent is actually edible. I bet it's just a small bit . . ." I ventured.

"Oh!" Our sponsor ruffled his hair as bits of dust and even food flew out. We all stepped back to give him a wide berth. Our mangy minor god continued when he was done. "It's dangerous, be careful when touching it."

We were getting somewhere. I stared at my hands. "Then it'd be a good idea to have some sort of protection."

"You'd better wear gloves." Tala unloaded her pack and rummaged through to find a pair. I slipped them on only to find my hands swimming in them. Tala noticed too. "I'll need to modify them."

Kama accompanied Seon and followed the crowd. "We'll meet you two at the arena then."

Tala took out her needle and thread. She instructed me to sit beside her with the gloves on while she tailored them to my hands and forearms. "I treated these with oil so they'll protect against water. Poison is a different beast though. I can't make any guarantees."

"Thank you for doing this."

"A dead or maimed candidate does me no good."

The way she said those words made me wonder what was underneath that gruff exterior. For all I knew, she was a sea urchin—spikes on the outside, golden treasure on the inside. Her motivations matched mine regarding self-preservation. I kept my focus on her methodical stitching.

She finished off one glove and began working on the other.

"What will you do with your peach?" I asked, unable to contain my curiosity.

Her lips formed a thin line. I tried another tactic.

"I want to open a restaurant." After that obvious disclosure, I should say something more personal. I decided to take a risk. In a lower voice, I continued, "I'd use the rest of the money to keep the Peninsula free from the Empress. Our armies aren't even close to ready or big enough to—"

A sharp prick stopped my words, and I doubted she slipped by accident. There were nicer ways to get me to shut up.

Tala finished sewing the final glove, then tucked away her needle and thread. I tested out the fit of the gloves. They were made of Bataan hide—thick enough to protect yet thin enough that I retained full mobility of my fingers. "Thank you."

In reply, Tala just stood and walked toward the arena.

I flexed my hands and steeled myself. The next challenge awaited, and I hoped I wouldn't die of poison.

Slicing and dicing is the prowess of the Blade Guild. The members engage in secret rituals, sharing techniques for the trickiest ingredients, so they may cut through any obstacle, no matter the hardness or texture.

All members are required to pass the arduous three days of testing to gain entrance. This guild partners with the Smithing Association to create the best knives in the world.

—*THE WAY OF THE KNIFE*, SIXTH SCROLL, MASTER ARCHIVES OF THE ALCHEMY GUILD

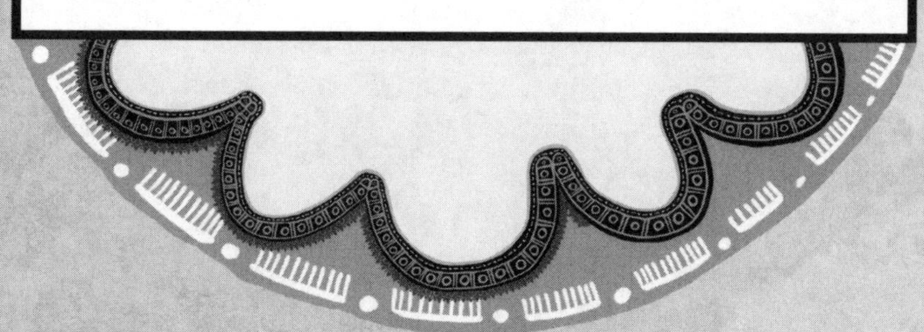

ELEVEN

Capturing the serpent had been a group trial, but this was a chef's task. I headed toward the arena alone while everyone else headed to the arena's seating to act as our audience. Our sea serpents would be delivered to our stations by Luck. As I approached the entrance, I noticed Songwon just ahead of me. Our eyes met, and I raised my hand in a tentative wave. He ignored me.

At least I tried.

Zi Rui, Chan-yeol, and Daichi huddled together, strategizing as usual. I edged a bit closer until I could make out what they were saying.

"The iron sea serpent doesn't respond to knives, but there is a way." Zi Rui smacked Chan-yeol's arm. "The eight-star formation will work. How many times must I tell you?"

"But the lore says the skin is impenetrable, yet it can be cooked—"

Daichi cuffed Chan-yeol's mouth to silence him. "Don't give out valuable information, you fool."

I couldn't help but feel a twinge of sympathy for the bruised Chan-yeol. The information confirmed what Kama had told me. I turned to Songwon to relay the gossip. "The pattern is the eight-star. We can use that to get through the skin! Zi Rui will demonstrate it. You might need gloves too. Better to be safe."

If Pubu's candidate heard me, he gave no sign of gratitude or even acknowledgment.

Luck's dual voices echoed in the maw of the underpass. "Competitors, please make your way to the ring. Make haste, make haste!"

We marched into the arena where five granite stations were marked with our sponsor's names—large, elevated tables the width of my arm span. The surface was bare except for a very sharp, curved paring knife. I stepped up to the one that matched the tattooed symbol on my forearm. The raven cawed and flapped its wings on my skin in approval.

The seating for the audience was in curved, spoonlike niches positioned near their candidate's table.

Songwon was to my left, and Daichi was to my right. Looking around, I was the only one wearing gloves, despite my warning to Songwon.

"Welcome to the stage!" Luck and Luck greeted us from a raised round pedestal in the center of the arena. "This is a beautiful day. Why don't we make it more interesting?" Their arms extended upward. The heavens rumbled, and the desert sky soon darkened with thick clouds.

Luck on the left snapped their fingers, and a large, fringed parasol materialized over their head, held aloft by invisible hands. The pit of my stomach sank to my ankles as the sudden deluge soaked me and the other candidates from head to toe. All of our teammates remained dry in their covered alcoves.

"Rain in the desert is considered a rare blessing, and may even prove crucial as you prepare your serpent." Luck on the right shook their hips and danced. "Be careful to preserve as much of the precious ingredient as possible. You must taste it first. A chef needs to know what they're cooking!"

The heavy rain plastered my hair against my scalp, as I readied myself for this task. The abject misery of this situation wasn't lost upon any of us chefs. Doing precise work under these conditions would be challenging at best. Not to mention, if we were correct that much of the serpent was poisonous, that taste test would mean everything.

"Are you ready?" Luck in their two forms clapped in unison.

The sound of the torrential rain drowned out everything but the sound of Luck's dual voices.

Our respective iron serpents materialized on the stone tables. Mine thrashed, thankfully with Tala's rope muzzle still in place. It wriggled, skittering across the surface, bucking until it threatened to escape the confines of the table.

"Don't let it get away!" Kama yelled from his seat. "If it escapes, we lose."

I danced to avoid its swinging tail and elbowed the serpent in the face. "Tell me something I don't know," I shouted back.

"Hold it down so you can watch Zi Rui for his blade work!" Seon raised his voice.

Great. Easier said than done. To either side of me, Daichi and Songwon had subdued their creatures—Songwon had managed to get his in a tight headlock thanks to his superior strength—waiting for Zi Rui's next move. Mine was curled in the corner like a cobra. My food was taunting me. I pulled out my cleaver and took a step forward. The sea creature hissed and by sheer instinct, I brought the side of my cleaver across its head with a thwack—the way a stern auntie would berate a disobedient child. Somehow, I stunned it and was rewarded with black goo spraying across my face—into my eyes and up my nose. Thank goodness I kept my mouth closed.

"See!" Kama exclaimed. "You'll be fine."

The liquid was stickier than squid ink. I tipped my face up to the downpour and rubbed the residue away—at least the rain could save me some time cleaning. Of course, the smell was as foul as the temperament of the fish. I grabbed its head and used Tala's harness to my advantage to hold it still.

In full view of his allies, Zi Rui pulled out his paring knife and made a shallow carve of an oval underneath the jaw of his serpent. In the center of this oval, he cut an eight-pointed star pattern before driving the hilt of the paring knife through, into the skull. The act sent a shimmering cascade of scales all the way down to its tail, shining through the curtains of rain and revealing the vulnerable skin beneath it.

This was the magic of the Blade Guild. It made my ambition to join one burn brighter. There was so much left to learn and I couldn't do it by staying in Lupong.

Daichi and Chan-yeol showed no hesitation in following Zi Rui's example. Even if Zi Rui wanted to keep this a secret, it would have been difficult since he had to show his allies, and he couldn't do that without me or Songwon seeing too.

I had no other ideas but to follow suit. It didn't feel like cheating when he had every advantage I didn't. I made the particular cuts and nailed the now dead serpent onto the table. As I readied the paring knife to begin butchery, a primal scream almost made me drop it.

To my right, Daichi was shrieking and holding his bare hands up before him. I drew closer, and so did the others. From a distance, it appeared as if nothing was wrong. His hands were pristine and unmarred, yet his howls were harrowing.

"What in eighteen hells is wrong with you?" Zi Rui grabbed his shoulders. "Have you lost your senses? Stop that damnable . . ."

The subtle shaking loosened the fingertip off Daichi's left index finger. The small piece of flesh slid off, revealing a blackened stump and bits of bone. Zi Rui jumped back while the rest of us gave Daichi a wider berth. His hands were melting away. Songwon and Chan-yeol ran to the perimeter, heaving their morning congee and Pu'erh tea.

I was frozen in place. My stomach turned, yet I couldn't look away as Daichi's hands disintegrated into his forearms—tissue and ligament purpling into black, then falling away as the bones remained until whatever was holding them up vanished. Daichi's high-pitched screeching never stopped. As his team finally led him away, the ghost of his terrified voice still lingered in my ears. Muyang, their team's noble representative and now the only mortal left on the team, bowed to his sponsor god and took his candidate's place. In the Celestial Banquet, a team hadn't fallen until all its members were out of commission.

This task had ensured that Daichi might never cook again.

"The fish is poisonous! Bring me gloves!" Zi Rui shouted to his team.

The other candidates echoed his call as their teams scrambled for protective wear.

Daichi's fate could have been mine.

Tala's gloves saved me.

"Cai, you've got this!" Seon whooped in encouragement.

My fingers trembled. I couldn't stop now. I closed my eyes and allowed Seon's cheers to fuel me as I began to carve into the serpent's now scaleless flesh.

The rest of us candidates fell into a quiet routine as if one of us hadn't lost their hands minutes earlier. Muyang, at the table to my right, clearly had little culinary skill. Songwon, to my left, held his paring knife and walked around to examine the sliced body of the serpent. Like the others, he was pacing, trying to figure out how to proceed.

I touched the tip of my knife to the skin and cut with even pressure through a thin film of mucus. My instincts told me to retrieve a thumb's width of meat near the spine. Every sea snake I had encountered had the best pieces in this location.

After I'd peeled away the layers, I understood why the others were paused in thought. Every ordinary fish, especially eels, had a conspicuous spine connected to the skull, fins, and tail. While this monster was considered a sea creature, its innards were closer to those of a jellyfish. Pinkish balloons of organs floated in its gelatinous body within an intricate network of scarlet blood vessels. The spine wasn't visible to the naked eye. Even if I did somehow find it, trying to extract it without disturbing the blood vessels, thus corrupting the meat, would be a towering feat.

Taking a deep, steadying breath, I submerged my gloved fingertips into the body. The wobbly insides squelched to my touch. Everything was as soft as it looked and without much structure. If it weren't deadly and poisonous, it'd be interesting to experiment with the jelly. But in Celestial Banquet tradition, the major gods did not allow for any ingredient to be smuggled out of the feast.

I continued to feel my way without disturbing any of the fragile scarlet blood vessels. With the blood being toxic, it was a wonder any bit of it was edible.

What would Baba do? Something unexpected. My father's mind worked in unconventional ways. He embraced experiments with a gusto I only hoped to live up to. He advocated for using all of one's senses when evaluating food, even when it might seem ridiculous.

Then it hit me. If I couldn't cut into it the traditional way, I had to feel for it. I chose a spot where I could slip my wrist in without disturbing the bloodstream and closed my eyes. More squishing and sloshing.

Until my fingers found something solid—a tubelike structure with a strip attached to it, almost like a flag. I yanked on the tube and almost shrieked with joy as I carefully pulled it through the opening. The tube must be the spine—and the attached meat measuring the width of my two fingers, the only piece of edible meat on this fish.

I pushed the rest of the carcass off the table and stretched out what I needed to trim. I made quick work and piled the cut pieces to the side. Luck said we had to taste the fish before we could proceed. I picked a small piece, popped it into my mouth, desperately hoping I wouldn't poison myself.

It had the tough texture of cured meat, which was astonishing considering the soft environment I found it in. The smoky taste surprised me too. The possibilities for this fish were endless; my mind started racing through methods of how to cook it and what to pair it with.

A minute passed. And then another. Raindrops mingled with my tears of relief as I turned my face to the darkened sky. My heart pulsed, racing with joy at my triumph. I had survived.

Over my shoulder, I saw Songwon had also extracted the spine and was preparing to taste. A speck of scarlet glittered on the piece he was holding.

I called out, "Wait!"

Poison is typically avoided in the kitchen—for obvious reasons. However, some scholars have fought to keep certain poisonous ingredients viable, so long as the amount is regulated. A famous example of this is stinging royal jelly. A full portion can and will paralyze the eater. But under the advice of herbalists and culinary advisors, the once forbidden honey is now allowed, in moderation, in certain beverages, to the delight of many who enjoy the tickling numbness that accompanies a spiked drink. But those who imbibe do so at their own risk.

—***CULINARY COMPENDIUM***, **SIXTH SCROLL, GREAT LIBRARY OF XIANLING**

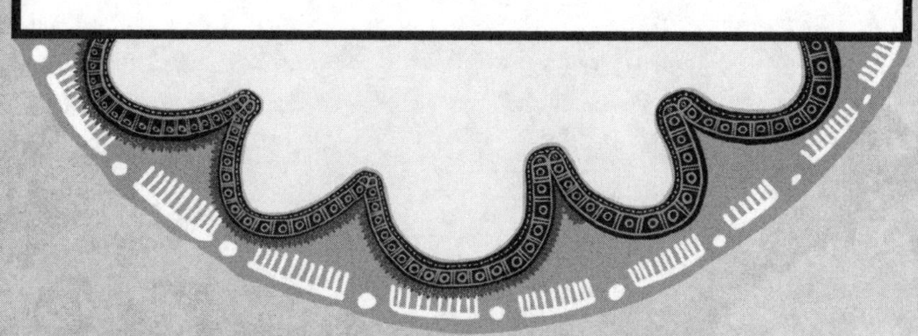

TWELVE

The speck was no bigger than a sliver of a fingernail, yet the amount could and would kill him. There wasn't time to engage in a debate or reason with him. He could thank me later. I ran to Songwon's side to swat the piece from his hand, sputtering rapidly about the poison blood.

Songwon stayed silent. He cut another piece, inspected it thoroughly, and then popped it into his mouth—thus moving on from the trial.

Oh well. At least I saved his life, even if he didn't appreciate it, and Bo would get to advance in the competition.

I gathered the remaining viable meat into an oiled, waterproof basket under the table. Given Luck's subtle warning about the necessity of moisture for the serpent, I made sure to collect enough rainwater to submerge the filleted pieces.

My team waited for me outside of the arena, where the weather returned to its normal arid state. Being out of the downpour was a blessing, and finishing my task was even more so. Seon rushed to my side. His arms were outstretched as if to embrace me, but he hesitated and held my bare hands instead.

"Well done!" He beamed and squeezed my fingers. "I never doubted that you'd do it."

I blushed. "Thank you."

Kama wriggled his eyebrows and smacked me on the shoulder. "Aren't you glad that part's over?"

"Yes, I am." I returned his playful smack with one of my own.

I approached Tala next and bowed. "Thank you for the gloves. They saved my hands."

She simply nodded in acknowledgment. Even in a moment of success she was surly. She'd be a tough nut to crack. Good thing I was a chef. Before I could prod her for a verbal reaction, Bo came over and swept me into his arms.

"You did it! Great job out there!"

I pulled back to notice he was covered in sweat. "Bo?"

"It's just hot. You know it was raining and . . ."

His forehead was burning, and his skin pale. He wasn't like this before we entered the arena. Without warning, he slumped into my arms. I had to take a step back to brace myself against his weight. Seon and Tala quickly came to my aid, and the three of us lowered Bo onto the ground.

"Perhaps it's the heat." Seon reached for Bo's wrist and checked his pulse.

Kama leaned down into a squatting position. "Check his leg, the one with the mended tear."

I rolled up the fabric and gasped. Bo's entire calf was mottled in purple and blue. The scaly, undulating pattern spread upward to his torso. He'd lied when I asked him if it had been from the sea serpent. Of course the idiot would, making sure I wouldn't worry about him. I should have checked anyway.

"Bo, wake up." I lightly smacked his cheeks. "Come on."

He groaned and kept his eyes closed. My pulse began to race. I couldn't believe this. I couldn't lose him. Not here, not ever.

"The poison's spread too far," Kama said. "If the wound weren't so small, he would have died instantly like his teammate. But he doesn't have much time left now."

No.

Not Bo.

I wasn't going to lose my best friend. He had to return with me to Lupong. This wasn't happening. He was coming home alive, damn it. He wasn't dying because of me.

What was the point of the peaches and the restaurant if it meant losing him?

"Bo?" I shook him as tears tumbled down my cheeks. "You can't leave me. Who's going to bully Lian's future boyfriends? Mei wants you to teach her how to dance for the harvest festival. You can't do this. Who's going to make sure I don't do something stupid? You just got here! You can't do this to me." I shook him and smacked his chest. "People are counting on you. They need you. Bo, *I* need you."

Seon dropped Bo's wrist. "I'm sorry, Cai. I can't find a pulse."

"No, no, no." I turned to Kama and grabbed him by the neck of his shirt. "Do something! He can't die like this. You're a god. Steal him back from Death! Do this for me. I'll give you anything."

Kama sputtered, "Even if I wanted to, I don't know if I have enough power. It hasn't been done before. As if the other minor gods would ever risk their own youthful glow to save a mere mortal . . ."

I crumpled against him and pressed my forehead against his chest. "Please try. I can't lose him . . . I can't. Kama, he's one of your people."

My sponsor rubbed my back and then gently pulled me away. "Give me some room, then. Let's see if I have enough to make this happen."

Kama stretched out his arms and cracked his knuckles. He held his arms over his head, turning his face to the sky, fingers reaching for the heavens. Seon, Tala, and I craned our necks and searched for a sign. Pubu, Songwon, and the rest of their team hovered nearby, watching and waiting.

My chest was hollow, as though all my vital organs had been scooped out and only the withered rind remained. Each painful breath reminded me of the emptiness. Kama *had* to work his magic. This vagabond of a minor god was capable of miracles like the others. Of anyone, he could trick Death and reclaim its prize.

Thunder boomed in the distance in a cloudless blue sky, followed by bolts of lightning connecting with Kama's fingertips. Our sponsor levitated off the ground as bolt after bolt struck him, convulsing his body, yet he didn't cry out from the agony. My ears strained against the noise, my eyes from the radiance.

The dark shadow of Kama's body hovered at Bo's side. He pressed his crackling hands against my friend's chest, transferring the collected energy into Bo's lifeless body—the light diffusing into his limbs and then coalescing again around his heart.

Once Kama removed his hands, I crouched down on my knees on the other side of Bo. "Breathe, by the gods, breathe. I don't want to have to drag you out of the underworld myself."

I pressed my head against his chest and waited for the symphony of life—the inhale and exhale of his lungs and the thrum of his heart pumping lifeblood. All that answered was silence. Until, one beat, then . . .

"Cai?"

It was a voice I'd never thought I'd hear again.

Bo's dark eyes fluttered open, taking a few seconds to focus on my face. For someone who had just escaped Death, he looked fantastic. His skin had recovered its healthy glow, and no trace of the sallowness remained. He was alive. If anything, he appeared more so.

His forehead creased as his deep voice came in a whisper. "Cai? Where am I?"

"We're at the Celestial Banquet in Xianling." I cradled his cheek, peering into his deep brown eyes. The short stubble on his skin tickled my palm. "Kama saved you from sea serpent poison. The Lord of the Peninsula brought you back to life."

He stared at me in disbelief.

Before he could say anything, I reached down, cupped his face, and kissed him.

The kiss was an unexpected tidal wave that swept me off my feet and left me breathless in its wake. I didn't know why I did it. I guess it was the only thing that made sense in that moment.

When he pulled away, the self-satisfied smirk on his face made me flick his collarbone. He laughed. "If I'd known that's how you'd react, I would have died sooner."

Blushing, I got up and covered my face. Bo's teammates gathered around us to check on him. I turned to Songwon. "Please look at his head. I think he must have hit it pretty hard. I have to go check on Kama."

A short distance away, Tala stood with our sponsor, just managing to keep him upright. Our minor god's hair had turned completely white. He'd aged decades, became an image of what his father probably looked like. How much had he sacrificed to save Bo?

I knelt at his feet and bowed, pressing my forehead against the ground. "Thank you for what you've done, Lord of the Peninsula. This daughter of Lupong is grateful for your act of grace."

"I accept your gratitude." Kama placed his hands on my shoulders. Though much dimmer than before, I was relieved to see the spark of mischief still present behind his white eyes. "Rise, my daughter."

Meal preparation is a dazzling showcase of a candidate's talents. If the candidate can't make the ingredients sing, their team fails. A candidate's life and skills are tested in this stage.

The best teams aim for the major gods' blessing, while the mediocre strive to prevent the major gods' wrath. And it's not only the gods' punishment that the chef must fear. On more than one occasion, a team has executed their own failed candidate without immortal intervention—such is the danger of serving an inferior dish.

—***CONCERNING MINOR GODS***, **SEVENTH SCROLL, GREAT LIBRARY OF XIANLING**

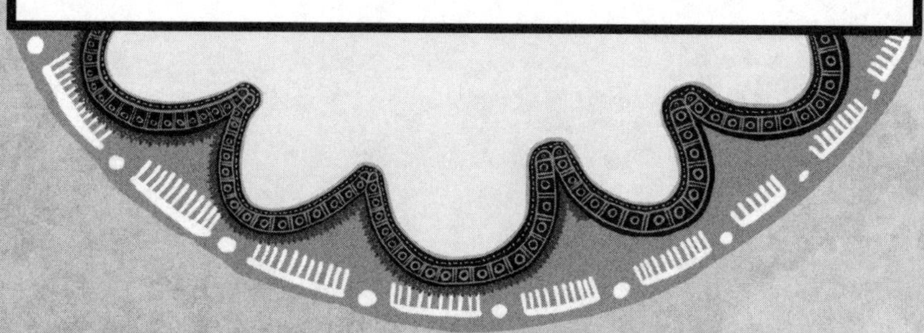

THIRTEEN

My palms always itched when it was time to cook. Baba often reminded me that I'd known how to wield a wok before other children could walk. It was a complete exaggeration, yet I embraced it.

Focusing was much harder than I expected when intrusive memories of Bo's kiss kept popping up. It had been half an hour since, and I couldn't stop thinking about how clueless I was about his feelings. I was caught between wanting to pull all the answers out of Bo and sticking my head in the sand, pretending it never happened.

I shook my head to clear my thoughts and concentrate on cooking.

Tala swung the large doors wide open to the banquet hall.

Underneath rows of floating paper lanterns were seemingly endless aisles of glorious ingredients—tables upon tables showcasing harvests from land and sea, expensive spices and herbs housed in glass vessels, along with racks of various wines, sauces, and other fermented goods.

"They have entire markets in here," I declared with hushed reverence.

We gawked at the bounty before us that was far more than anything we had ever seen in Lupong or anywhere else. Even Seon and Kama were beyond impressed. Tala was Tala—ever frugal with her words and emotions.

Baba and I used to spend hours in our little room combining and experimenting. He'd wanted to expand my tongue's vocabulary, not through words, but through taste. And he'd walk until his shoes had holes in order to tuck away a little coin to fund our shared passion. I wished he were here to see this.

I clapped my hands to break everyone out of their spell. "We can look later. Let's find our kitchen first."

Beyond the grand market, the teams had set stations equipped with cooking fires, butcher blocks, and work tables. I chose an empty one farthest away from the others. I needed to concentrate.

Seon offered to help Tala with setting up the fires while Kama joined me in hunting down just the right ingredients to accompany the serpent.

Kama could barely keep the drool from his beard as we sifted through stands of perfect juicy fruits, crisp vegetables, marbled meats, and every spice imaginable. "This is heaven. I keep forgetting how much I wanted to live in the banquet hall just for the food alone."

I picked up two small pink-speckled silver fishes.

"Meadow flower breams?" He scratched his head. "Wouldn't that be too rich in taste?"

For the people of Lupong it might be. But I was in a different league now and I wasn't going to let myself forget it. If I knew anything about the gods, let alone the Empress, they'd value luxury over taste. So, luxury they would get. It wasn't enough to satisfy an immortal palate, I had to succumb to the tastes of the old hag with the crown on her head. Kama was too far removed to remember this.

"No. The bream is perfect. I've heard it's the latest trend, we just don't get the chance to use it back home."

He shrugged. "This is why you're the cook. I'm only good at eating."

I moved to the rainbow section of roe and found the tin containing the golden-pink singing carp's eggs. Tondo the Tall would pay an empress's ransom for this cache. I popped one into my mouth, and as soon as my teeth punctured the thin membrane, a buttery, sweet liquid flooded my tongue. Perfect.

"If I didn't know any better, I'd say you're aiming to make the priciest meal. Good thing it's free," Kama said, rubbing his hands.

"The best of the best," I replied.

He wagged his eyebrows. "Is this in any way a celebration of a certain boyfriend coming back to life?"

I ignored the comment, moving toward the rows of produce to pluck out golden song mushrooms and diamond dust rock sugar. I touched my lower lip, and Bo's kiss resurfaced again. If Kama wanted me to win this, he'd better keep his mouth shut about my love life.

When we returned to the others, Kama made himself at home by sitting on a wooden barrel and acting as our overseer. I unloaded everything on the table, grabbed my father's wok from my pack, and joined Tala and Seon, who were in the middle of a conversation.

Tala gave me a curt nod. "Do you want me to help cut anything?"

I directed her toward the ginger and shallots and asked for them to be minced while I heated Baba's wok. Tala moved to the farthest end of my kitchen to do her work.

"What do I need to do for you to kiss me that way?" Seon asked.

Blood rushed to my face and to the tips of my hair. I busied myself with filleting the silvery pink meadow flower bream. "I got carried away. It was just a happy moment."

Seon moved beside me and began sorting the singing carp roe by size and color. "Kama gets happy every time he gets his tankard refilled. I doubt he gives Shuyi, the tavern owner, those types of kisses."

"Maybe he does when he has enough potent plum wine in him."

"But does Bo hold your heart?"

This halted my blade. The assumption that Bo and I were together wasn't uncommon. Part of it was society's inability to see that a boy and a girl could be friends and nothing more. Part of it was our familiarity with each other, and how we always seemed to be physically connected—whether we were linking arms or bumping hips. A lot of habits from childhood endured. Bo's protectiveness wrapped around me like a blanket, same as with his sisters.

After the kiss, I doubted anyone would easily believe that Bo and I were just friends, especially Seon.

"We're childhood friends," I replied, refusing to think more deeply about it. Besides, I didn't want to talk about this with my longtime crush, of all people. The small fish emitted speckles of pink light as I carved them open. The glittering faded in a few seconds. The trick to preparing this fish was to produce the same effect for the diner.

"You didn't answer my question."

My knife slipped, nicking the edge of my thumb. I sucked on it to staunch the bleeding.

"Pretty boy." Kama wagged his finger at Seon. "She needs to concentrate."

Our sponsor god's intervention, for once, was welcomed. I turned to Seon and, with a wink, barked instructions. "Make diagonal cuts into the flesh to tenderize it, please."

Seon smiled and got to work. Less than a minute into the task, he stopped and stood back. "I can't cut it. It's too tough." I peered toward the other teams, the closest of which, Pubu's, was ten feet away. He sighed. "We're too far away from the others to copy a technique from someone in the Blade Guild. I'm sorry, Cai. I don't know how to do it."

There were other ways to break down tough meat.

"Seon, find a deep basin. The meat will need to be completely submerged in liquid. Kama, come with me." I set down my cleaver and half-dragged our minor god back into the markets, toward the large ceramic jars, flasks, and bottles. Every possible liquid ingredient could be found here. But faced with written labels, my heart sank. I wouldn't be able to tell which was which. However, Kama, without prompting, began reading each one aloud. He was really starting to grow on me.

"What exactly are you looking for?" The old god tugged on his earlobe.

I replied, "The most potent vinegars available. We can marinate the iron serpent. The acidity level has to be as high as possible while still retaining flavor."

Within minutes, we narrowed our choices to Demon's Breath, Wine of the Diyu, and Petty Revenge. The creative names were given by the inventor, an old smelly hermit who lived up in the Guolin Mountains with a deep obsession with pickling and vinegar. No one ever doubted his dedication to the craft or his talent. However, his smell was apparently so offensive that he wasn't allowed to set foot in the jeweled city.

I tapped the stretched rubber lids of each jar. "Let's see . . . My guess is that the smellier, the better."

When we returned to our kitchen, Seon and Tala had finished the preparation work I'd tasked them with.

"Before you ask, you're very behind already. Guolin's and Xi's teams have already served their dishes. They've fed the Qilin and advanced to the judgment chamber." Seon took the jars from my arms and transferred them onto the counters.

I tied my apron around my waist and ladled some of the vinegar into a bowl. The color was a glossy black, and the moment I dipped my finger into it, my skin pruned. The taste was complex, with sweet notes and quite a rich, earthy flavor. This old Sour Master was a genius.

I poured the vinegar into the basin with the iron sea serpent. The dual strips of meat reacted with a hiss. Foaming bubbles began to form along the surface. Taking this as a good sign, I raised my cleaver to finish filleting the exquisite meadow flower breams.

Pubu is the waterfall minor goddess and her familiar is the fantail goldfish. She is the only minor goddess, though it is rumored that two others have faded into memory. She prides herself in her unparalleled beauty and sharp mind. Though she has many mortal male admirers, she prefers immortal company. Her latest failed dalliance with Senlin left her in a precarious position for the upcoming banquet.

—*CONCERNING MINOR GODS*, EIGHTH SCROLL, GREAT LIBRARY OF XIANLING

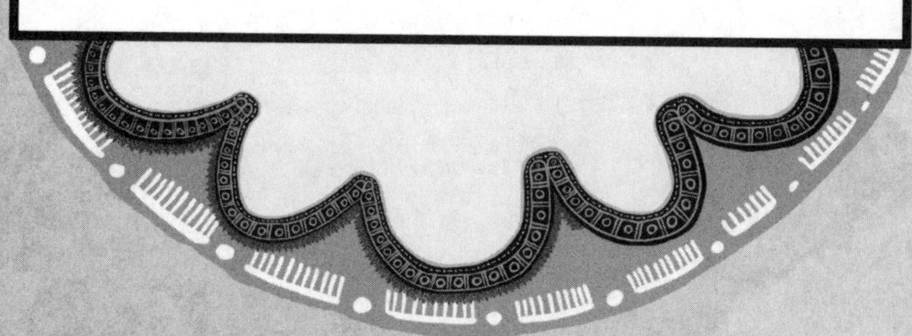

FOURTEEN

The dish with the iron sea serpent for Luck and the Empress of Wan was done.

I had delivered all the luxury that they could ever want, showing them that Lupong could do fancy food just as well.

Now, I just needed to whip up a humble yet comforting plate for the Qilin. I decided on an apple dish I'd first tasted when I visited Bo's farm. His sisters had picked the bright fruits straight from their own orchard, and their mother had prepared them with oats from the field and precious cinnamon from the market. I vividly remembered how the meal had made me feel: warm, taken care of. Bo's family didn't have much, yet they were willing to share what little they had. And without Baba or Mama, it meant the world.

Baba's belief was that good intentions created better flavor. "If you cook from the heart, your food will always taste good," he said. Passion was my fuel, my guide.

Now it was time to deliver the meals.

Tala cradled Ulan in her arms while I finished plating the dishes, setting them up on the ornate tray we'd been provided.

"Let your food do the talking." Seon embraced me and whispered in my ear. "Remember who you are." To my surprise, he brushed his lips across my cheek.

I searched his eyes for any indication of a motive. Did his constant flirting mean something? Or was he just jealous?

Kama bid me good luck next. "When presenting to Luck and the other major gods, speak carefully." He patted my arm with reassurance. "You know they'll take any excuse to penalize us, so, while I truly hate to say it, keep that fire within you dimmed. It will be well worth it."

Panic swarmed like mosquitoes. I wasn't used to this sort of scrutiny.

Kama placed the tray in my hands. "Focus on the task at hand, and the rest will sort itself out."

I dared not look back as I marched toward the gilded doors. Luck's Qilin guarded them with a majesty that the Empress lacked. I bowed before the incredible creature. Its dragon head contrasted with its scaled equine body. Golden flames appeared near its hooves, its beard, and its tail. The mighty antlers at its crown were sharp. Its every breath sounded like a vibrating snare drum.

The steaming bowl of oats and apples warmed my palms as I pushed it toward the legendary beast. I waited with bated breath as he sniffed the bowl. He paused for just a moment before diving in and devouring it in a few gulps. *Yes*, I thought. The Qilin gave me a slight bow. I had its approval to proceed.

Thank you, Bo's mother.

I clutched my tray to my chest and waited by the doors. Cooking demanded all my attention, so I never saw the other chefs embarking on this stage. Still, I was determined not to let anything in the room that lay ahead surprise me. Kama had taught me to expect the unexpected. And just a few hours with Luck had confirmed that.

A brass gong sounded, prompting me to take a step back. The massive doors swung open, revealing nothing but bright light that burned my eyes. I squinted and walked forward, hoping there wasn't some sort of steep cliff on the other side.

The blinding light faded as soon as the doors closed behind me. Luck, in their two forms, was seated at a high table with a floating stone staircase leading up to it. The Empress of Wan sat next to them. Behind them was a split room—one side was splashed in gold and jewels from the gilded furniture and overflowing chests, while the other stopped me in my tracks. It was a perfect rendering of my room at the boardinghouse in Lupong, exactly as I'd left it. I knew anything was possible when it came to the gods, but how could I have known to expect this?

If they were trying to send a message about how they could get under my skin, it worked. I dared not let the tray wobble as I ascended the steps.

"Ahhh, come, come. I am hungry." The left Luck patted the table with their fingertips.

The right waved me forward. "Yes, I need to eat. I've been waiting a decade."

I reached the table and presented my dish. "The plate features seared sea serpent with poached meadow flower breams."

The acidic bath method had worked. The flesh of the sea serpent had transformed yet again and changed to a very iron-rich deep red. The taste was reminiscent of fatty tuna, with a stronger metallic edge. I'd set the filets in shallow clay bowls and bathed them in a marinade made of coriander, minced ginger, chilies, kalamansi, and my signature soy sauce.

I'd toasted black sesame seeds and combined them with crushed pink peppercorns as a rub—the crust to create a contrast for the tender, almost jellied meat underneath. On the side, I added the poached filets of meadow flower breams in a rich golden sauce with singing carp caviar.

"Looks like you're a peasant cook who chose the richest ingredients possible." The Empress of Wan narrowed her beady eyes at me. The powder on her face caked within her deep wrinkles—which were plentiful given her unnatural age. "We are supposed to be impressed by this display of garishness?"

She took a small bite with her chopsticks and made a face. The Empress turned to Luck on the left. "It's too rich for my delicate palate and far too heavy-handed. It's barely edible."

"Perhaps. I will be the judge of the dish." The one on the right pinched a morsel of the marinated sea serpent with their wooden chopsticks.

Luck on the left poked the meadow flower bream. "You could have chosen a better fish to complement the richness of the roe. Such expensive choices. Is it because of your own humble beginnings?"

"The meadow flower bream is highly coveted right now, and it complements the flesh of the iron sea serpent." I ensured there was no edge or whiff of defensiveness in my voice, despite my growing panic. Had I totally miscalculated? "The roe is powerful as a garnish. As a cook, I have to be able to make my dishes sing."

The left version of Luck asked, "And what song should they be singing?"

"One that will soothe the beast of hunger."

The left and the right turned to each other and exchanged looks.

The Empress of Wan leaned forward and laughed. "What makes you think you belong here? You're the youngest and the only female candidate. You also lack the pedigree. Not a culinary guild to be found in that backwater town of Lupong."

I swallowed my pride, remembering Kama's advice. I was here for something greater. I could take these jabs. Besides, it's Luck's opinion that really mattered.

"Kama deemed me worthy. I am just asking for an opportunity." I stood firm, raising my hands up in supplication.

After a painfully silent minute, Luck on the right pointed their chopsticks at me. "Kama's a poor excuse of a god. He lost any sense of power or respect when he fell in love with a mortal woman." The left narrowed their eyes. "Unspeakable."

I held back a sigh. It seemed that Luck was just as much against us as Empress Wan was. Kama didn't deserve this just for falling in love. No wonder he hated the Celestial Banquet so much. I hid my hands behind my back so I could wring them.

The gods acted like being mortal was a disease one could catch and be killed by because we humans were the ones who walked with Death. But here they were, holding this competition to taste the dishes that only we could make with our hard-earned experience, memories, and ingenuity.

"Kama will never win," the Empress harrumphed. "You might as well leave now."

Luck tsked. "True that her dish was far too rich for the tongue, yet I detect a spark of potential. Something that could be great with the proper amount of experience and training. It's very intriguing." Luck on the right commented, "What interests me is why you're not ashamed of your pedigree and your homeland."

I kept my hands clenched behind my back. I could take a lot, but this dismissive talk of my homeland infuriated me.

"Keep the Peninsula out of your mouth," I spat.

Their eyes, all-encompassing, held me firm. I braced for a bolt of lightning to incinerate my flesh and bones. The room filled not with the sound of my skin crackling, hissing, or popping as I was immolated, but with laughter.

I cracked open one eye to see both versions of Luck doubled over in glee.

"Why haven't you killed me yet?" I asked.

"Because now, you're interesting," the left answered.

The right added, "Let's see if you survive to cook the next feast."

Before I had the chance to retort, I was swept toward the opened doors by a sudden whirlwind. On the landing, I stumbled forward, almost bumping into my team, who were waiting for me.

"How did it go?" Kama asked.

I looked back at him, ashamed. "My dish failed; far too rich, like you said, and I lost my temper. This may be the first and last meal I ever cook for the gods." Each of the three nights, one team was kicked out of the competition. I was left with no confidence that we would make it to see tomorrow.

Seon looked horrified. "I'm at least glad Luck didn't kill you. Are you sure you failed?"

I'd been briefed about the consequences of failure. Seon had mentioned lore of potent, creative ways gods loved to punish the losing teams. The gong sounded again before I could answer, a warning, and I herded my team out to the courtyard, where the rest of the players loitered looking far more confident than I felt.

My dish was unworthy.

I had chosen what I thought would impress the elite and was unsuccessful in my task. Cooking for others instead of for myself—something Baba would be appalled by. I realized that the only dish I had done right was Qilin's.

My mistake could cost all of us our lives. Perhaps I could bargain with Luck to restrict the punishment to me because the others . . .

Just then, the two versions of Luck floated out on miniature clouds. The Empress of Wan was nowhere in sight, a small solace. A grand stone wall rose from the trembling ground. The Qilin stood atop the high ledge, looking down at all of us.

"I have tasted all of your dishes." Luck on the left steepled their fingers. "They were interesting, to say the least."

Luck on the right made a signal to their Qilin. "Three were outstanding. Two were not."

The mythical beast tipped its head down to breathe fire as three silk banners unfurled marking our rankings—Guolin's umber signaled his dominance in first, followed by Xi's gold, then Pubu's seafoam.

At least Bo was safe.

Now, it was between us and Senlin's team for the final slot in the next round. With excruciating agony, the final banner was revealed, and I screamed.

Kama's gray.

I collapsed to my knees and muttered my grateful prayers to Baba, who I knew was watching over me. We were still in.

The dual Lucks moved to seek out Senlin's losing team, who trembled in their emerald uniforms. Muyang, who had taken over for the maimed Daichi, cowered behind his sponsor. The forest god shivered, the embroidered squirrels on his silk robes retreating into the seams. But it was Daichi, standing to the side with his bandaged stumps in makeshift slings, far less jolly than when I first saw him but with his chin held high nonetheless, who the two variants of Luck approached. I was struck by their cruel nature. Hadn't Daichi suffered enough?

Luck on the left tapped their temple. "What shall I do with you?"

"He didn't even manage to cook anything! The punishment must suit the crime." The right wagged their finger.

Seon moved to my right, and I asked him in a low whisper, "Is Luck one god or two? I was never sure when I was addressing them."

"In my studies, I believe it's one god but two incarnations—Bad Luck and Good Luck." His pinky finger drifted over and brushed against mine.

I blushed in spite of the very grave moment.

"Ah, I have the perfect solution!" The left clapped their hands. "And it matches your dismal performance."

The right leaned forward and placed their index finger in the center of Daichi's forehead. "My judgment is as follows. You have failed in my feast, and so, you'll all be stricken with the bad luck of spilling liquids for the rest of your lives. Begone with you. You now are banished from my sight."

Another whirlwind force blustered, gathering the group into a spinning tornado, including the mortified and flailing minor god Senlin. They spun and spun in a dizzying pattern. Daichi turned greener than the glow of his sponsor.

"Oh, here it comes." Kama rubbed his palms together with glee. "This is going to be ugly."

The tornado turned into a spiral of contained vomit, screams from those trapped, especially Senlin's, echoing in the distance, until they vanished from sight.

Their run of bad luck had begun.

After what felt like the longest day of my life, we finally returned to our lodgings. A still withering Kama had hoped we might be able to move into Senlin's superior accommodations, but this was not offered. That was fine by me, though. The rooftop view gave us a superior view of the upcoming feast.

After a much-needed trip to the bathhouses, we dined on a picnic of leaf-wrapped sticky rice, beef satay skewers, and young coconut juice with grass jelly. It was likely much simpler than what the other groups were eating, but gathered around the fire pit with the symphony of cooing pigeons in our ears, we were all content. It had been a hard day, but we'd learned a lot. I felt readier for whatever would come next in the second meal I'd be cooking, this time for Temperance. We'd do better. We had to.

"Today brought deaths, tomorrow will likely bring more." Tala portioned off some of her meal for Ulan to eat.

I threw aside my two empty skewers and began unwrapping my parcel of sticky rice. I wasn't ready to let her burst my bubble. "If we all made it through today, there's a chance we make it through tomorrow too."

"Then, the next feast, more people will die," Tala countered in a monotone voice.

"Yes," I said, "but it's only two more left to go." I gestured toward the glittering palace in the desert. "The fact that we're still here means so much."

Seon nodded. "Cai's right. We're still in the game."

"I have to cook better. But if today taught me anything, it's to follow my instincts. It was a mistake to cook what I thought they wanted to eat. I need to cook them what I'd cook for my family, my friends, my people. I think I can do this."

"That's right," Kama said, beaming through his recently acquired wrinkles. He still looked very weak, but seemed to be holding it together. "These major gods need to learn what it means to be a daughter of the Peninsula." He bit a chunk of beef and slid it along the skewer. "We are not Xianling—no offense, pretty boy."

Seon grinned. "None taken, Lord Kama."

I *was* a daughter of the Peninsula, and I proudly claimed this.

But Kama wasn't done. "We of the Peninsula are a proud people where each pretty girl gets at least two suitors."

I rolled my eyes, but then I caught sight of Seon. There was something unreadable in his expression. I'd have to worry about that later. Right now, I needed to stay focused on getting us through tomorrow.

Temperance is the second major god that contestants have to face in the Celestial Banquet. They are the most friendly of the three and are known to be kinder to mortals than their siblings. They are known for their moderate nature. This major god is powerful enough to bring stability to those around them under any circumstances.

—*ORIGINS*, FOURTH SCROLL,
GREAT LIBRARY OF XIANLING

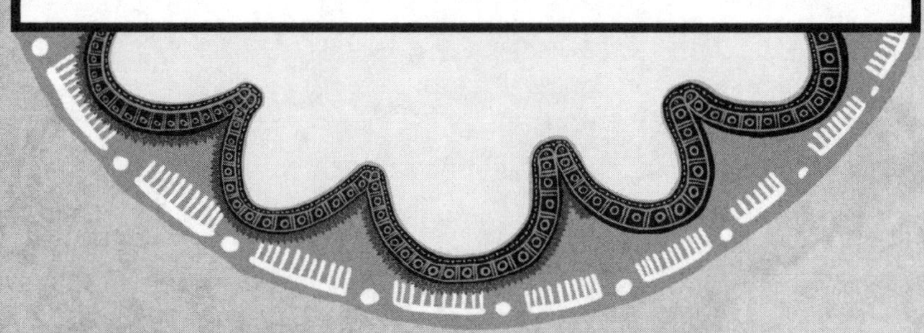

FIFTEEN

Kama woke us again for the grand restructuring of the palace—each day it would take a new form, dictated by the god in charge. I watched the swirling sands carefully as they unveiled Temperance's updated building. The biggest difference from Luck's palace was a giant archway, even taller than the Imperial Palace, with a shimmering veil under it. What did this structure mean? That, and the banquet hall was made even bigger. The lake and the open-air arena from yesterday at least gave us a bit of a hint of what to expect. Temperance seemed far more stingy than Luck was with clues.

I looked over to Seon, who watched from a perch a few feet away. Since last night, he had been avoiding me, remaining oddly quiet during the morning chatter. And with Tala being her usual aloof self, the team felt scattered as we headed into day two. It worried me. We only stood a chance if we were united.

I wanted my father here so I could turn to him for advice.

Finally, the telltale gong sounded, and we all headed to the palace. The contagion of silence seemed to have infected even Kama, who muttered to himself but shared none of his usual jokes or bluster. I reassured myself that everyone would snap out of this strange spell when the competition started. They had to.

Our four teams gathered just past the open gate, waiting for the grand entrance of the next major god we had to cook for. The buzz around us echoed my bewilderment about what the upcoming trial would be. Bo waved at me from his team. For once, I was grateful we were on separate teams. I had no doubt he'd want to ask me about the kiss when I had no satisfying answers to give. Hurting him was the last thing I wanted.

Ten minutes passed. Then another ten. Temperance was taking their time and testing everyone's patience so that even the minor gods were grumbling. Kama had slipped into an impromptu nap while standing upright, his quaking snores rising above the din. I was about to ask Seon, who had been studiously looking toward the sky, if he had any ideas about the arch, when the gong sounded again.

Citrines, bright yellow jewels capturing the sunlight, rained down into a cascading waterfall before the doors of the banquet hall. And through them emerged Temperance. They had similar masculine and feminine features to Luck, but they came in a singular form. Their robe was the deepest shade of jade, accented with pearls and various gems. A Pixiu, a hybrid creature in gold and jade that resembled a winged lion, paced beside them—its formidable presence instantly silenced the griping of the crowd. A powerful roar echoed through the space.

"Ah, welcome, welcome!" Temperance's harmonious voice ranged from high to low. "I hope you haven't been waiting too long. Ah, four to cook for me. I'm ever so delighted to be fed."

The calm nature of this god was infectious—literally. I noticed the corners of my lips tipping upward, everyone else mirroring the same eerie smile. On Tala's face, the happy expression appeared almost horrifying when combined with her angry eyebrows. I looked from Bo to Seon, who both also seemed perplexed.

"And what do I want to eat today? I want to have something very rare and tasty. Only the best for my table! A delicious ingredient that will make one glorious dish!" Temperance paused and clapped their hands. "Let's see if you all survive the acquisition of the goods, then we'll worry about the preparations. Gather your teams, and head for the arch. Quick, quick!"

The paved pathways underneath our feet began lighting up, guiding us stone by stone to our next destination, and Temperance followed on their Pixiu. As we approached the grand arch with its glittering portal, I noticed the surprised expressions around me. This made me even more grateful for our vantage point on the rooftop. I might not know what it meant, but it was nice not to go in completely unaware. Once we had all arrived at the foot of the arch, the Pixiu once again roared everyone into silence, its golden mane shaking.

"Each team will venture into the grand expanse of the Xi Desert to seek a valuable culinary treasure. Stepping through this special door will take you to separate areas where there is no chance of collusion." The major god blew their lips, and fine grains of golden sand swirled like smoke before us until they began forming an image of an unusual fowl with a wicked curved beak and puffy tail feathers. Before I had so much as a moment to exchange confusion with my team, Temperance continued.

"The desert silkie chicken is unusually illusive, so prepare yourselves to spend some time out there. Only if you manage to complete the undertaking will you be given the privilege to return. And if you fail?" They gestured at the steaming sands. "The desert can have you."

At Temperance's direction, we headed to a pile of rucksacks we were meant to fill with provided supplies.

Tala wasted no time digging through them. "They didn't provide poultices or balms for burns," she said, tossing a tied package at me, hitting my legs. "You'll need to wear the robes in the pack for the day."

I picked up the bundle. "If you meant to hit my face, you missed."

"I don't miss." Tala threw on her robes roughly, muttering Mutyan curses under her breath—some of which I recognized. Was it just me, or was she getting more ornery by the day?

I turned to Seon. "Please tell me that you know something."

"I'm sorry, but I don't. I haven't seen anything about this creature or how to capture it." He was still avoiding my gaze.

I yearned to ask why, but hesitation dried up my questions. I told myself it was because I wanted to stay focused. But was I also afraid of the answers? What a conversation with him might expose? All of a sudden, the deepest of weariness weighed down my bones—a sense of exhaustion I hadn't felt since Baba died. I quickly shook it off. I didn't know what that feeling was, I just knew that if it ever caught up to me, it would devour me whole.

The Xi Desert lies south of the Yang River. It is fabled that the minor god Xi's jeweled palace rests deep in its dunes—but no mortal has ventured far enough into the desert to find it. An offering to Xi is customary for desert wanderers, ensuring them a chance for him to guide them through. It is said that those who become lost may be lucky enough to spot a golden eagle flying above to lead them to safety.

—*GUIDES TO THE CONTINENT*, THIRD SCROLL, LIBRARY OF LUPONG

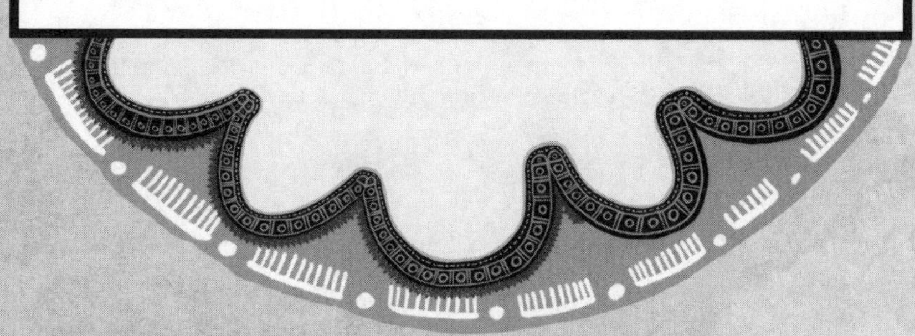

SIXTEEN

Tondo the Tall once told me of a terror that plagued sailors. When faced with the full expanse of endless open water, a wild panic and fear could take root. "It's the realization of how easily you could disappear in the vastness, be devoured whole," Tondo the Tall explained. "It's about confronting your mortality and fragility in one moment."

I felt this now as I looked upon the sand dunes. We'd been walking all day, looking for some sign of life. Now, under the guise of night, the golden hillocks resembled the dark shadows of the still sea—terrifying and beautiful at the same time.

With Tala's consent, Kama cradled Ulan while scanning the vicinity. "Sand, sand, and more sand. How are we going to find anything here?"

Seon produced a small compass from his robes. It was lacquered and decorated with many symbols and characters. The center contained a glass window with a tiny red needle. "Perhaps this can help us." I'd noticed him furtively checking it throughout the day, probably to avoid any unnecessary conversation with me, but I was glad he was now ready to share it.

"That will always point north, right?" I leaned over and took a closer look. "Tondo the Tall has one. He told me Mutyan sailors have used these for centuries."

"Yes, it's a relatively recent adoption by the Continent. I bought this in Xianling a few years ago." Seon held the compass in his right palm.

I hoped Bo was safe out there somewhere.

"Unless that can track down the desert silkie, it might as well be useless," said Tala, blunt as always. A gust of wind blew a plume of sand our way, and she wrapped a thin, gauzy fabric over her nose and mouth. "Be prepared for sudden sandstorms. Only Xi's team is safe."

The desert god's team had the full advantage over any of us, like Pubu's team on the lake. Kama appeared far more diminished than before, yet the sparks in his devious pupil-less eyes remained—weak in body, strong in spirit. He hadn't let go of Ulan, and the cormorant didn't mind its new keeper.

I followed Tala's example and covered my face with the fabric. "Other than sandstorms and running out of water, what else should we be worried about?"

"Lava geysers." Seon tightened the straps of his sword. "And who knows what else. There aren't that many explorers who venture here and return to tell the tale."

Great. We already knew we were doomed to be desiccated and lost. And now, we could also be broiled by lava. "Does anybody have any ideas on how to catch this chicken quickly so we can leave?"

"There is no record of this fowl in the Bestiary scrolls in the Great Libraries," Seon said. "It's possible that Temperance created it for the trial. Lord Kama, do you ever remember seeing the desert silkie before?" Seon tapped our sponsor's arm to divert his attention away from Ulan.

"This bird is new. Never heard of it before." Kama narrowed his eyes. "When they do this, there's always something tricky about the animal. It can belch fire, for all we know."

I scanned the horizon for anything that wasn't sand, searching for a clue about what direction we should be traveling in. This wasn't meant to be an impossible task—challenging, yes, but Temperance would remain hungry if there were no possibility of success. Achieving new levels of excellence was the goal of any feast.

"Why don't we split up, two by two, but stay in each other's sight? That way, we can scout without losing anyone," Seon suggested. "North is the most natural direction to start. I can go with Cai. Tala and Kama can walk together."

Tala grunted her approval, with Kama and Ulan joining her.

Seon and I headed east while they headed west, and once they were visible specks in the distance, with a wave we all turned north as planned. He and I still stepped around each other in a careful dance.

"Can we talk?" I asked. "This is getting awkward, and I miss how things used to be."

He paused for a moment, considering something. "Well, actually, I want to pick up where we left off last time. You never did answer my question about what I needed to do to get you to kiss me." His voice was surprisingly calm. He kept his eye on the compass in his hand. "Cai, what I really mean is . . . I care deeply for you, have for a while. I guess I just want to know if you feel the same."

I had dreamed of hearing these words from him, and yet, I still found myself momentarily speechless. How could someone like Seon have feelings for someone like me? But the sincerity in his voice wore down my defenses. I spoke my truth.

"I don't know. And I can't imagine trying to figure out my love life on top of everything else we have going on. I do know Bo means the world to me, but I'm not sure if that's just because he's the only family I've had for years, or if there's more to it."

"Well, maybe that's because you don't have anything to compare it to. You still haven't kissed me yet." The gauzy material failed to conceal the shadow of a grin tugging at his lips.

I couldn't deny the thrill buzzing under my skin, but I covered the energy with a snort. "You would know. There isn't a pretty girl who doesn't know your lips in the Peninsula. Do you ever get tired of charming your way through the womenfolk? It must be exhausting. You'd solve the sewage problem in Lupong if you applied half as much effort."

Seon chuckled and gave me a sly wink.

I cleared my throat and tried to brush his flirtations away.

The sea of sand stretched in endless waves with the crescent moon rising over the horizon. It was a relief to have the sun off our backs. Being in the kitchen, where steam hissed and the flicker of flames was ever present, I was used to sweat painting my skin and dampening my tunic, but even I was shocked by the heat of the sands.

"Wait." I spied our huntress, waving her arms. "Tala sees something."

We converged on the dune where Kama and Tala stood. Downhill and about a hundred paces away was a cave with an arched opening. As we approached, what we thought was a much smaller opening from a distance became a cavernous maw.

"Shall we?" I waved us forward.

After lighting a torch, Tala, the fearless huntress, plunged ahead of us into the cave. Kama followed her into the narrowing tunnel with Ulan honking in his arms. I went next, with Seon taking up the rear. Cooler air and darkness awaited us inside. Whether this was a natural structure or not, I couldn't tell.

After a few minutes, when Tala's torch became the single source of light, Seon stopped moving. His breaths came ragged—a disjointed sound that, when accompanied with his hand pressed against his heart, was concerning.

"I can't do this . . . I can't." He repeated under his breath. "Too dark. Tight spaces."

I walked to his side. "Are you all right?"

He shook my head. Seon's pupils were dilated, and he continued to take shallow breaths. I took his clammy hands in mine. I'd heard that the fear of enclosed spaces was similar to how I felt staring at deep water. The panic he must be experiencing was all too familiar.

I squeezed his hands tighter. "Focus on me, Seon."

Tala noticed our situation and made a gesture saying they'd wait for us, and moments later, deep in the cave, the torch held still.

I cupped Seon's cheeks and positioned my face before his. "You're safe. It's only a cave, and we'll stick together. I promise I'll do everything to keep you safe."

The trembling in his limbs increased to violent shakes. All he must have been thinking about was darkness and suffocation. If I didn't do something, he'd end up struggling to breathe soon.

I did the only thing I could think of—I kissed him. I took in the comforting scent of sandalwood. He had always smelled good from afar; up close it was so much better. I almost sighed with contentment. He tasted like the sweetest of nian gaos, but without the stickiness. His touch burned through my skin as he cradled my cheeks in his hands. I didn't know whether I was drowning or flying. I wrapped my arms around him, clinging for balance.

When he pulled away, the panic had receded.

"You don't know how long I've wanted you to do that." His voice was quiet. "I'd have rather it been under different circumstances."

"I told you I'd do anything to save you." I reached up to touch my lips. "You gave me no choice."

He winked and held out his hand.

Creatures from the Xi Desert are known to be tough because of their environment. When the major gods conjure beasts from the sands, they tend to have fiery elements—a reflection of the punishing sun over the dunes. When cooked, the fire elements manifest both in temperature and spiciness.

—*BESTIARY VOLUMES*, THIRD SCROLL,
GREAT LIBRARY OF XIANLING

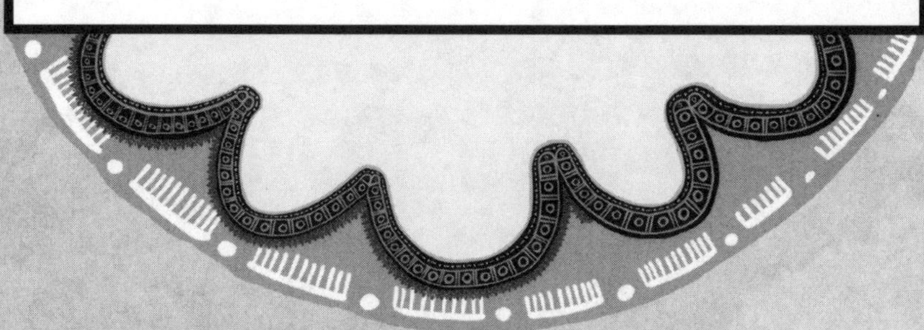

SEVENTEEN

This wasn't what I signed up for when I entered the Celestial Banquet. My plan was to win the peaches, save the Peninsula from war, and open my own restaurant.

And yet here I was now, in a cave leading underground, holding the hand of a boy. A boy who wasn't the one I'd kissed the day before.

"Thank you again." Seon squeezed my fingers. His other hand carried a torch. "We'll grab the chicken and be out of here soon."

Tala stopped a few paces in front of us. She held her torch against the wall of the tunnel, examining something. We approached and found the rocky wall covered in inscriptions. The writing wasn't anything I'd seen before—it seemed ancient. Relief carvings of the desert silkie decorated the lower half of the wall.

"Does anyone know what the writing says?" I asked.

Tala shook her head. I realized it was likely she also didn't know how to read. Seon mentioned that oral traditions were far more emphasized in Nomad culture than a written language.

Seon leaned in closer and inspected the strange lettering. "This is the old language—one meant for the gods. Lord Kama should be able to decipher it."

Our sponsor tilted his head, narrowing his eyes at the inscription. "Give me a minute. I haven't seen this in a while."

"The sooner you tell us what it says, the faster we can leave." Tala's testy tone even startled Ulan, who had until then been calm despite being underground.

I held up my hand to defend Kama. "He's trying. He's still recovering from saving Bo."

"*Right*."

I'd finally had enough of Tala's attitude. We were all stuck in this position, and she hadn't even been the guardian I wanted. "What is your problem?" I blurted at her angrily.

"You." She stepped toward me with a pointed finger. "We barely made it through the last feast. We're here because you convinced Kama you could win this. But you aren't up for the task."

I anticipated words, not venom. "Look, Tala, I am trying. This competition is nothing like I expected it to be. I'm a cook! Not a wrangler of mythical beasts. I am trying as hard as I can."

"Mistakes cost lives. Until you get that through your thick, lovesick skull, we all might as well be dead." Tala stalked off farther into the tunnel until her torch disappeared from sight.

I reached out to touch the carved desert silkie. The grainy rock was a comforting texture under my fingertips. Tala's last barb hit a nerve. "She's not wrong. I failed all of us in the last feast. If I don't redeem myself in the next one, we'll get eliminated, or worse, killed."

"Ah, I think I know what this says." Kama clapped his hands, as though he'd heard none of what just happened. "*A sacrifice must be offered*."

"But what does that *mean*?" I asked him frustratedly.

"Hell if I know, child." And with a giant weary shrug, he walked off after Tala.

I covered my eyes and sighed. "Great. Seon, you better follow them before I push you away too."

"I'm not going anywhere," Seon said comfortingly, guiding me forward. "Let's keep searching. There's got to be more to find."

"How can you be so optimistic?"

"Someone has to be." He offered his hand, and I took it.

As we headed deeper into the tunnels, my apprehension still lurked. Seon tried his best to distract me with stories about his adventures while studying in Xianling. I imagined what it would be like to have such an opportunity, to study with the finest teachers in the finest city. I was proud to be a woman, proud to be Baba's child, but it would be a lie to say I didn't resent the inherent limitations of my life.

"I've been trying to think about types of sacrifices. There are blood sacrifices, sacrifices of food, sacrifices of self. Which do you think it is?" I wondered aloud.

"I don't think Temperance would want us to take a human life . . . the gods prefer to do that themselves. It's what makes them almighty." He rolled his eyes, lifting his torch occasionally to check the walls for any inscriptions.

I felt surprisingly at ease despite the circumstances. It was almost as if Seon, with his information and books, had the ability to make things less scary just by naming each monster. He made the world feel limitless, whereas Bo reminded me more of home, of what I had. Which did I need more?

I noticed Tala and Kama had finally stopped walking. We caught up to find them at a fork in the tunnel. All of us looked at each other, no one quite sure how to pick a direction.

A subtle hissing noise caught my attention. The steamers at the Golden Lotus made a similar sound when the woven bamboo lid was dislodged. It was important to listen to its call when making dumplings, especially when there were two other hot woks vying for my attention. Where was it coming from? The tunnel itself had no visible holes or vents.

The soft sound was constant and growing louder by the minute. Tala, Kama, and Seon didn't seem to notice as they discussed which route to take, their backs to me. Ulan jumped out of Kama's arms and waddled in a circle around his feet. She headbutted Tala's left knee and was met with an absent pet on the head.

"Psst!" I called to the cormorant. "You hear it, too, don't you?"

Ulan made her way to me. I stroked her feathers and was rewarded with demands for more. "This sound, where do you think it's coming from? Should we try and find out?"

I wandered near the group and peeked down both corridors. The left was mustier than the right, which had a distinct smell of burnt noodles. I'd follow my nose. There must be something related to the hissing sound in that direction. It wouldn't hurt to take a look.

Ulan and I wandered down the right path for a few minutes. Under us, the sandy floor gave way to shiny, textured glass. A kaleidoscope of brilliant colors splashed against the walls of rock and sand. The cormorant swayed her head, marveling at the display of moving lights.

"It's pretty, isn't it?" I cooed to the bird. "I didn't think we would see something so beautiful down here. Come on, let's see where this leads."

The passageway led to a greater cavern with the same transparent glass floor suspending us over a lake of bubbling lava. It extended forward, equivalent to the size of the lake where we had to catch the iron sea serpent. Straight ahead was a smaller frosted-glass replica of the arch we stepped into aboveground, which was likely to be the way out. Finally, in each cardinal direction was an ornate altar to Temperance begging for a sacrifice. By Kama's scratchy beard, I knew what we had to do.

I was about to head back to report what Ulan and I had discovered when I spotted Tala emerging from the passageway in a fury matching the bubbling lava below.

"You had no right to take Ulan and wander off. What do you think—"

A geyser of lava shot up behind her, expanding and solidifying to block the passageway we came from. I gasped as I realized what this meant. Seon and Kama were trapped on the other side, and us, here. Tala and I didn't get along, and now she was the only help I had to complete this task.

She snatched up a startled Ulan and confronted me. "What have you done?"

"I didn't mean to wander off—"

"You got us trapped here. Kama and Seon won't be able to help if we need them. I doubt that you . . ."

I placed my hands on my hips. "Tala, I think we're supposed to be here. Look." I pointed at a few other dark pathways that led out of the room. "There are ways out of here, but see how many there are? Four. One for each team. And see those altars? Also four. One must be ours." I walked to the closest one and unloaded my pack. "It fits with the whole 'make an offering' inscription. And it looks like, for once, we're the first ones here."

I expected Tala to soften, but she continued glaring at me. Though I wanted to hate her as she clearly hated me, what I felt was the opposite: I admired her. She was a formidable warrior. But I wasn't the type to beg. And I wasn't going to let her poor opinion of me get in the way of winning this thing.

"Come on. The sooner we solve the sacrifice problem, the faster we get out of here with the special chicken." I stood before the southern altar, which I chose because of proximity, and examined it at every angle.

The altar was a true and spectacular likeness of Temperance's rounded face, with an open mouth complete with perfect teeth and a sloping tongue with a flat tip. It was made of textured limestone. This contrasted with the glass under my feet, which was so transparent and smooth I could see each bubble of the red-gold molten lava below.

A few beads of sweat trickled down my hairline, confirming the rising heat in the chamber.

Tala ignored me. Meanwhile, the other teams had started to trickle in, each centering around one of the altars. I noticed that they, too, had two members each in the chamber—I was disappointed not to see Bo among them.

We had to work together, or we wouldn't escape this underground prison. I tried another tactic—clearly pleasantries and civility weren't working.

"Tala—do you want to burn to death in here with Ulan? Help me figure out what to sacrifice so we can leave with our chicken." I tapped my temple. "The sooner we figure this out, the better."

Tala set down her pack and sat on it. This seemed like a good sign. I followed suit.

"It won't be anything too obvious," I continued. "Not like food, drink, or paper money offerings like they take at the temples—though a monk will swindle you out of every coin if you let them."

"In Mutyan culture, the gods accept dances and songs."

I scratched my temple, something nagging me. "For a Nomad girl, you seem to know a lot about Mutya."

She reacted with a dismissive grunt.

Everything about Tala was prickles and vinegar. "The way you swim is unlike any Nomad. And that spice you fed me. Pretty rare. God-given even . . ."

She narrowed her eyes. "Get to the point."

"What's your Mutyan connection?"

Her lips remained a thin, closed line, but I wasn't going to give up so easily. I knew a thing or two about Mutyan culture, having been practically raised by Tondo the Tall. She was hiding something, and I was going to find out what it was.

"And if you're a Nomad, aren't you supposed to have a Zhenniao? That's something that even a backwater country bumpkin like me knows. Personally, I think Ulan is much better than some poisonous eagle, though." I kept my mouth moving, hoping to provoke her out of her semi-silence.

She groaned through her teeth. "Can you ever be quiet?"

A reaction was better than the passive-aggressive rage she'd been marinating in.

"You're not even a Nomad, are you?" I tried. "I know about Mutya because of my adopted Mutyan uncle. He was my father's best friend and kept an eye on me since I was orphaned. What's your excuse?"

Finally, something softened in her dark eyes as if she had sheathed the sharpness of her gaze.

"My uncle wasn't as honest or honorable. He killed my parents. All because he wanted power."

I put my hand over my mouth to cover my excited shriek at realizing she was a famous princess. She was one of Tondo the Tall's stories from home. It also didn't escape me that we were both orphans all this time. As tragic as this was, I was comforted that I wasn't alone, making the best of my life without the presence of those I wanted most.

"The Empress stole my baba from me." I pressed my lips into a thin line. "If I could, I would have killed the Empress already. But poisoning her is out of the question."

"Get in line." Tala cracked a wicked smile. "She funded my uncle's rise to the throne. I hold both of them responsible and won't rest until I get my vengeance."

This was it. Something we agreed on with our full hearts. Something we could fight for, side by side. I wriggled my toes and found my feet were warm. I reached down to press my palm against the glass floor to confirm my suspicions. Hot. There must be a time limit to solve Temperance's puzzle. I grabbed Tala's hand.

"Let's take her down together."

The way to the Mutyan Isles is perilous! Only the most skilled sailors from the Continent have successfully navigated the whirlpools of the unforgiving Singing Sea to reach Mutyan's shores. Some scholars have theorized that the major gods have no power past the lands of the Continent, but only the Mutyans themselves know the truth.

—*ON MUTYAN HISTORY*, ELEVENTH SCROLL, LIBRARY OF LUPONG

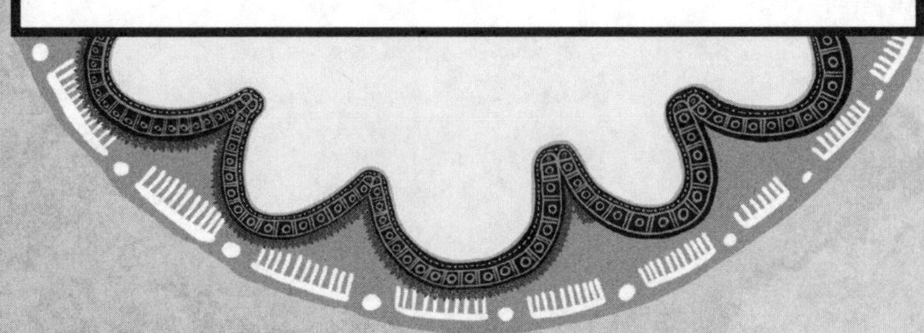

EIGHTEEN

"I now know what a dumpling feels like." I wiped the line of perspiration from my brow. "Kama and Seon better thank us that they're not here roasting in our place." Another ten minutes had passed, and we still didn't have any bright ideas about how to make this offering.

"Tell them when we get out."

Tala's answers were still terse. Considering the environment, I didn't blame her. But she had also revealed something very personal to me. In order to keep our truce, I had to return the favor. "Ask me anything. Nothing is taboo."

Her dark brow arched, distorting the red tattoo on her forehead. "Anything?"

I stretched out my arms, giving her permission.

"Fine." She cut me off. "I'll start. Who would it be if you had to choose between Bo and Seon?"

I puckered my lips and breathed through my nose. Of course she'd ask. Her tone wasn't accusatory or hostile. It might be from heatstroke, but I swore there was a twinkle in her eyes. I sighed and answered with honesty. "I don't know. I like them both for different reasons. Though with Bo, I didn't see him this way until . . ."

"You're not answering my question."

I almost choked on my spit. "I'm trying to. So, uh, what's it like to be a princess?"

"Shhhh!" Tala hissed. But after looking around and confirming that no one had heard, she answered. "It used to be great. I had my family and it was all I needed. But now I really do feel just as much Nomad as I feel Mutyan. I was smuggled out of my country and adopted by my aunt who married a Nomad. They raised me from the age of five. This is an important part of my history. Anyway, I barely tasted royalty before it all fell apart. Now if you tell anyone, I will murder you and throw your carcass into the deepest depths of the Singing Sea."

"Okay, okay." I laughed. "But seriously, your secret is safe with me until you're ready to share it." Then, a commotion pulled our attention elsewhere.

A desert silkie shot out from Songwon's altar, but before he could catch it, Zi Rui pushed him away to embrace the flying ball of feathers. A shouting match between Zi Rui and Songwon ensued.

"Thank you for your contribution." Zi Rui stood with Zolzaya, the fearsome Nomad warrior. He held a dark fowl with golden-tipped feathers by the legs as the arch portal, a small replica of what we stepped through, flickered to life.

Songwon raised his fist. "You stole that from me."

The expression of anguish on his face broke me. I'd seen that expression before when Baba was robbed on his way home from work. He ate very little until his next pay to ensure that I kept growing. Fire burned my bones remembering that feeling of helplessness.

I rose to my feet and ran toward the arch; my index finger pointed at the dirty thief. "Zi Rui, you give that back, you dirty cheat!"

Tala positioned herself in front of me and, with a gentle yet firm hand, pushed me back. She raised her chin and addressed

Zolzaya. "Honored sister, will you please return what has been stolen?"

The tall warrior with the striking face had tattoos similar to Tala's—the large red points marking her brow and various others with intricate geometric patterns covering her bare muscular arms. Her ink-black hair was in plaits with colorful ties at the ends. She stood at least a head and a half taller than my teammate.

"Little sister," she said, addressing Tala, "I cannot do what you ask. My duty is to the one who has paid the competition price. I must protect his interests. If I need to kill you, I will, but I do not desire it."

I had no doubt that she could massacre us all in no time, with Tala putting up the biggest resistance. This exchange only proved to me how much respect these two women had for each other.

Tala lowered her chin. "Then I will not have your hands stained by the blood of your kin, honored sister."

Zolzaya nodded to Tala and shoved Zi Rui through the portal before disappearing herself.

"I'm guessing you saved our lives?" I asked Tala.

"We live by a strict code. She would have killed all of us if I insisted."

All the anger I had had burned out, and what was left was empathy.

Songwon and his noble, Yoshihiro, slumped their shoulders. They returned to their altar, where Yoshihiro then withdrew something old and rusted from his pockets. He placed what appeared to be a bracelet onto the offering plate. The plate simmered, making the piece of jewelry disappear. Moments later, the desert silkie shot out of the altar, and Pubu's team left through the portal.

The sacrifice must be something of value. To anyone else, what Yoshihiro offered was some old junk. Worthless. But clearly it wasn't. I might have solved this puzzle.

"If we want the desert silkie, we need to give it something of personal value." I declared with a clap of my hands.

"You mean a blood sacrifice?" Tala rubbed her forehead. "But we are not feeding Death. We're dealing with Temperance. They represent moderation, humility, and prudence. Not violence and death."

"You're not listening to me." I stomped my foot to get her attention. "The value is individual, and it depends on the person." I picked up my father's wok from my pack. I'd been bringing it with me each day, as a talisman of sorts. "This means the world to me while you see it as an old, ordinary frying pan."

This was the only thing I had left of Baba in this world, and normally I would risk my life for this dented piece of metal. But there was only one thing more important. Winning.

I picked up the wok and readied to set it down on the tongue pedestal.

"What are you doing?" Tala asked. "We're not even sure that is the right offering."

"Yes, it is. It's the most valuable object I own," I argued.

Tala shrugged and threw her hands up in the air. "Do what you want."

I placed the piece of cookery on the pedestal and waited. I had to be right. There was no other . . .

"Did you hear that?" Tala whipped her head around.

"What?" Before I had a chance to ask again, my ears detected the very distinctive sound of a cluck. The elusive desert silkie came shooting out from the altar like a lit firecracker. Tala sprinted and caught the fuzzy projectile in her arms. Ulan wandered by my feet and squawked from what I guessed was jealousy.

As Tala secured the chicken, Temperance took Baba's wok away.

I had cradled it so many times when I was lonely or needed my father. It allowed me to be fooled into thinking I wasn't alone;

otherwise, I was like any other impoverished orphan in Lupong. It was my father's legacy.

No, *I* was his legacy. Baba would have wanted my team to advance to the feast. He always insisted that I needed nothing but my memories of him to keep his spirit alive.

Tala handed me the desert silkie, and by the time she picked up Ulan to soothe her, the blasted chicken had pecked me at least half a dozen times. Wincing, I held my prize by the legs and waited for the portal to appear. I looked around. Xi's team must have gotten their silkie and headed out while we were arguing. We were the last to leave.

"Look, we didn't die after all. Are you disappointed?" I asked Tala.

She grunted.

The portal shimmered before us. The other side showed the courtyard with Seon and Kama waiting.

"I mean, come on. We did it, and we ended up not killing each other."

Tala rolled her eyes, but I saw a hint of a smile on her lips.

"After you, Your Highness." I bowed, then gestured for her to go first.

She playfully shoved me forward, causing me to arrive on the other side on my ass with the squawking chicken in my hand.

After returning from the desert, it was already morning. I only wanted a nice bath to purge the sand and sweat from my skin, maybe even a nap, but I had to cook first.

Kama and Seon entered the banquet hall first to help prepare. Our sponsor god had Seon stoke the cooking fires and ready the kitchen for our arrival. As much as I wanted to chat about what happened, there was no time. I enlisted Kama's help in gathering ingredients.

When we returned, Tala eyed the loot. "What are you going to cook?"

"I'm not sure yet. It's a fowl, so a broth would be a good start." I checked the chicken that she had prepared for butchering. The feathers were plucked and gathered into a pile to be repurposed for her arrows.

I started cutting and found that the desert silkie had charcoal-black meat. Without any further information, I assumed that its properties were otherwise similar to that of the common silkie served in stocks, soups, and stews. Silkie meat wasn't as plentiful as that in a typical chicken, but its flavors were far more complex.

"What are you going to make?" Kama appeared at my side, lifting the lid of a boiling pot and stirring the contents with a ladle. The pungent aromas of dried chilies, peppercorns, ginger, shallots, and spring onions spiced the air.

"A hot pot stew, I think." I deboned the silkie chicken breast and sliced the meat. "Then I'll serve it at the table with glass noodles."

I'd made this dish for Bo's family when I last visited the farm. Their kitchen was so full of laughter that day. Bo's sisters had helped me prepare while he brewed a tea made of roasted brown rice for his mother. This dish was a staple in Lupong.

Kama creased his lips and bobbed his head. "Interesting choice. Very Peninsula. Make sure you use the dragon stones as the heating element when serving." Then he left me to my work.

Once the soup stock was underway and infused with the desert silkie chicken, I dipped my spoon into the bubbling broth to test it. Warmth filled my stomach as I sipped. The rich, gamey flavor of the chicken rose above the simmering spices. A pleasant numbness tickled my tongue, and a puff of smoke emerged from my nostrils. The spiciness had a sour, savory dynamic that, combined with the ingredients I'd chosen, created a wonderfully complex profile.

This broth had a deliciously sour note that would raise eyebrows in the most luxurious district in Xianling. And this was my special touch—the tartness was a signature Mutyan influence Tondo the Tall had taught me. Being a cook didn't always equate to having full access to the food I was making. It was a job, first and foremost. I went to sleep every night with a growling, angry stomach as a companion. But this competition could change that.

The desert silkie should be tender and ready for tasting soon.

A flick of my paring knife transformed carrots, cucumbers, and radishes into roses and chrysanthemums as a garnish. In Lupong I supplied Yi Feng, the local expert in decorative carving, with the best-dried fish maw in the city in exchange for lessons in his craft. I bartered with the only currency I had—my time and my ingenuity to trade with those in the same position as me.

I returned to the market area to fetch the dragon stones Kama recommended. I'd only ever seen two of them before, and they were in the kitchens of the most prestigious restaurants. They were the size of a palm, oval with a flat bottom and domed top, and provided constant heat—the brighter the stone was, the hotter the temperature. Dragon hunters found these in ancestral nests among eggs and often died trying to steal them.

I wrapped the two in heavy burlap cloth and transported them to my station.

As I prepared the stones, a loud explosion erupted. The floor shook, and the guttural screams coming from Xi's team halted the activity in the hall.

The metallic scent of blood hung in the air.

King Lapu and Queen Kassia were the last monarchs of the Golden Age of Mutya.

Riza, the king's brother, won the throne with a violent coup. It is suspected that his armies were funded by a secret alliance with the Empress of Wan.

The sole rightful heir to the throne, Princess Ligaya, is suspected to have been murdered along with her parents by King Riza himself.

The massacre of the royal family is one of the bloodiest in Mutyan history.

—*ON MUTYAN HISTORY*, FOURTEENTH SCROLL, LIBRARY OF LUPONG

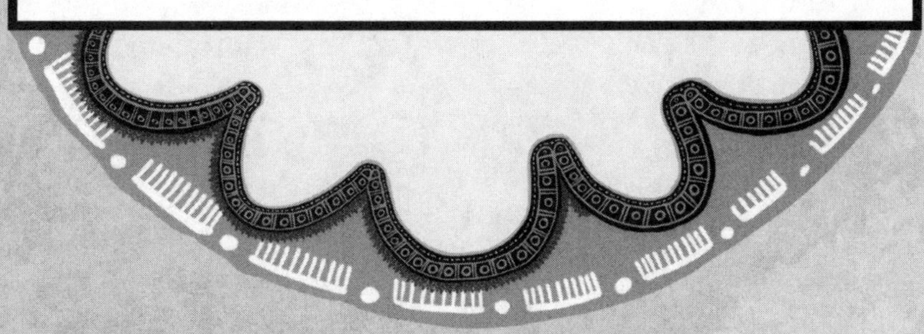

NINETEEN

Everyone rushed to Xi's kitchen, crowding the area to assess the damage. In place of the stove was a dark crater next to which the minor god wore charred, bloody pieces of his candidate all over his golden silk robes.

"What in eighteen hells happened?" the bearish Guolin asked.

Xi blinked but didn't answer. He was the desert god, so this was meant to be their challenge, but now . . . His once immaculate ink hair stood on its singed ends. His hands trembled as he reached up to pop his ears. If he had been mortal, he'd also have been blown to bits.

"Speak!" Guolin shook him and then smacked his cheeks. "I don't want my own candidate's body in pieces. What caused all this?"

"Chan-yeol was making a stir-fry. He was there, and then, suddenly, he wasn't. I don't know what happened."

Zi Rui stepped up beside Guolin and lowered his voice. "He was a renowned culinary scholar. There must be some property of the desert silkie that he never expected."

He then shook his head disappointedly, retreating to his kitchen with his bearish sponsor god in tow. Bo shot me a look of concern before escorting Songwon back to his kitchen. He mouthed, *Be careful.*

It shouldn't have been a surprise that the desert silkie, like the sea serpent, could be deadly.

My team walked back to our station, and I automatically headed toward my pot.

"Wait!" Seon grabbed my arm. "Not until we figure out how to make sure you don't explode. That was awful back there."

"No boom," Tala grunted in agreement.

We all looked at each other somberly. There wasn't a clear solution because there was nothing out of the ordinary with the meat by appearance. There were no clues as to the cause of the explosion.

"Let me just experiment with it a bit. I'll be careful," I told them.

With the utmost care, I slowly fished out a piece of the desert silkie and brought it to my mouth. I didn't even make contact, yet the heat and spice radiating from the meat scalded the tip of my tongue. A tiny blister formed from the exposure.

Seon brought me a cup of cold water to soothe it.

"Okay, so we know it's superhot, but that doesn't explain a full explosion. Frostbite berries might work to balance it out. I think I saw some in the market," I said, then finished gulping down the rest of the water.

Seon nodded and went off to fetch what I requested.

My tongue throbbed from the pain. The broth itself was delicious, but if the silkie meat was inedible, I had a problem. As much as I'd love to attempt an assassination of the Empress, I didn't want the rest of my team to suffer as well.

The frostbite berries should work. They'd been used before when dealing with volatile, fiery ingredients like dragon's breath fungus, firebird nests, and ruby treasure arowanas. The berries, which were harvested in the northern Nomad territory, were a common staple in their diet and a big export. The properties of the fruit neutralized the dangerous aspects of powerful ingredients in temperature and spice level.

Just as Seon presented me with a basket of light blue berries, Bo ran up and shoved it away. "Don't use those. Songwon found traces of them in the explosion."

"That explains that." Kama puckered his face. "I suspect that Chan-yeol, like you, was trying to counteract that potent effect." Wow. I had almost walked into exactly the same trap. Clearly us chefs thought alike.

"Let me go see what else I can find out," said Seon. He walked off, Kama and Tala in his wake, leaving me and Bo alone.

"That means I'll have to find another solution. I don't want bits of me sprayed everywhere." I pressed my fingertips against my temples. "It needs to be soon because my dish is almost done."

"Now that I'm here, can we talk?"

"It's not the time. I have to cook and—"

Before I could finish my sentence, he scooped me into his arms and kissed me. The fierceness of his kiss left me sagging against him. Bo had never shown this much confidence in anything in his life. This was not the same boy I once knew.

"If we don't get out of this alive, I'd never forgive myself for not doing that. We can talk later, but I just needed you to know how I feel. It's always been you." He pulled away, stared at my face as if he were memorizing it, and then returned to his team's kitchen.

How was it possible for two kisses from two totally different boys to both feel so good?

After shaking my head to dislodge every thought that didn't relate to cooking, I ran down a list of known substances with similar qualities to frostbite berries. Kama, who had apparently returned to our station, raised his hand to offer a suggestion. Had he seen what just happened?

"If you're going to say anything, need I remind you that I'm the one holding the cleaver." I lifted the mentioned blade to show him.

He scoffed, then rubbed his belly. "I'm not interested in that. I was going to ask you to make me some noodles while we waited."

I thought to the last time I made him noodles back at my stall. I could certainly pull together my Lupong classic here. I just needed eggs and flour. And then I remembered. There was an auction that morning, and Tondo the Tall had rewarded me with . . . icy spicy peppers! This might be the solution we needed. And I could afford to give Songwon an extra one to help Bo's team to advance too.

"Hot and cold, hot and cold, hot and cold," I repeated to myself, then filled Kama in.

I still had three peppers left in my pack. Kama sent Tala to our lodging to retrieve them, summoned Seon, and then we all gathered again. "Do you really think this will work?" Seon asked nervously.

"Only one way to find out," I said.

"I would use the whole pepper instead of cutting it," our sponsor god chimed in, making a scattering gesture. "Everyone move away from the splatter area."

I winced at the possibility of being overcooked into a bursting human sausage.

I dropped one tiny, bicolored pepper into the stone bowl of simmering silkie hot pot. I closed my eyes and waited. No boom.

My heart raced in my chest as I used chopsticks to pick up the small morsel of silkie chicken. I touched it again to my tongue; it didn't wither. Instead, it was blessed with a very delicate, flavorful meat, sending fireworks of delicious prickles in my mouth. The desert silkie's fiery spiciness lingered and still packed a forceful punch. The dish was everything I'd hoped for.

"No boom," Tala declared with a hint of a smile on her lips.

I laughed and danced on the spot. "It worked!"

"Are you ready to serve it to Temperance?" Seon asked.

I checked over my shoulder to see that Songwon hadn't finished cooking yet. The chopped portions of desert silkie remained on the counter. "Not yet. I'm going to help him first."

My fellow candidate stood alone by his stove with his hand cupping his smooth chin. I approached him and gave him a tentative wave.

"I'm here to help if you want to accept it." I held out my hand, revealing the icy spicy pepper. "Add it so you can safely neutralize the desert silkie. Make sure to add the pepper in whole."

The tension dissipated from his narrow face. "Thank you."

"I want to formalize our alliance."

There was no hesitation when he offered his open hand. I grabbed it and shook it.

"May we reach the final feast together." He lowered his head in a slight bow. "You're an honorable cook, Cai. You make a worthy opponent."

"As do you."

I returned to my kitchen to put the final touch on my dish—a splash of black aged vinegar to the broth. The acidity provided a better balance in the overall flavor. Black pieces of the desert silkie floated like ebony islands against the rich cinnabar shade of the hot pot broth. Amidst the bubbling broth, the vegetables—deep green leaves with orange, dark pink, and light green blossoms—created a kaleidoscope of tropical colors.

It told a visual story of Lupong surrounded by the turbulent Singing Sea—how the humble Peninsula was a vibrant place, despite the Continent's view that it was a desolate backwater. It was the defiant testament that we existed. Our sovereignty was important, and the Empress had no right to invade our land and our home. This dish was a reminder that winning the peaches of immortality would mean freedom for the Peninsula. I wanted the Empress to eat my defiance.

I shouldn't keep Temperance waiting. Zi Rui, as usual, was the first to finish.

I served the Pixiu first. I had prepared raw cuts of liver, kidneys, and filets of sweet plains bison for it upon Kama's advice. With its coiled mane and fearsome roar, this creature was far more intimidating than the gentler Qilin. Its massive chest expanded and contracted with each heavy, echoing breath as it ate the bowl with great gusto.

Thank you, Kama.

The gong sounded when I reached the spot before the massive doors, and I was allowed inside. If I had been asked what I envisioned Temperance's table to look like, I'd imagine the god squatting on a mound of gold like a smug hen over a cache of eggs. Instead, I was greeted with two larger-than-life busts of Bo and Seon. The carved stone faces were as tall as Zolzaya. Multiple beams of light illuminated the sculptures and the floating stone steps leading to the major god's platform.

Between them, Temperance sat on a stone throne before a matching table with carved Pixiu for legs. Their living Pixiu had followed me in, promptly falling asleep at their feet. The soft snores echoed in the dark chamber. Temperance's robes were ever-changing, one moment lavender silk embroidered with gold lilies, and the next, liquid silver with golden vines of jasmine blossoms snaking across it. The prune-faced Empress sat beside them, staring me down. I would never give her the satisfaction of flinching.

"Such a serious expression for such a young face." Temperance clucked their tongue.

The corners of my mouth turned up despite my internal objection.

"You carry such a heavy burden. I might say that the weight of the Peninsula is on your shoulders." The major god chuckled to themselves and licked their lips as I unloaded the stone bowl hot pot and accompanying platter. "This is quite unusual, very much so. How will it taste, I wonder?"

"I've never seen such a dish," the Empress sneered. "It looks terribly common. What makes you think you have a chance here with this?"

"Because you've never tasted anything from the Peninsula before."

She squinted at me and frowned. "Nor do I care to. Your uncivilized land is nothing but a bridge to the Singing Sea. The sooner I conquer it, the closer I get to securing the *entire* Continent."

"The Peninsula is stronger than you think."

"Now, now. This isn't a political arena. We only care about food here." Temperance pursed their lips.

I silently savored the pained expression on the old bat's face.

Temperance dipped their finger into the simmering broth and tasted it. Of course, had they been mortal, they'd have been more cautious and used a spoon instead. "Do you recognize my decorations? Such lovely boys, don't you think?"

I held on to my silence like a shield and prepared to be analyzed against my will. I came away from the last feast more cautious and less chatty. If these major gods wanted to pry anything else other than a meal from me, I'd be kicking and screaming about it. The smile plastered on my face thanks to Temperance's strange power masked the growing irritation building between my arched brows.

The major god pulled out a few pieces of the desert silkie from the broth. "The one on the left is Bo, am I right? Handsome and rugged. Your childhood friend—not a towering intellectual by any means, but whatever he lacks, he makes up for in his perfect physique. The farm boy is as sweet as sakura mochi."

My shoulders tensed, my cheek muscles ached from the unnatural smile, and my teeth and gums were dry from being exposed to the air. Still, I clung to my silence.

"And the other one, very pretty. A wonderful specimen of male beauty, I must say. Very learned and, more important, quite wealthy. Correction, *was* wealthy because he's been disowned by the House of the Crane. I highly doubt he has a coin to his name after paying the tithe, though who knows, as the standard for richesse is so meager in the Peninsula. And with a face like that, I'm sure the lack of coin won't be an issue. He could always make his way as a humble culinary scholar, or as a hired swordsman if he chooses the bolder path. If he were to be a cut of meat, he'd be a delectable marbled wagyu."

What Temperance had said was nothing I hadn't heard before. If this was a ploy to get a reaction out of me, the major god hadn't counted on my infinite amount of stubbornness.

"Why haven't you decided? Or have you? Mortal decisions are fascinating to me because of the unintended consequences."

When I stayed silent, Temperance snapped their fingers, and Bo's and Seon's faces changed, shifting, sliding slices of red sandstone in such a way that they both formed the same face—mine. The scraping, grating, gravelly sound almost drowned out his question. "Still not going to say anything?"

I balled my hands. My short fingernails dug into my palms while my knuckles gleamed white.

"This child knows nothing about love. If she's lucky, she can be a fourth or fifth concubine of some country lord." The

Empress steepled her bony fingers. "She is dust. She only stands before you because she was chosen by her perennial loser of a minor god."

"Take Kama's name out of your mouth," I threatened, before I could control myself. "He loves the people of the Peninsula—"

"Yes, love is important." Temperance held up a finger interjecting, and both mine and the Empress's mouths closed. "Let's return to the matter at hand."

The major god plucked a black silkie chicken wing from the broth and nibbled, then sucked the fragile bones dry noisily. "You don't want to choose because you're selfish. You're in an enviable spot of holding a heart in each hand. Do you enjoy squeezing them to see how much blood runs down your fingers?"

That was my tipping point. Between the Empress's imperial ambitions and this unwanted interrogation into my love life, anger bubbled within me as I chose my words. After already challenging an earthly tyrant, defying gods, major or minor, didn't seem too different. "You should talk. You're a major god, and you force your will on others. You accuse me of manipulation when *you* are the puppet master." I pointed to the painful smile on my face. "How is this any different?"

Temperance arched their thin, drawn brows. "You question that I want to bring happiness? Such an impudent little mortal you are. Need I remind you that you are here competing for my peaches of immortality? Lucky for you, I am feeling forgiving today."

Temperance picked up the stone bowl with their bare hands and drank the broth in gulps. Droplets splashed onto their beautiful robe. Once empty, they turned their attention to the carved flowers, even going as far as to lick the banana leaves clean. They wiped their mouth with their sleeve.

"Good meal. Quite satisfactory. You can cook, mortal."

The Empress scoffed but didn't protest.

I swallowed the praise as if it were a spiky fishbone scratching down my throat. My manners prompted me to utter the requisite "Thank you."

Temperance flicked their wrist in a dismissive gesture. "Pray that you impress Indulgence next, and that you learn to hold your tongue. They're not as congenial as I am."

I stumbled out of the room, reeling over everything Temperance had said to me. I knew they were just trying to break me—the gods were known for toying with humans, meddling in our affairs despite supposedly disdaining us—but it still hurt.

It wasn't until I was back outside that I realized what had just happened. They had liked my dish.

The Pixiu is a fearsome yet noble creature—the lion-dog companion of Temperance. When not by its master's side, the beast is known to wander the Continent protecting people from wild animals of the mortal world. It is common to see a humble altar and offerings to the Pixiu in isolated villages.

—*BESTIARY VOLUMES*, SECOND SCROLL,
GREAT LIBRARY OF XIANLING

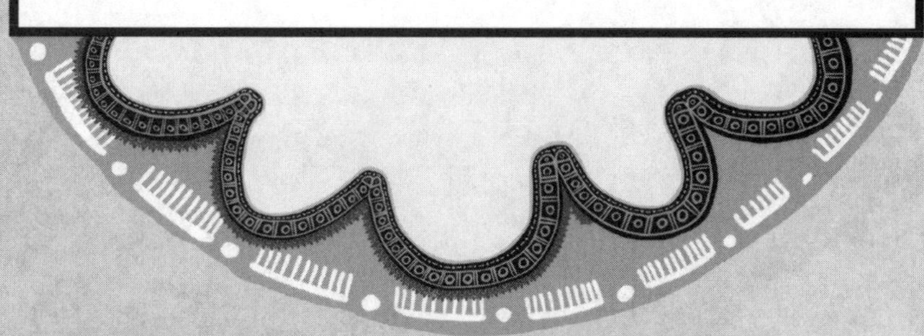

TWENTY

After all the chefs were officially dismissed, we filed out into the courtyard for our rankings. Though I had the verbal reassurance that I'd done well, and a dead chef on Xi's team meant almost certain elimination for them—they had apparently barely managed to cobble a dish together without their chef—I couldn't brush away the seed of worry.

Bo gave me an encouraging smile as he stood by Songwon.

Tala and Seon flanked me from both sides in solidarity.

The grand stone wall emerged from the trembling ground. The Pixiu hopped onto the rising ledge, snarling at us from above. Under its massive paws were the four remaining bound banners.

Temperance appeared, as did the agonizing smiles on our faces. "Your dishes for this feast were interesting and better than I expected. Three were outstanding. One of you served something inferior."

The legendary lion-dog roared, the tremendous sound unfurling the banners—again Guolin's umber was first, next was Pubu's seafoam, and third, Kama's gray. I screamed and raised my fist while Seon and Tala whooped. Even tired Kama managed to clap. Xi's golden banner was, as expected, last. I bowed my head thinking of Chan-yeol perishing in the kitchen so violently. The competition was so intense that we moved past these deaths as though they were nothing. But they all meant something. My fire to win burned brighter.

As if rubbing it in, the major god laughed and addressed the losing team. “Ah, team of gold. Your reward for failure is quite lovely indeed. Everything you consume for the rest of your days will taste like your favorite food and drink. Aren’t I such a generous god?”

As with the previous losing team, Xi and his minions were swept up and away from the palace in a whirlwind. I knew better than to take Temperance’s curse at face value. I couldn’t imagine eating the same thing for the rest of my life. I’d be miserable. All of us here loved food, its variety, its exciting combinations. Those poor souls.

With one last feast to go, I vowed to see Kama’s gray ride high above the others.

The Celestial Banquet might offer the greatest of rewards, but it also snatched lives and limbs. Five teams started this, and there were only three of us left with Indulgence’s trial and feast to come. What would be my sacrifice?

Tala bumped my elbow as we all walked toward our quarters. “Where is your head at?”

“Everywhere but here.” I followed her up the rope ladder to our rooftop.

As soon as we reached the top, she put Ulan into my arms. “Pet the bird.”

The cormorant settled into the crook of my chest and nuzzled my chin. With each stroke, the tension drained from my body. Ulan’s soft feathers tickled my skin.

"The last meal you served was phenomenal," said Seon, emerging onto the roof and approaching me, Kama huffing behind him. Seon's eyes helped make everything feel a little less bleak. "That was the real you. The chef whose noodles the people of Lupong dream about."

"Very good food," Tala echoed.

The sincerity of their praise touched me. Baba had taught me to never ask for compliments when cooking. To be able to serve and express my creativity was gratitude enough.

As I thanked them, I noticed the prepared meal laid out for us by the fire. Various grilled meats, fish, and vegetables accompanied packages of lotus leaf–wrapped sticky rice and pots of jasmine tea.

"Why don't we all get something to eat and chat?" I lowered Ulan to the ground. The cormorant waddled away to perform her hobby of harassing the pigeons.

"Is it okay if we join you?" Bo asked, emerging onto the rooftop. Hearing his voice instantly brought me home. I nodded excitedly, ignoring the surly expression that had come over Seon's face. Bo gestured down the ladder and soon, the rest of his team followed, with Pubu last, floating upward on a misty, watery cloud.

After a brief set of introductions, we all gathered and sat down, sharing the meal. Talk quickly turned to what had happened in the desert that day.

"We need to neutralize Zi Rui," Songwon declared, staring into the flames of the fire pit. "He's far too good a cook to discount."

"He's the only one the Empress will allow to cook for her outside of this competition." Yoshihiro, the noble representative of Pubu's team was a quiet, soft-spoken older gentleman who embodied respectability. "And he is the only one with membership to two guilds—Blade and Palate. He has no equal in the kitchen."

Bo raised his teacup. "There has to be a weakness. He can't be perfect." I had been thinking the same thing.

"He might as well be." Seon muttered, "Cai is an amazing cook, and I'm sure Songwon is as well, but Zi Rui has the upper hand. Those guilds give unfettered access—to ingredients, to information. He has experience that just isn't possible to get elsewhere."

Tala flashed me a warning look as she fed Ulan bits of fish.

Bo didn't miss a beat. "Fancy qualifications mean nothing. Songwon and Cai are in this competition, and they actually worked for it themselves. Are you saying they're less worthy because they're not part of a guild, because if you are . . ." Bo made a fist and pounded the roof.

Seon jumped to his feet. "I'm not diminishing their skills. All I said was that being a part of a guild is an advantage we can't ignore. To dismiss Zi Rui as a common cook is foolish."

"Of course you would think that! You're a noble. You've never had to work hard at anything in your life. All you needed was bags full of gold to get to the Celestial Banquet." Bo stood to his full height and towered over Seon by at least half a head.

"And all you needed was to ask for a favor from our sponsor god," Seon fired back. "If Kama hadn't decided to use you as a pawn, you'd be back in Lupong."

I glanced over at Kama and Pubu, willing them to come break this up. But they were oblivious, deep in their own conversation. I wedged myself between Bo and Seon. Fighting now when we were so close to the peaches of immortality was not an option. "You two need to stop before you say something you can't take back." I slowly pushed them farther apart. "We're allies. We need to work together."

I shot a glance at Tala, who chose to stare up at the stars instead of meeting my eyes.

"We're all nervous right now, and it's probably a good time to take a breath."

Bo reached for my hand. "Can we go for a quick walk? We need to talk."

Seon looked at me, asking me to stay with his eyes. But Bo was my best friend.

I decided I'd deal with Seon later. Bo and I excused ourselves and headed down to the street. The neighborhood around the building was quiet. It might have been designed this way to prevent distractions for the competitors. Tea shops, acupuncturists, and herbal shops populated the street. The persimmon trees lined the way with their golden-orange fruits glowing under the streetlamps like miniature evening suns. The air was sweet with an underlying earthy scent from steeping tea leaves. Such a beautiful city and no time to enjoy it. Before the banquet, everything in my life was already figured out—it was a simple life, yes, but one with clear purpose. Now, I found myself with more questions than answers.

Bo offered his arm, reminding me of our routine in Lupong.

"Do you like Xianling?" I asked him.

"Not really. From what little I've seen, it's noisy, there's too many people, too many voices. There's not enough room to breathe for my liking. It's like people are insects living in one overcrowded hive, just waiting to be stomped out." He tugged at the collar of his uniform. "All I want to do is take you back to Lupong with those peaches. I'd even give you mine if we won. It'll be you though. I feel it in my bones."

I blushed at the open display of affection and laughed. "I don't know if I'll win. Bo, I . . ."

"If you're still wondering or unsure about how I feel about you, I can kiss you again. What I need to know now is how you feel."

The quick change of subject took me by surprise. I found myself babbling, "We've been friends forever. After you died, I was so happy to see you alive. I acted on impulse. Kissing you then felt like the most natural thing in the world. But . . ."

My feelings for Bo were complicated. I wasn't ready to decide what they were. Especially with Seon in the picture.

"I can't get distracted by anything," I finished. "I want to win those peaches because the Empress is set on conquering the Peninsula soon. War will kill us." I tucked a stray dark strand behind my ear. "We have to win. Your team or mine."

"You didn't answer my question. When I got a second chance at life, I realized you are the most important person to me." He stopped and placed his hands on my shoulders. "I can't believe it took me this long to act on it. Do you feel the same way I do? I need to know."

The true answer would crush Bo. How could I tell the boy who had begged a god to join a deadly competition and then died for me that, at best, I didn't know how I felt? Not to mention that I had kissed Seon too. I didn't want to have to choose or change the way things were. I was terrified to lose two of my only friends, whom I considered family, to face the brutality of being alone yet again.

"Bo, it isn't that I don't feel the same way about you. I just need time. I don't want to hurt you, and I'm sorry I don't have the answer you're looking for."

"It's him, isn't it? Seon." His jaw tightened. "You know that he'll only break your heart. You know that he'll grow tired of you eventually, then move on to the next girl. That's who he is, Cai."

Bo told no lies. It was what scared me the most about choosing Seon. It was why I could never seriously consider any relationship with him.

"It's not him. It's not anyone. I'm in the middle of the bloody Celestial Banquet!" I threw my hands up in the air. "This isn't the best time to have this discussion."

"Then when would that be, Cai? Right before I die again? Is that the only way you're able to show me how you feel?" The rage and frustration simmering in his deep voice surprised me.

"I'm sorry that I can't give you what you want. If it matters at all, I'm not choosing Seon either. There are bigger things to worry about."

"It will always be *something*." Bo's voice hardened. "Talk to me when you're finally out of excuses."

With those words, he turned away and jogged back to our building, opting to take the main entrance instead of the rooftop ladder.

I shoved my hands into my pants pockets and craned my neck upward to the starry skies. At least in this position, my tears would stay in the lakes of my eyes instead of becoming streams down my cheeks.

Lupong is the capital of the Peninsula and home of the infamous minor god Kama. It is a modest-sized city whose primary trade partner is the island nation of Mutya. When Kama and his mortal wife settled down, their homestead became the center of what became a city. Though Kama's direct mortal descendants no longer live, he considers citizens, visitors, and travelers to Lupong to be his own children.

**—*OUR FREE LAND*, SIXTH SCROLL,
LIBRARY OF LUPONG**

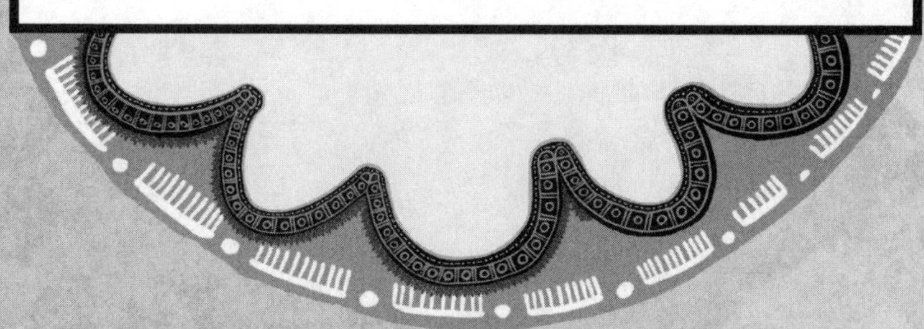

TWENTY-ONE

I returned to the rooftop and gave a vague excuse for Bo's absence.

Our two teams had sunken into an easy camaraderie with Kama sitting on his pack, regaling everyone with an outlandish story. I cracked a half-hearted smile and took a seat at the edge of the group beside Tala and Ulan.

"I take it that your talk with Bo did not go well," she stated in a low voice that only I could hear.

I nodded. "He wants me to choose him."

"And you haven't."

It wasn't that I never would. "Not right now, no. How is Seon?"

The object of my question was busy talking with Yoshihiro and Songwon. They seemed to have forged some sort of friendship. At the moment, he debated with the two older men about how to feed the dragon at the next feast. The dragon was the third god Indulgence's familiar, and like his master god, the most intimidating.

"He's fine. Don't worry so much," Tala replied as her voice lowered, glancing meaningfully at Seon, who was now approaching.

I closed my eyes and exhaled. "I feel guilty for putting Bo through this."

"Why?" she asked,

"He wanted to come on his own, Cai. It's not your fault." Seon sat beside Tala and me. "Would he have stayed home if Kama's candidate wasn't you? Probably. But that's on him."

Was it? Why did I feel so responsible for pulling Bo into this mess? Because at the end of the day, any of us could die; he followed me to that inevitability—setting this romantic headache in motion. I poured myself some tea and took a sip, hoping it'd calm my nerves.

"Seon makes a good point." Tala poked my elbow. "He chose this."

"Tomorrow, Indulgence's final feast will start. We're so close to the end." Seon rested his hands on his lap. "Soon, we can resume our lives."

We all watched the flames in silence.

I was so lost in the tide of my thoughts that I barely remembered saying good night as the group started dispersing.

"Stop thinking and get some sleep." Tala nudged me as she got up. She moved her mat from the farthest edge of the rooftop closer to mine and Seon's.

I was grateful for her support and for Seon's. The final trial was likely to be the most trying, and I had to admit, I was terrified. This truce would make the difference in winning this competition—or, at the very least, surviving it.

While Tala's soft snores filled the air, I rolled over to face Seon. A few strands fell over his brow as he rested his cheek against his hand. "What's eating your thoughts?"

I replied, "This competition is brutal. I hate how much it's taken from all of us. How much is left for us to give?"

"How are you feeling right now?"

"Overwhelmed." A scattering of stars in the sky above us reminded me of spilled rice grains against a dark marbled floor. "This is nothing like our lives in Lupong. Gods, monsters, beasts, treachery . . ."

"But there's also the food. Everything you've cooked is only possible because of divine intervention. It must be exciting to taste and handle such luxurious and rare ingredients. From a culinary scholar's point of view, all of this is a wonder. I can't even imagine how you feel as a cook."

With all the shadows I'd been dancing with, he reminded me that there was still light. The experience of the Celestial Banquet was equal parts torture and triumph. I couldn't deny how each meal from my hands made me proud, and the honor of serving a major god, no matter how rude they might be, couldn't be easily dismissed.

I still remember the joy of walking on water—the freedom of overcoming a lifelong fear and seeing how beautiful the lake was without worrying about being swallowed whole in its depths. All my emotions were distilled in a breathless run across the impossible. I also couldn't forget the thrill of solving the altar puzzle and watching the desert silkie shoot out from it like a feathered dart.

"It's funny; I'm usually the one who is considered an optimist. Thank you for reminding me about the good in all this. I'd almost forgotten."

Seon poked my shoulder. "Come on, let's go. I've got a surprise for you."

"Shouldn't we be getting our sleep?"

"Oh, I guess you're not hungry. What a shame, because I've called in all my favors—"

My stomach growled despite the meal I had earlier. "Fine, let's go!"

We snuck past a sleeping Tala cradling Ulan and a snoring Kama. Our scroungy sponsor was shifting from side to side like usual. If we weren't sneaking out, I'd try to comfort him.

"Lyka . . . No, you can't go. Lyka!"

It was the same name he'd uttered before.

Seon tugged me onward, holding my hand in his, and the thrill of a surprise overtook me.

We headed in the opposite direction as I had with Bo, toward the public market. Things were quieting down now, though we managed to grab some morsels at the stalls that were still wrapping up—crispy bite-size cubes of tofu decorated with red chilies and pink rock salt, deep-fried chicken skins wrapped around skewers crackling with perfection, stewed short ribs topped with sweet sapphire snapper roe.

Seon laughed as he bought everything I pointed to. As we walked and ate, I counted the red ribbons I found tied to certain stalls. I had to ask Seon about them.

"Are they indicating that they belong to the same clan or family?" I asked in between bites.

Seon gave me a secretive look. "I'll tell you when we get to our last destination. Make sure you leave room for dessert."

We ducked into a small restaurant down one narrow alley. Another of those red ribbons decorated the colorful lanterns hanging by the open door. The interior was cooler than the night air because of the block of ice behind the counter.

We were guided to a table with a bouquet of rare starlight peonies. Seon pulled out my chair for me before he took his seat. The flower petals radiated tiny pink, blue, and violet lights as they opened and closed. I touched one with my fingers and was surprised to feel warmth.

"I wonder if they're alight because of the heat in the petals." The words dried up in my throat when I realized he was staring. "They're so beautiful, thank you."

He reached across the table to squeeze my hand. "I love seeing the world through your eyes."

His fingers intertwined with mine, brushing against my sensitive fingertips. He rubbed idle circles in the space between my thumb and index finger. I didn't think I'd ever get used to his touch without my insides trembling. I cleared my throat. "So, about those red ribbons?"

"They represent a popular charity for widows and children." He lowered his voice and cupped the side of his mouth. "It's also the sign of the resistance to the Empress. The movement is alive and well here. I encouraged them to reach out to friendly contacts in Lupong."

I couldn't hide the growing smile on my face while I whispered, "There's hope, then!"

He nodded as another server placed a heaping plate of bingsu on our table—snow topped with condensed milk and slices of princess mango. Seon pointed to the cook behind the counter, who wore a tattoo of the Blade Guild insignia on his bare muscled shoulder. He worked with two cleavers to create a mountain of fluffy snow from the block of ice.

"When we win the banquet, I will reestablish my mother's noble house and try for a council seat. I'm staying to do everything I can for the resistance effort."

I had to admit, I was envious. The idea of life in Xianling was tantalizing. It was more than I had ever dreamed of for myself. I imagined opening my restaurant here and even to join the fabled guilds, which I'd never even seen as an option. There was so much I could learn from the culinary world, and I'd have a friend, or something, in Seon. The scariest part was how tempting this future was. This version of myself felt unrecognizable from the one who had plans to never leave Lupong and Bo. But could it be a possibility that I return here one day? I almost hoped it wasn't, for if it was, I would be faced with an impossible choice.

Indulgence is the eldest and most powerful of the major gods—and the most feared.

Their great hands opened the chasm in the world that trapped their brother, Death.

Indulgence's temple in the great plains north of Xianling is the largest of the three and boasts the most monks in service. Glory is theirs while the mortal world kneels in supplication.

—*ORIGINS*, SECOND SCROLL,
GREAT LIBRARY OF XIANLING

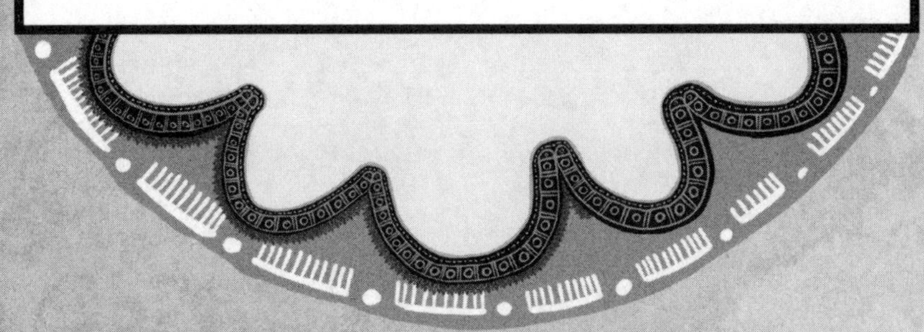

TWENTY-TWO

For the third and last time, we lined up along the edge of the roof and observed the palace. Temperance's round structures were unceremoniously decimated, leaving only the banquet hall untouched. A craggy, snowy mountain peak erupted from the sands behind it. The height of it worried me as I wondered what lay in store for us at the top. In the other direction, a wide path led from the banquet hall to a new rectangular courtyard bordered by living quarters. This meant some sort of extended stay. My shoulders slumped. I wanted everything to be over with. Even though barely a week had passed, it felt like a lifetime. The weariness weighed down my body. Finally, a massive, circular arena with seating for hundreds of people formed on the opposite side of the mountain. My instinct told me this would be where we would cook.

The song in the air created a melodic frantic, frenetic pull. The tension and friction between the bow and the strings created heat and smoke to manipulate the sands. This accompaniment was new, marking the importance of the day. My heartbeat matched the agitation, galloping at breakneck speed against the cage of my ribs. I pressed my hand against my chest and took deep breaths in an effort to slow it down.

Everyone was serious; the gravity of this final day was settling in. Beside me, Tala stared off into the distance, a slight furrow between her brows. Seon narrowed his eyes, gripping the hilt of his sword.

I missed Bo. We'd had spats before, but they'd passed quickly, never interfering with our friendship's constant rhythm. This time felt different, and I had not a clue where we stood with one another.

The gong rang out, and we readied ourselves for what was to come.

If Luck was fickle and Temperance was manipulative, Indulgence was known to be outright cruel. The obstacles this major god cooked up would be ghastly. My guess was based not on pessimism but pragmatism. Save the best for last and all that. We filed into the courtyard, led by Guolin, Pubu, and Kama, then each of the three teams headed off to a different corner. From afar, Bo avoided my gaze and busied himself with his team.

Kama leaned on a wooden staff, which he'd adapted as a walking stick. His movements were slow—before, it had been out of indolence, and now, it was from weakness and age. His voice had ripened into a raspy, hoarse whisper. "Have your wits about you, children. Indulgence is a right bastard of a major god. They'll have you twisted in a way you never thought possible where your head would be close enough to lick your—"

"We get the point," I interrupted. Better not to visualize our potential punishment too clearly.

We waited three torturous hours until a ribbon of burnished red and gold streaked the afternoon sky. Gasps erupted among us.

A dragon! I held my breath and drank in the flying wonder as it approached—large as the two-story tea shop in Lupong.

The dark ruby scales shifted with each of its movements, accompanied by hisses and roars. Tufts of golden hair decorated the dragon's head, legs, and tail. Its enormous nostrils puffed out clouds of smoke. The acrid aroma of brimstone made us cough.

The dragon was as fierce as I'd imagined, and the paintings of it paled in comparison to the living being. I wished Baba were here to see this. Everyone was as awestruck as I was, save for Bo, who remained expressionless. I itched to ask him what disappointed him. There must be a reason why he wasn't excited. Ever since he was a child, he'd wanted to see a dragon up close. We'd talked about it many times, on our walks in Lupong, day-dreaming. Something inside him was broken. I feared I was responsible.

Finally, the dragon curled into a resting position, almost like a giant cat. It laid its head on its arms and fell into a nap. A figure in jewel-encrusted robes materialized before the mythical beast bearing a harsh androgynous visage. Deep frown lines settled into their cheeks, and the downward slashes of their brows conveyed displeasure. Indulgence.

"Welcome, welcome. I see that there are three of you left." They turned their eyes to each team and their sponsor gods. "Kama, you mangy dog, is that you? You've made it this far?"

Our sponsor winced, mustering what he thought was a congenial smile, but which manifested instead as a maniacal grin. "Indulgence, long time no see."

"You look like a pile of dung left out in the sun for too long." The major god guffawed and clutched their belly. "Let's hope you win those peaches. I doubt you'll last long after the competition. Your losing streak has cost you."

Kama narrowed his eyes, dropping the charade. "Perhaps if I win this time, I won't have to see your sour face until at least a century from now."

"Tsk, tsk." Indulgence tapped their lips and winked. "You're probably wondering what's in store for today. I had originally intended for a three-day survival competition for you all. A scant selection of food and resources to battle over. A bit bloodthirsty, but still quite amusing."

I grimaced.

"What changed your mind?" Guolin's voice boomed, the only one who dared to ask what we all were thinking.

"Wounds and broken limbs, especially death, are predictable, basic. It's far more interesting to watch what happens when you draw blood you cannot see." The major god climbed onto the back of the sleeping dragon. "To begin, I bestow upon a chosen one in each group a curse, one that is not to be taken lightly. Pick this team member well, for you have only tonight to prepare for your mountain trek. In the meantime, try not to harm yourselves. I am still hungry, after all." With those words, the major god took to the sky with his great dragon and headed east.

The large housing complex was split into three sections. Inside each was a set of living quarters and sitting rooms. The communal areas were the bathhouse, the large kitchen, and the dining hall. The pantry and cellars were well-stocked. And for our team, at least the lodgings were relatively sumptuous. I was grateful for the change.

After staking out our rooms and transferring our belongings, Tala, Seon, Kama, and I gathered in the sitting room.

Everything in the room was luxurious—from the silk cushions, vases of fresh roses and peonies in painted ceramic vases, red lacquered furniture, and sandalwood incense burners. The air of serenity must have been meant to lull us into a false sense of security.

Indulgence's words left us all wondering what he would curse us with and how it would work. So far, no one has sprouted extra limbs, turned feral, or changed into another animal. We all stayed quiet, scared to make the first move.

"Indulgence isn't one to create curses with no teeth. They revel in chaos and pain. When they mentioned wounds, they meant it. This major god is known to be far more bloodthirsty than their siblings. This will be a lifelong curse." Kama leaned back in his chair.

Feeling safer that speaking wouldn't be dangerous, I ventured, "They said someone has to be 'chosen.' Is it us who will do the choosing?"

"It has to be me or Seon. You have to cook the final feast." Tala shifted to the right to accommodate Ulan hopping onto the sofa. "I'll bear what I must if it's my burden."

Seon clasped his hands together. His gaze switched from Tala to me before declaring, "I volunteer. I'm ready to bear what's to come."

I turned to him and placed my hands on his shoulders. His light brown eyes bore no hint of doubt. "You don't know what he has planned. This major god is serious trouble. Are you sure?"

Indulgence wouldn't let Seon off easy. He could face anything from dismemberment to disfiguration to disembodiment. I shuddered imagining such a fate for Seon. The previous curses by Luck and Temperance were severe enough to ruin the lives of the two teams who received them.

"Are you sure?" I asked again, leaning in and taking his hands in mine. "What you're about to do for us is . . ."

"It's a price we all have to pay. That's how these trials work. We're so close to the end, and when our team wins, then it'll all be worth it." He squeezed my hands. "I believe in you."

I blushed in spite of myself. Out of the corner of my vision, I swore Tala rolled her eyes.

"Well, pretty boy, make your formal sacrifice. We'll see if you sprout another head." Kama rubbed his hands together. "In all seriousness, be prepared. We'll let you know if we notice anything."

Seon closed his eyes and took a deep breath. His beauty was unquestionable in the angles of his face, the bow of his lips, and those enchanting eyes that made you feel as if you were the only being in existence. There was more to him than that—his kindness and intelligence. His adventurous spirit. His loyalty to his mother. I couldn't imagine losing any part of him.

I couldn't help but ask him one more time. "Are you certain about this?"

He nodded. His full mouth formed a thin, determined line.

Something in my chest squeezed.

"High lord Indulgence, I am ready to receive your curse," Seon declared with his palms open to the ceiling.

Not a moment had passed before a wisp of golden smoke materialized above his head, thickening into a slithering dragon. It split into seven entities before entering through his eyes, ears, nose, and mouth. Seon shuddered as golden light burst from his orifices. Then, nothing—it had disappeared just as suddenly as it began.

I was the first to grasp him by the shoulders. "Are you all right? Tell me how you feel."

He blinked, and his brown eyes focused on my face. "I love you and have been in love with you since I met you at my family compound. You are the only girl for me, and I intend to ask you to move to Xianling with me when this competition is over."

Surviving a Celestial Banquet is quite rare—and is reserved for the most talented.

It is far more prevalent to see former participants afflicted with a variety of curses from the major gods. These range from the absurd—one team quacking instead of speaking; to the deadly—another team having their mouths permanently sewn shut. The wrath of the major gods manifests in unspeakable acts.

—***CURSES, HEXES, AND OTHER AFFLICTIONS***, **SECOND SCROLL, GRAND LIBRARY OF XIANLING**

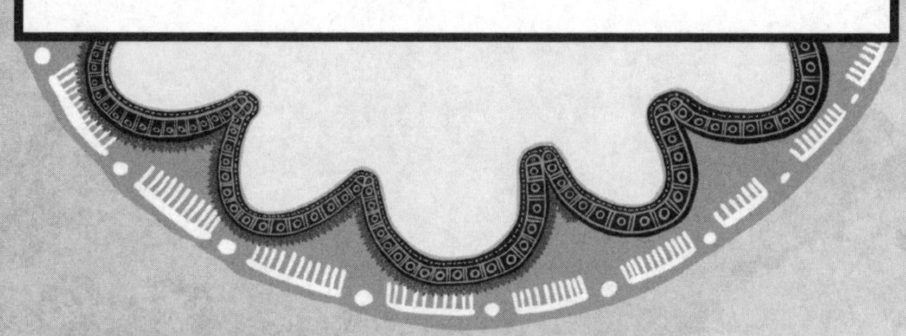

TWENTY-THREE

After Seon finished his confession, a deep flush spread across his cheeks.

"Indulgence's curse is real." Kama wagged his finger at everyone. "It seems that extreme honesty is the dagger with which he'll injure."

My heart thudded from his words. All this time, I assumed Seon was busy with other girls, despite our flirty friendship. Even over the last few days, I had thought his love was borne of convenience; I was the only option for him here in the competition. But this changed everything. He could have his choice of anyone in Lupong, yet for some reason, he *loved* me?

I creased my brows and searched for a hint of sarcasm, a chance Seon was joking.

"Do you mind if I talk to Seon alone?" I asked the others.

Before our sponsor god could object, Tala plopped Ulan into his arms and pulled his ear to usher him out of the room. Kama was grumbling the whole time he clutched the cormorant. He even dared to take one last peek until Tala shoved his head back.

I waited until it was quiet again to speak. "Was it the truth, as Kama said?"

He didn't seem as worried or as shocked by the curse as I would have been in his place. If I had absolute honesty, more people would be educated about their flaws. Bo had always joked that speaking my mind could incite a civil war.

"It is." Seon didn't blush or give any hint of embarrassment. "If we don't get out of this alive, I'd never forgive myself for not doing that. I just needed you to know how I feel. You're the only one for me."

It felt like my brain was scrambled. "But the other girls. Literally last week, I saw you flirting with Anzu in a rickshaw! And then there was—"

He stopped my words with the touch of his fingertips on my lips. "I'm ashamed to admit it, but I only did that to make you jealous." He laughed ruefully. "Seems like it didn't work."

Seon traced his way down the line of my jaw with his finger. In spite of myself, I leaned in to his touch. He moved in and captured my lips with his.

The first time I tried huangjiu, my head swam. It was from Kama's personal stash, and the powerful alcohol tasted sweet, bitter, and savory. It had been enough to make me light-headed with warmth bubbling under my skin. This was how Seon's kisses made me feel—they lit a wildfire inside me with every breath stolen.

At that moment, I allowed the possibility of being with him—exploring Xianling together, making a home in the glamorous city, ascending heights as a chef I could never reach at home. I was starting to think this was my destiny after all. It was everything I could've ever dreamed of.

It was Kama's raucous chuckling as he returned to the room that broke us apart. "I should have known how this would end."

While Seon smirked and shook his head, I seesawed between outrage and mortification. I covered my face with my hands and groaned.

Tala snapped her fingers, but a smile played on the edge of her lips. Clearly she was team Seon. "All right. You had your moment. We need to discuss the plan. This is the last feast."

Kama settled into his previous seat. "Yes, children, it is not the time to lose sight of our goals. I can assure you that this will only be the first of Indulgence's tricks. And while you were busy enacting a teenage romantic opera last night, I was talking to Pubu, who kindly gave me insight about the final feast. As you all know, this is my first."

"The last ingredient quest will be far more difficult than anything we've faced," Seon added. "I've read that only two people participate—the sponsor god and their designate."

Kama sighed with exasperation. He'd been looking forward to delivering that news. "Yes, Seon, that is quite right. Anyway, the trick is that I have to choose before I know what we're doing." The old minor god scratched his snowy whiskers.

Tala pointed north. "The mountain."

The craggy, snowy peak formed out of sand earlier this morning, just as predicted.

I turned to Kama. "Who will you choose to go with you?"

Our sponsor god squinted and scrunched his lips. He scratched his temple and made a big show of deliberation. I'd seen him perform the same dramatics when choosing what to order for dinner. Bo once described the expression as being between passing foul wind and smelling it.

"I need to know more about you all."

Kama and I had known each other the longest. He'd seen me at my start as one of Tondo the Tall's runners at the auction house. Even back then, we talked about food and the news around the culinary scene in Lupong.

Seon rested his hands on his knees. "Lord Kama, ask me anything if it helps with your decision."

His offer, considering his curse, was generous, and I hoped Kama took this with grace. The more people who knew about the curse, the more danger Seon would be in. I vowed to protect his sacrifice to the best of my ability. He deserved nothing less.

"In Lupong, there were rumors about your mother. Are they true?" Kama asked.

I sighed with disappointment. Of course he'd ask Seon about this. There were whispers about everyone. It was the biggest city on the Peninsula, and gossip was the cheapest hobby anyone could have. Everyone's business was borrowed, bartered, and sometimes buried with the right amount of coin. I had no appetite for the rumors that were spiced with malice. I especially hated those that concerned people I cared about—Seon's kind mother, Yoona, was one of them.

Seon closed his eyes and replied, "Yes. My father is known to lay his hand on my mother. It's the reason why she hasn't been seen outside of the family compound in decades. Not enough powder or prestige could hide his cruelty. I want to use my peach to help my mother escape Lupong and rebuild her family house here in Xianling. And before you ask, the more notorious rumors about my father are also true. He paid to have the old city counselor killed so he could take his position."

I lowered my head. I'd suspected the former but not the latter. When Lady Yoona had showed me her prized peonies, back upon my first delivery to their house, her sleeve had fallen to reveal a mottled trail of bruises on her pale skin. I was young enough at the time to not ask any intrusive questions yet old enough to know what the marks meant.

As for her husband, Lord Yeong-su, all I heard was speculation and nothing tangible. Plus, I stayed out of it—if you whispered to the wrong ear in Lupong, your tongue would get cut off. I trusted that both Kama and I would keep this news to ourselves. If it came out, it would mean ruin for Seon, either by his father's own hands or his father's enemies.

"Tala, please don't tell anyone about what Seon said. It's a dangerous piece of information."

"I won't." She nodded. "Kama, what do you want to know from me?"

"Why do you have the most charming cormorant instead of a dreadful Zhenniao? Such a better choice." Ulan cooed in response from her perch at Tala's feet.

I caught Tala's gaze, reassuring her that I would keep her secrets. She, of all people, would have hated the honesty curse the most. It was her choice now to answer with the truth or a vague version of it.

"Because a Zhenniao is only given to a true daughter of the Nomads." Tala wove her fingers together. "I was adopted through my aunt and her wife." It seemed that Tala was finally ready to open up to the group.

"This makes you a . . ." Kama narrowed his eyes.

She pressed her lips into a firm line and placed her hands on her hips. "I'm from Mutya. My parents were the late king and queen, and I am here in pursuit of justice. If any of you breathe a word about this to anyone, you will regret it. And for you, Kama, I'll make every moment of your immortal life a misery."

Our sponsor god blanched and made a motion to close his lips. Seon gave her a polite nod, though I saw the shock in his eyes.

I stood up, stretching my arms. "I suppose it's my turn."

My love life had already been an open subject this whole competition, my whole life in fact. I thought I might as well settle in and expect the grilling I'd get from the nosiest uncle of all.

Kama tapped his lips and asked, "Why do you cook?"

I was taken aback but not deterred. This question was easy to answer. It was as natural as breathing.

"Because it was Baba's wish for me, and I love it. Cooking is magic. I can't find anything else that can change a person's mood, bring back long-dormant memories, keep us *alive*, like food. Experimentation is the best part . . ."

My words spilled from my lips as I described my passion. Kama's innocent question seemed to have dissipated the tension in the air.

"Tell us about your father. Was he a great chef?" Seon chimed in.

The smile on my face faltered.

Baba was the center of my world. For the longest time, I believed he ran the kitchen of the Golden Lotus—cooking up a whirlwind of dishes with his trusty wok and thriving, shining as the central force propelling the delicious meals out into the dining room. Pride puffed in my chest when I greeted the exiting patrons of the restaurant. I was never allowed in the kitchen back then because Baba insisted that it was far too dangerous for little ones. I still remember the day I found out the truth, for it was the same day I got into my first fistfight. A fellow runner at the auction house taunted me with what I'd thought was a foul lie.

I swallowed the lump forming in my throat. Even still, the memory fills me with pain. Not because of the deceit, but because of Baba's sacrifice.

"My father was never a cook, at least not professionally. He was a dishwasher. He wanted me to believe that he was the head cook of the Golden Lotus. And he could have been. Easily. He cooked things in our wok at home that rivaled any restaurant I've ever been to. He wanted to be a hero to me." I touched my cheek and found it damp with tears. "I wanted desperately to believe him and felt betrayed when I found out the truth. In my anger, I wanted to confront him, and blessedly Tondo the Tall saved me from that foolishness. He explained why it was important for Baba to live his lie—that doing so fueled his motivation to live, to believe that his daughter's future could be better than his. So, I made sure that he lived his grand lie to his last breath."

My grief, which I had bottled and fermented for more than a decade, was unleashed. Crying was usually a luxury I couldn't afford, but now I gasped for breath while my shoulders shook.

Comforting arms enveloped me, and when I looked up I saw the person I least expected: Tala.

Beware the lures of the Continent, brother.
Do not forget the Singing Sea.

These foreigners do not understand
or respect our ways.

While this land has its own claim to beauty,
it can never rival the way the sun kisses
the honey hyacinths in full bloom.

I will return soon with profits from trade.
Home is where I want to be.

—A MUTYAN LETTER FROM THE CONTINENT

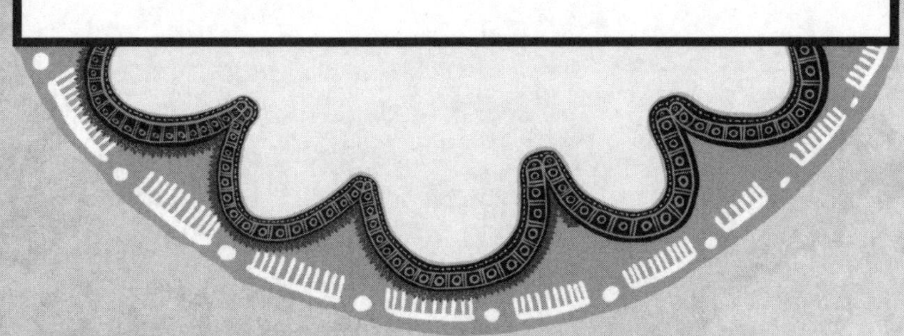

TWENTY-FOUR

When the tears subsided, Tala passed me an embroidered kerchief. "Need to get away for a bit?"

I wiped my eyes and nose. The rest of the company sat quietly, giving me space to grieve.

I suddenly had a strong, irrepressible urge to see Bo. He was the only one who had met my father. I needed my friend. I needed things to go back to the way they were. And yet, I doubted he'd want to see me. Perhaps after all this is over, we could repair what I had broken.

Kama held up his palm. "Pubu also warned me of a final challenge for the minor gods. Indulgence will test me."

Tala, Seon, and I glanced at each other.

Our sponsor god was diminished. He was a shell of himself when compared to the reckless vagabond on the throne of the Three Cranes Tavern. The telltale sparks emanating from his being vanished right after he saved Bo and hadn't returned.

I was responsible for his weakened state. I begged Kama to challenge Death.

I hated myself for what I'd done to my friends, but I hated this cursed Celestial Banquet even more. These sadistic gods with their trials and tests. I was beginning to wonder if their celebration of Death's defeat wasn't just a sick excuse to keep us mortals small, hungry, and complacent. Victories from the Continent enriched their war chests and funded their expansion. And the Celestial Banquet was picking off the best each province had to offer one by one—all for the chance at some rotten peach. The injustice of it all made my blood boil.

"Let's hope you're in for a celestial drinking game," Tala muttered, breaking the spell.

Seon and I burst out laughing. Even Kama grinned, puffing his chest without shame.

"In all seriousness, children, we should be prepared for the worst. Indulgence always wants their price in blood, immortal or mortal. Nothing like a little maiming for sport." Our sponsor god made a face. "They want us to *bleed* for those peaches."

After a half hour of collecting myself with the support of Tala, who had graciously let me keep her kerchief, Seon returned from a visit to the courtyard. "I ran into Songwon. He suggested that you two should cook dinner together for all of us. If you're wondering about Kama, he's resting. I suppose we should all take some time to ourselves before our meal."

"Cooking will clear your head." Tala patted my shoulder before heading to her quarters, with Ulan following her.

By the time I entered the communal kitchen, Songwon had every ingredient we needed to prepare four dishes. The bounty of the cellar decorated every counter while two woks were set by the stove side by side. The protein of choice was fermented tofu. The wiggly, pale blocks of carved soy jiggled when he smashed cloves of garlic with the flat of his blade.

"Vegetarian dishes would be calming for all our nerves, don't you think?" He tossed the flattened cloves into a bowl with sliced ginger. "There was enough proverbial bloodshed today. I had no appetite for more, so I invited Zi Rui, too, but he unfortunately declined. It would've been nice to remember that we're all human here—even Guolin's team."

I nodded in agreement before heading to the sink to wash my hands. I picked out a handful of dried chilies, white peppercorns, bitter melons, and bamboo shoots. "Vegetarian is a good choice. Who did you all choose for the curse?"

"Yoshihiro. He took it well, said he had enough privilege as an elder to speak his truth and to insult anyone he wants to. It'll be interesting how his family will react to it."

Family grudges were the worst from what I'd seen and heard. Back in Lupong, Poleng, whose stall was beside mine, had a long-running feud with her older brother, Anding. They would screech at each other at every encounter, embarrassing their relatives.

I chopped the bamboo shoot and reveled in its polarizing odor. "Seon took on that burden. He seems to be doing okay too."

"Speaking of your friends, I apologize if I'm overstepping . . . I did, in fact, see Bo die, yes?"

"Yes, he did. Kama brought him back to life."

"Ah, I didn't think that was possible." Songwon tossed a bowlful of shredded cabbage into a hot wok. My nose perked up the instant the sharp spices hit the hot oil. "Then again, we are all here because Death has been vanquished. Granted, usually that's just for the immortals, but perhaps something can be done for us after all."

As I cooked alongside him, the calmness in his movements contrasted with my frantic energy. Songwon cooked with precision and steadiness. He didn't possess a flashy bone in his body. It must be all channeled into his food.

"If you're wondering, the rumors are true, I have lost parts of my tongue. My father punished me for crying too much. From what my mother told me, I'd been sick with a fever at the time. It was the motivation she needed to move from our peasant village to Xianling." He tapped his mouth. "I'll let you see it if you ask."

I shook my head. "Thank you for taking me into your confidence, Songwon. That is enough for me."

After taking a deep breath, I volunteered my own secret about Baba. Now that I had said it once, it felt good to be honest. If I had any shame, it was for my part in concealing it and continuing the lie. I was proud of him and how he provided for me until his dying breath. Cook or not, he was the best father I could ask for.

Songwon tossed the stir-fried cabbage with a flick of his wrist. The crispy pieces flecked with red chili flakes floated in the air as if suspended in motion before tumbling back down. "Your father was good. Mine was not. Yet we stand side by side here at the Celestial Banquet. What would you do with a peach?"

I told him about protecting the Peninsula from the Empress, my restaurant, and following in Tondo the Tall's footsteps when it came to charity. To his credit, Songwon didn't seem the type who was fiercely loyal to the Empress, so I felt safe in disclosing my intentions.

"And you? How would a peach change your life?" I asked.

He wiped his brow with his sleeve and plated the cabbage into a deep round bowl with painted golden-scalloped edges. "Fund my second restaurant and help my mother with her dream—to start a house for widows and any women who need support. Our parents, at least the good ones, seem to trust us with their cherished hope."

He was right. Baba must have known I'd feed and nourish his dream. "Admirable. Not planning to join any guilds?"

"I might apply with my victory, only to turn them down. I wasn't good enough for them before, and all of a sudden, I'd be only because I won?" Songwon laughed. "Not the type of people I'd want to associate with."

We finished cooking with light chatter. I learned his philosophy on cooking, and he admired my approach to experimentation. He was roughly a decade and a half older than me. I couldn't help but consider him a big brother. By the time we finished preparing our plates, he already had the nerve to tease me about my messy love life.

"I'm invested now. Who will win?" He lifted his brows and loaded his plates onto my tray while I filled his with my dishes.

"I don't know. Maybe it's best I move to the Guolin Mountains and start a culinary nunnery."

"The idea has merit. The restaurant's name must be Sisters of the Wok."

"Don't give me viable ideas." I scrunched my nose at the suggestion.

Emerging from the hallway, the waterfall minor goddess walked on the tiled floor, with each step producing a puddle that evaporated seconds after it appeared. She was beautiful beyond mortal standards, yet all I could think about was how much she irritated me.

Pubu gestured for me to join her in the dining hall. "The others will join us soon. Can we have a little chat?"

Songwon lowered his voice. "She is complicated but kind. You'll see." He flashed me a confident grin before disappearing to gather the others.

I rolled my eyes.

The goddess clicked her tongue as I entered the room. She had taken a seat on the longest divan. The goldfish on her elaborate robes jumped into the air and dove back into the aquamarine silk with a plop. "Sit, let's talk."

This minor deity had nothing to peddle that I'd want to buy.

"I suspect your heart is torn and I have some valuable advice for when you decide your future—the one that involves choosing who you want to walk alongside."

I pursed my lips, frowning. "No, thank you."

"You know what happened to me before all this." She pressed her palm against her temple. "I'm trying to spare you more pain."

The rumors about her dissolved love affair with fellow minor god Senlin were everywhere. I sighed while asking, "What is your advice?"

Advice was like the chicken satay stick shoved in your face whether you were hungry or full. At this point in my life, I'd whack the skewer on sight. However, the beautiful goddess sitting across from me seemed determined to give wisdom.

Pubu had an ethereal quality that mortals lacked—no blemishes, perfect features, a sparkling aura meant to bewitch and enchant, and perfume reminiscent of mist-covered tea roses against a refreshing waterfall, her namesake. The goldfish on her elaborate robes jumped into the air and dove back into the aquamarine silk with a splashing plop.

"What is this life-changing piece of wisdom you have for me?" I asked.

She laughed, and it echoed like tiny jostling bells. "You certainly are full of century-old vinegar for such a young thing. How do you get to be so crusty?"

"With never-ending practice," I replied with a scowl.

"We minor gods were mortal once and chosen by Indulgence to oversee the world in their absence. This is a roundabout way to say that I've been around for a long time. I understand the perils of having to choose your partner. I've had many friends die while

I continue to live. Wounds like these don't heal completely. Love involves both joy and pain."

The deep-set frown loosened from my mouth. The genuine sorrow in her voice surprised me. I'd once assumed that these minor gods were above human emotions. Pubu and Kama were clearly not.

Pubu reached out to cup my chin before I could stop her. The gentleness in the gesture surprised me. "Choose well, Cai. Bo has shown the valor and dedication. He will make a devoted partner, husband, and father. That is what you want, isn't it?"

It was—before I left for the Celestial Banquet. Before I started imagining a different future for myself.

Bo would never want that. His heart lay with his family farm.

Seon offered me the future in the city and now, I had to admit I wanted to take it. But if I did, I'd break Bo's heart.

"Ungrateful child. He *died* for you." Pubu interpreted my silence as disagreement. "You don't deserve him."

She stood up to take her leave. The sound of rushing water over stones accompanied her exit.

My chest tightened from the truth of her words. I didn't deserve him. But he deserved the world. Maybe I could find a way to give him the world, even if it was without me. After Baba's death, I thought our side couldn't win against the Wan armies, but that changed when Seon showed me that the fires of resistance burned even at the Empress's doorstep. And with the peach, I could stoke this rebellion. I didn't get this far only to fail.

I would *triumph*.

Slapping my cheeks, I tried to bury all of my emotions along with the worries about crawling back to Lupong in defeat. What-ifs were a luxury I couldn't afford.

By the time I returned to the kitchen, I'd locked up my emotions under a ceramic lid.

Guolin promised Pubu the stars. He climbed the highest peak of his mountain range and jumped, ascending into the heavens to grab the lowest-hanging star. He then squeezed it with his great hands to break it down into a necklace of stardust. The gift elevated the status of the minor goddess even more and won Guolin her affections, though only temporarily.

Nothing about the gods is forever except for their lives.

—*AMORAL LIVES OF THE MINOR GODS*, THIRD SCROLL, GREAT LIBRARY OF XIANLING

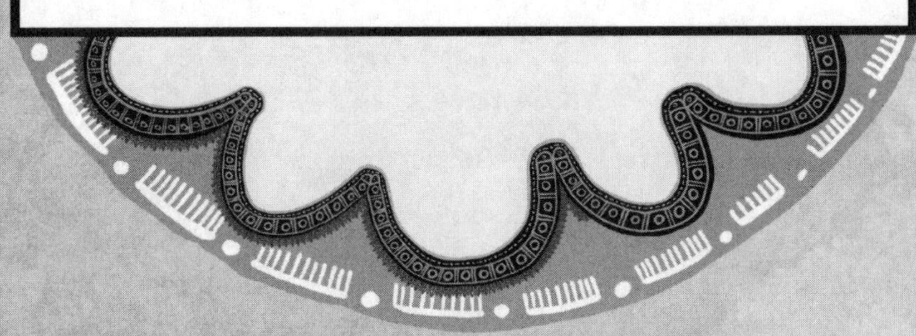

TWENTY-FIVE

Teams Kama and Pubu had gathered to occupy the long table in the dining room. Both minor gods were seated at the heads. Bo sat at Pubu's left hand, which put him the farthest away from my place next to Kama. When I raised my hand in greeting, he ignored me and turned his full attention to the beautiful goddess.

The meal was superb. Songwon's tofu soup was infused with a variety of mushrooms, giving it an earthy note, and the cabbage dish was a nice finisher. His dishes possessed a sense of finesse that was cultivated with the utmost respect and understanding of the ingredients. He wasn't a devout disciple of seasoning like I was. The difference between our dishes made me respect him even more.

I served steamed snapper with spring onions in soy sauce of my own formulation and conpoy congee. I wanted the dishes to complement the simplicity and comfort of Songwon's offerings. After I removed the spine and fish bones, the red snapper gleamed under lamplight and yielded easily to the snap of eager chopsticks. Blooms of steam escaped the large tureen of the congee, releasing the delicious aroma of grated ginger and the crispy fried-scallion garnish.

I slid into my chair and passed the spicy stir-fried cabbage to Tala. "Thank you. Let's see how well Songwon cooks."

"Good cook. No wonder he got this far." Kama slurped the delicious broth. "Very subtle with his spices yet still excellent."

Seon nodded. "The communal meal is a success then. It was a wonderful idea, Lord Kama."

"I thought it was Songwon who suggested it?" I refilled my cup of tea. "Am I wrong?"

"I may have hinted a few things before he made the formal request. I am cleverer than you all think." Our sponsor winked.

I reached out and grabbed the last of the cabbage. "Clever but not fast enough, it seems."

Kama puckered his lips. "I wanted that!"

"Don't ever say that I fail to respect my elders, right, Bo?" I said, raising my voice and handing the bowl to Kama, who tittered with glee. Bo gave me a curt nod and a pathetic excuse of a smile. The kernel of worry in my stomach grew until it took away the rest of my appetite.

I grinned, the corners of my mouth wobbling to keep the false gaiety in place. I could use Temperance's influence right now. Crumbling in front of everyone on the eve of the last trial and feast would be catastrophic. I took a deep breath and curled and uncurled my fingers below the table.

"*Baba, give me strength*," I whispered under my breath before turning to Songwon. "Shall we bring out dessert?"

Songwon winked at everyone. "This is our treat and Cai's lovely idea. We hope we don't disappoint."

We reconvened in the kitchen to make the final preparations, and it was there that I was able to reground myself in the magic of cooking. In the early years, when I missed Baba the most, I tried my best to navigate living life on my own while keeping my grief at bay. The solution was to cook, while talking to my father, using his wok. Miracles happened in the act of creating dishes that sang on the tongue and satisfied a gnawing hunger.

"Pubu has agreed to your request?" I asked Songwon while I ladled the honey passion nectar into a large, grand lotus-shaped bowl. In another deep bowl, I meticulously arranged a trove of blush-pink boba, taking care not to jostle them too much.

Songwon gathered the matching petal-shaped cups. "She has. Everything is set. Oh, everyone will be enchanted. I can't wait to see their reaction."

When we returned to the table, the needed space was cleared for the dessert. Songwon and I took our seats, and he gestured to me. "Cai will introduce her special treat."

"Back in Lupong, a clever auntie made a delicious discovery. Auntie Marikit taught me her secret, and I'm forever grateful. I present to you honey passion nectar with ethereal exploding white peach boba."

The rare nectar was another luxury courtesy of the Celestial Banquet. At the auction house, it would command at least three hundred silver coins by the jar. The taste was a perfect amount of sweetness tempered by a sharp tang. The nectar came from pink and blue tropical flowers found only on Mutyan soil. Perfumes from its petals were a noble favorite on the Continent.

On the other side of the table, Songwon whispered to Pubu.

The goddess lifted her wrist and made a spinning motion with her index finger.

A golden ribbon of nectar flowed out of the bowl to hover above our heads and make a looping chain design, with one end dipping into the smaller bowl of the boba. The nectar took the shape of a stairway to carry a string of obedient pink boba upward into the suspended design. The air filled with the fragrance of the honey passion mingled with the soft scent of white peaches.

One by one, each of the boba exploded into tiny pink blooms like New Year's sparklers above the petal cups. A cheer rose from the table, along with claps of delight. Bo remained expressionless while his dark eyes met mine. How do I tell him that I was starting to see myself in Xianling?

"Everyone ready for the trial?" Indulgence jumped off the dragon's back and clapped their hands. It was the next morning after a sleepless night. Finally we could get the rest of this competition over with. Bo continued to avoid my eyes as we stood in the courtyard. "I'm craving something unlike anything you've seen or even thought of. I'd love to see you take away something that is fiercely protected. Trickier that way! Guard your eyes lest they be plucked out. Get me Jian bird eggs. There are only three such eggs, guarded by a pair of full-grown Jian birds, of course. They are on those mountain peaks." Predictably, the major god pointed to the snowy mountain that stood high behind them. "Before I set you off, one last matter to attend to."

The dragon breathed a wall of fire upon Indulgence. I let myself dare to hope that it had just deep-fried the major god, but when the fire retreated, Indulgence was, of course, unharmed and standing by three waist-high pedestals. A glowing oval jewel was suspended above each. "This part of the competition is what we call the sponsor evaluation. I need to see if these minor gods are up to the task."

Seon nudged Kama in the ribs. Like usual, our sponsor god had managed to drift off while we waited for Indulgence, making a snuffling noise hungry pigs make when they shove their heads into the trough. Tala reached over and pinched Kama's nose shut until he was jolted awake.

"Present!" Our minor god raised his hand as if Indulgence were taking attendance.

Tala, Seon, and I exchanged looks of fond embarrassment.

"Kama, Pubu, Guolin, come, let's see how well you three fare against each other." The major god stepped to the right side of the three pedestals. "This godly test is to see who has the strongest immortal essence."

This wasn't good.

Guolin sneered and swaggered his imposing body ahead. Embroidered mountains decorated his umber robes with three snarling black bears roaming the rocky terrain. He pushed his way past the others, causing Kama to stumble. Big bully. It would be even sweeter if Songwon or I were to triumph over his precious Zi Rui.

Once all three had positioned themselves in front of their respective pedestals, the enchanted jewel floated upward, stopping at their eye level. Guolin placed his hands on both sides of it without touching it. He grunted as the gem began to fill with a silvery brown liquid. Pubu followed suit, straining to raise the silvery seafoam levels, while Kama grunted, groaned, and grumbled, yet his jewel remained empty, though if it were measuring the amount of creative swearing, our sponsor god would have won by now.

It was a foregone conclusion that Guolin would take the prize, with Pubu coming in second. Kama never stood a chance, but especially not after what he did to bring Bo back to life. Indulgence clapped their hands and squealed, "Good, good! Guolin, you get to choose who you want as your companion for your mountain adventure. Pubu will be next."

Guolin surveyed his team. "Zolzaya," he announced before crossing his arms over his chest. It was the natural choice. She was the fittest and most seasoned among the three. The Nomad warrior walked to Guolin's side with her fearsome Zhenniao perched on her leather-strapped arm.

Pubu glanced over at her team. "Bo."

Bo was the wisest choice. He was young and could endure the brutal climb more than Songwon or the elder Yoshihiro. Pubu would take care of him as she had at the lake. I repeated this to myself for extra reassurance.

"And now, Kama." Indulgence grinned. "You came in last, which comes with a penalty, for I will decide who'll be your companion."

Seon and Tala stood at my side as a pit in my stomach formed. Normally, I'd be ready to volunteer, but this was a challenge that both my teammates would be better at. Seon was an expert swordsman, and Tala, like Zolzaya, was familiar with mountainous terrain. This would be perfect for her skillset. Could Indulgence possibly choose either of them? But this was a punishment and Seon was already cursed . . .

"Cai."

Tala gave me a gentle nudge as I scrambled to join Kama.

"We'll be fine, just fine," I muttered to myself. "A mountain isn't that bad."

"You have a few minutes to confer with your team before you must go. You don't have time to waste to steal those Jian eggs." Indulgence rubbed their palms together. "It's cold and getting even colder by the minute. I don't need to set a timeline on this task, as those who do not retrieve the bounty in time will most certainly perish from the elements."

Seon offered me a thick coat and helped me strap on the climbing supplies provided by the major god. "You and Kama will get those eggs. You've got this."

"I appreciate it." I grinned. "And I know you actually mean it, so, that helps."

He laughed. “True.”

Tala tugged on my sleeve. “We’ve hunted those birds. They are very dangerous and can create winds with their wings. Remember that they travel in pairs.”

“Thank you.” I then bent down and gave Ulan a ruffle. “Take good care of each other while we’re gone.”

I glanced over my shoulder, and Bo had already retrieved his pack and was heading toward the path to the mountains with Pubu. He’d have to face me at some point. Our alliance with Pubu ensured we’d work together.

I linked my arm with Kama, and we trailed behind everyone else.

A thin dusting of snow covered the paved path to the mountain the closer we got to it. Lupong had the occasional snowfall in the winter. I loved the way it looked as if the major gods themselves sprinkled sugar over the buildings and the trees.

“Wait, wait.” Indulgence appeared before us, shimmering into existence to bar our way. “Your punishment isn’t complete.”

I asked, “Punishment?”

“Yes, for Kama’s failure. Because I’m a merciful god, it will be temporary.” They snapped their fingers. “Now . . . it’s complete.”

Then everything in my vision went black.

Jian birds are associated with eternal love and marriage, for they mate for life. Couples often use this motif in their wedding feasts and garments. A carving of these mythical birds is a staple on the tables celebrating anniversaries.

Jian birds are native to the northernmost Guolin Mountains and to Nomad territory.

—*BESTIARY VOLUMES*, SECOND SCROLL, GREAT LIBRARY OF XIANLING

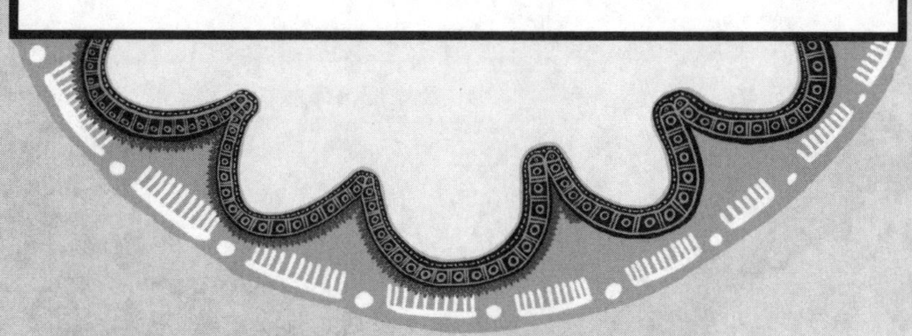

TWENTY-SIX

I took a deep breath to steady myself. "You'll need to be my eyes."

The rising panic in my throat made my voice hoarse. The absence of sight felt like being in an enclosed space. There weren't even shadows for me to follow.

"For the love of plum wine, don't even think of passing out. I'm in no shape to kick your body up the mountain," Kama grumbled. "Learn to breathe first instead of gulping air down like koi."

It took a few minutes for me to calm myself down. When I did, I took a few tentative steps forward. Kama and I found a rhythm where he'd nudge me in the right direction if I were deviating too much. After a bit, we had transformed from a drunken-looking duo to something more like dance partners.

The growing wind whipped powdered snow in my face. I clutched my coat tighter. "Where are Bo and Pubu? How far ahead are they?"

"Not too far."

"And Guolin and Zolzaya?"

"Much farther. If I could transform into a bear, we'd be up the mountain by now," Kama declared with a sigh. "Or perhaps, more fittingly, a dragon."

"If you could turn into a creature, I always pictured you as a drunken chicken."

I was rewarded with a hearty chuckle from the old minor god. Then I heard the unmistakable sound of a flask opening. If Kama were mortal, he'd be dead by now with the amount of drink he consumed.

My curiosity got the best of me. "Why do you drink?"

"You ask this of me when I can push you into the nearest snowbank?" My sponsor god's tone remained jovial, so I dismissed the threat. "It's a temporary way to forget. Though distant, the past can be far too painful to bear."

His voice took on a dreamy quality. "Ah, Lyka. The beach is better, but this will do. So nice to take a walk together again."

I asked him, "Lyka. You've mentioned her before in your sleep. Who is she?"

"Cai, I'm sorry. My mind is scattered. It's like I've been trying to gather spilled rice, grain by grain. I'm so tired."

"Once we get those peaches, we'll fix you up." I infused all of my optimism into my voice. "This is almost over."

"Memories remind you what is lost. I don't want to remember anything."

I didn't understand him. Memories were precious. This was how I kept Baba with me all these years. How else could I banish the loneliness that threatened to drown me at every turn?

"Don't you want to remember people who were important to you?" I kept trudging forward in the darkness, waiting for Kama's voice to guide me.

He let out a long, drawn-out sigh. "I prefer the shadows. I'd give anything to return the world to what it once was."

"That I understand. I'd do anything to see Baba again. So, is Lyka your wife?"

He tipped his head in confusion. "How do you know her name?"

"You've mentioned her before in your sleep."

"She was beautiful and came from the islands to the Peninsula . . ."

Though he had mentioned before that his memories hurt him, I allowed Kama to luxuriate in his past. Telling me about her seemed to be bringing him joy and comfort somehow, despite his ramblings. I didn't want to take that away from him. My sponsor god told me of their time spent on the Peninsula long ago. I made the mistake of asking him to describe her, and true to his nature, he went into too much detail that I had to cover his mouth.

"Have we caught up to Pubu and Bo yet?" I asked him.

The loud voices in the distance signaled that we had. I was surprised to hear that Pubu was midconversation with Guolin, whom I'd expected to be on his way back down with an egg by now.

"This is a once-in-a-generation offer. Join me, and we are guaranteed to reach the final feast together." Guolin's gruff voice defied the whistle of the wind. "I'll even let you ride on my back. With the both of us, we can finish this challenge quickly. An alliance to get us through the final challenge will be mutually beneficial."

"Tempting, very tempting, even if this offer is only because your other comrades have fallen. You're guaranteeing me a Jian egg?" Pubu asked the bear god.

"Yes, I'll steal two."

Of all the double-dealing, hypocritical . . .

"You have no honor!" I shouted in what I hoped was Pubu's direction. "You are an ugly cheat of a god if you renege on your deal with Kama!"

Instead of admonition, my outburst was greeted with laughter. Guolin's guffaws were ground-shaking while Pubu's giggles were resonant and musical. Blood rushed to my cheeks, and I scowled.

Kama squeezed my arm and whispered, "You won't stand a chance against these gods even if you could see them, let alone blind."

"But she's going to abandon us. She promised," I hissed between my teeth.

"This isn't as easy for her as you think. Patience, little firecracker."

"Why? Is there a penalty for breaking alliances? If—" Kama's hand covered my mouth.

"I accept," Pubu announced with a flourish. "Come, Bo."

"I'm not moving. You made a vow to Kama." Bo's voice was unwavering and emotionless.

"Don't be childish. This will save us the effort of stealing an egg." Pubu's cajoling tone was angelic. "This way, you can also get back at your traitorous girlfriend."

I steadied my breath to quell my increasing anxiety. If Bo used this as his reasoning for joining Pubu, I'd forgive him. I had to. I'd deserve it.

"You made an alliance. You should honor it," Bo repeated louder.

The roar of a massive bear echoed in my ears. "You had your chance."

The scraping of snow and the subtle shaking of the ground implied that Guolin and Zolzaya had moved on.

"Foolish boy," Pubu chastised Bo. "Now all we have are two invalids slowing us down."

If I weren't so annoyed, I'd pity her situation. A quick way to get ahead had been snatched away. Ruthlessness was as much a currency as diplomacy in this competition.

"Can you transform into a creature that could carry us?" I asked her.

The goddess scoffed. "Do I look like a horse and carriage to you? Perhaps your mind is gone like your vision."

"Her powers are restricted to water and water creatures, which wouldn't help us." Even though Bo's tone was flat, I still flinched.

I lowered my chin and busied myself crunching the snow under my boots while the three of them discussed our meager options.

The snowfall covered the sleeves of my jacket, and the dampness irritated my nostrils. An idea took root in my brain.

"Kama?" I tugged on his ragged sleeve. "How much snowfall did we have? Is there a lot of it around?"

"There's more than enough for anything you could have in mind," my sponsor god replied. "It's about boot-high."

"Snow is water! If Pubu can shape the snow into a vehicle, we can get to the top, provided that there is a clear path. If it's too narrow, perhaps she could try making a rickshaw with water people?" I made a vague gesture miming my ideas.

The goddess snorted. "You do realize we can hear you just fine. As for the snow, I suppose it's worth a try."

I couldn't see what Pubu was doing, yet my other senses whispered that something impossible was happening, a prickle on my skin. Magic. I had never noticed it before.

"Well, well, you truly are a talented goddess." Kama whistled and then addressed me. "She made a rickshaw—wide enough to carry all of us while narrow enough to navigate the path. The water man pulling it is a fine specimen—tall, brawny, with flashing pectorals. Of course, it resembles yours truly."

I laughed at the absurd picture Kama concocted.

"What is everyone waiting for? Let's go." Pubu's impatience powdered her musical voice.

My father had taught me manners after all. "Thank you, Pubu, goddess of the water."

If she had given me side-eye, I was thankful not to witness it.

Kama guided me into the ice rickshaw, sitting beside me, while Pubu and Bo sat behind us. I could hear her whispering but couldn't make out what was being said. The sound of water conveniently muffled their conversation.

I yearned to speak with Bo, yet I still couldn't find the right words to say. Privacy was also another matter. But with my visual impediment, waiting for the right time would never happen. "Oh, to hell with it," I muttered under my breath. "And you never told me how you felt because . . . ?"

Silence.

"If I knew how you felt earlier, we maybe could've figured it out. Before things got so complicated."

A low whistle followed Kama's muffled chuckle. The vagabond godling was enjoying every moment of this. I gave him a jab with my elbow.

"Bo, you can't stay silent forever. Anger is a poison. Believe me, I know. I don't care if you want to curse me. Please, just say something, anything." Now Pubu joined the chuckling.

I should be charging coin to these two immortals because they had front seats to my personal drama. "If this is how you want to end things, that's fine. It's not what I'd choose. You figure out how to explain to your family why we're no longer friends."

I conjured up the last image I had of Bo. It was at the base of the mountain when he was preparing his supplies. The stubble on his square jaw had thickened and almost covered his lower face like a beard, aging him ten years. He didn't have the softer features of his father. His mother, Ai, always predicted he'd be a heartbreaker with his choice of a wife.

"What matters now is that you know how I feel yet you still choose to look the other way—in Seon's direction." A thread of anger wound its way around Bo's deep voice.

"I don't know, Bo." I clenched and unclenched my hands, threading my fingers together then apart until I settled on picking at my fingernails. "After . . ."

"We've been over this, Cai. There's no time like the present, and now I'm starting to think you're just making excuses." His voice softened to a whisper. "After all these years, how can you not be sure? If you care about me at all, you'll at least be straight with me."

I owed him honesty, yet it stuck in my throat as if I was choking with it. Confronting his feelings for me—and being unable to reciprocate them—was a point of no return. And I had to admit it, I did want Seon more. "This thing, this thing with Seon, it took me by surprise, but your friendship means the world to me. I don't want to lose that."

Dead silence. He wasn't going to respond after that, nor did I expect him to.

It felt like a lifetime ago when he and I would linger by the bridge and watch the monks at the temple light their lanterns and incense for the major gods. Prayers then were to faceless deities that existed only in name.

I'd cooked for two major gods and was about to serve my food to the third.

These major gods were real.

Dragons were real.

Death was real.

What wasn't was the childish hope that everything broken could be fixed.

The minor god Kama took on a mortal wife against the counsel of the major gods. The union was an abomination. Dalliances between minor gods and mortals are conventionally tolerated and overlooked by the major gods, but a marriage defiles the sanctity of godhood.

—*OF MORTAL AND IMMORTAL RELATIONS*, SECOND SCROLL, FORBIDDEN VAULT AT THE GRAND LIBRARY OF XIANLING

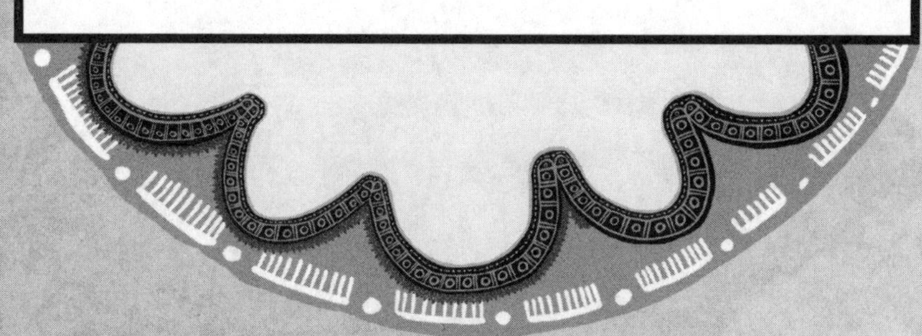

TWENTY-SEVEN

By the time we reached the summit, a blizzard had whipped the mountaintop into a frenzy. The cold specks of snow lashed my exposed skin. As soon as we all disembarked, the distant, frustrated sounds of a growling bear rose above the howling blasts of wind.

"What's happening?" I asked Kama.

"We're all blind now thanks to this storm. But it sounds like Guolin hasn't made any progress. The grumpy bear is powerless against the storm." My minor god cackled. "He'll have no choice but to wait it out with us."

Pubu altered the rickshaw into a large tent to shelter us. The goddess had her admirable traits, yet they didn't quite cover up her capacity for treachery. If Bo hadn't spoken up, she would have gone along with Guolin. Still, there must be something there that Songwon found endearing. However, I didn't possess the time or inclination to dig through a dung heap to find gold.

"Is there an act two to the drama?" Kama asked, breaking the silence. "Pubu and I would be grateful for any form of entertainment while we wait for this to pass."

I covered my eyes and sighed. Impudent minor god. If Bo had any objection, he didn't say a word. At least the goddess had sense not to join in.

Pubu and Kama soon resorted to gossiping about their peers, filling the silence. Judging from the salacious slander, these minor gods were as flawed, if not more, than mortals. Dalliances, double-crossing, and dirty deeds were the standard when living for so long.

The winds abated when night fell. We ventured outside, and the others scouted the area. The moonlight would have changed the snow into shimmering stardust like it did on winter nights in Lupong. I wished I could enjoy the view.

"Any sign of the nest or the birds?" I asked Kama.

Baba told me about Jian birds once. My mother believed in them because she was a romantic, and these birds were paired for eternity. I often pictured my parents together in the afterlife. Though I never met my mother, Baba reassured me that I was her mirror image. To me she was a beautiful dream, in contrast with my very real father, whose callous hands I held as he took his last breath.

"There is a nest with two Jians. One is dozing while the other keeps watch," Kama whispered in hushed tones. He then described what they looked like.

The two Jian birds huddled together, protecting three golden eggs. Apparently, the mythical animals were as strange as they were elegant. Each possessed one leg and one eye. They acted as one, moving in unison, compensating for their mate's sight. They boasted ruby and sapphire plumage.

"Wait, I just remembered something important. Someone told me once that they'll get lulled into a trance if you sing a love song," Kama declared in triumph.

I coughed. "Maybe you and Pubu can perform the duet. I can't sing."

It was true. Even the drunken singing at the Three Cranes Tavern sounded much more pleasant than my creaky mangling of a traditional song. I preferred to use my precious free time at the markets, scouring for ingredients and honing my ability to bargain.

"We are only allowed to escort you to the challenge. We're not supposed to interfere after that," Pubu cautioned. "At the moment, Zolzaya is approaching the nest on her own. She's using her Zhenniao as a distraction. The eagle is circling above the nest and has caught the attention of the waking parent. The Jian is flying up to investigate while Zolzaya battles the second one to steal the egg." A few taut minutes passed. "And she's done it. Guolin is now carrying her away and down the mountain."

I was disappointed, but unsurprised. If what Tala told me was correct, Zolzaya could hold her own against a small army. Meanwhile, I didn't even have my basic senses intact.

Kama's method was our only shot. I'd never heard Bo sing before. Songs about cats and ducklings for his younger sisters were chanted aloud rather than put into complicated melodies. He had never shown any inclination to burst into song or even whistle. It wasn't as if we both avoided music—there were many summer nights when we sat on the tea shop rooftop listening to the night market buskers—we just weren't the ones producing it.

I tugged on Kama's sleeve. "Should we practice first? I'm not even sure Bo can sing."

As if to prove me wrong, Bo cleared his throat and *sang*.

His deep, baritone voice sent shivers down my spine. Tiny bumps erupted from my skin, and it wasn't from the cold. My best friend had been hiding this incredible talent along with his feelings for me. He was either very good at secrets or I was completely dense. I sensed it was the latter.

"That was incredible, Bo." I clapped.

"Let's get this over with." The crunch of his boots followed his words.

And there it was. He still didn't want to talk. I wanted my best friend back instead of this cold stranger. My heart constricted. I never thought Bo was capable of coldness. His boyish grin was more reliable than the morning sun.

"You two will need to sing a love song," Pubu instructed. "I suggest 'When the Star Fell in Love.'"

The song was familiar to those on the Continent and the Peninsula. It was far older than anyone could remember, uttered on the lips of old men and women, their children, and their children's children. The words might have changed, yet the lilting melody of the ballad endured. The grand forbidden romance of a mortal and a star stoked the dreams of generations of romantics. Every year, it was performed as a duet at the harvest festival. The songstress playing the star always had the most elaborate costume and makeup. The two performers received the city's accolades in the form of applause, small gifts, and most important, bragging rights for a full year.

Pubu and Kama became my patient teachers for the next half hour. They corrected my ineffective warbling into something passable. I by no means matched Bo in skill—but it was no longer quite so shrill. If I were a dish, I'd be covered with a delicious sauce to hide the horror underneath.

Kama gave me a nudge forward. "Go on, it's time."

We trudged forward, singing softly, Bo holding my arm to guide me. All of a sudden, there was a terrible screech and a surge of wind, and the force of it made me stagger a few steps backward.

"What's going on?" I screamed into the wind.

My sponsor god yelled back, "I think they just found out they've been robbed by Zolzaya."

"We need to keep singing then," I announced. "We need to keep them calm until we get our eggs."

Bo cleared his throat and resumed our song but louder. With no walls and endless echo, his deep voice surrounded the mountain and all its glory. "*Memories fade as the dawn clears the sky, the old day gone. Once, loneliness enveloped a man as he walked under a canopy of stars. The hollowness of his lifespan.*"

It was working. The wind was dying down. I hoped my participation wouldn't break the spell.

"*I have my sisters with me always. I'm never alone. This mortal has no other and I want to cure my malaise.*" As I sang, my modest offering brought on another gust of wind. How could I do better, make this feel more real . . .

The rest of my words of protest evaporated from my mind when he kissed me. His strong arms held me as I went limp, feeling like I was falling. I had been so sure of Seon, but how could he be the one if I could still feel like this with Bo? But just as I let myself give in to it, I noticed something was off. There was no emotion behind it, unlike Bo's previous kiss in the kitchen, which echoed with hope and yearning. It was as if a living stone statue were kissing me. The act might as well be something like washing the dishes or wiping down a table. It hit me. He was doing this to make the song work. Some mythical animals were known for their emotional intelligence, and who other than creature-obsessed Bo would know that best?

Still, the poor excuse of a kiss seemed to convince the Jian. The air around us was settling back down. I tried my best not to fail and act as a wobbly bridge to Bo's next part.

"The star fell from the sky tree,
She landed near the waves of the sea.
He found her, at first in silence,
He taught her to speak, whence

From him, she learned of love,
To love."

The pairing of mortal and immortal had always been shunned and considered taboo. This is why Kama's mortal wife was such a stain on his reputation.

I thought back on my conversation with Kama as we trekked up this hellish mountain, and I understood the longing the star must have held—easier to think about his love story than my own.

"Then this is how I defy
That being mortal is worth
Losing an eternity of sky."

As I sang, I pictured Bo stealing the two remaining eggs in the nest. I hoped he was successful because the end of the song was approaching.

"Memories fade as the dawn
clears the sky for a new outcome.
Loneliness no longer haunts them
As they walked under a canopy of stars."

"It's done, child." I felt Bo's hand on my arm guiding me back to the magical rickshaw while he completed the ballad. I was handed one of the eggs, which was very warm in my arms. The goddess then warned us, "Hold on. We're getting off this mountain as fast as we can."

I instinctively joined arms with my old sponsor. "How did you know the love song would work?"

"Because true love endures. Ever wonder why the Three Cranes Tavern is my home? Because it was at one point. That was where Lyka and I built our homestead. I'll never leave that place."

To my relief, my eyesight was restored the instant we returned to the courtyard. The golden egg in my arms was roughly the size of the dragon stone. I looked all around me, cherishing the view.

Indulgence waited in the courtyard with their dragon, as did the rest of our teams. I greeted Tala and Seon with quick hugs and even gave Ulan a few pets on the head. They were jubilant to see us return with the egg.

Indulgence lifted their hands up, palms to the sky. Kama, Guolin, and Pubu were compelled to stand before them. The devious smirk on the major god's face sent shivers across my skin. The climb up the mountain had Kama looking frailer than ever, especially in contrast with youthful, muscular Guolin.

Indulgence wagged their finger. "Kama, you don't look too good. Your immortality is draining from you."

My sponsor god held up his index finger. A tiny ball of energy, the size of a rambutan, popped into the air. "See, I still got it."

Kama flashed a proud grin before he fainted.

Pubu might be the only remaining minor goddess, but this wasn't always so. Whispers of missing goddesses have rippled from the North. The Nomads uphold the tradition and belief that there is an all-powerful goddess who created the world, the mother of the major gods themselves. The name of this goddess is a closely guarded secret.

—*THE TWO MISSING GODDESSES*,
FIRST SCROLL, FORBIDDEN VAULT AT THE
GRAND LIBRARY OF XIANLING

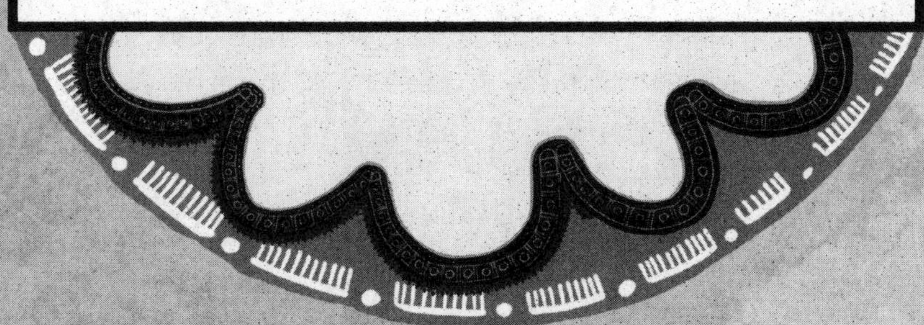

TWENTY-EIGHT

Indulgence made a face and snapped their fingers. A jolt of energy coursed through Kama's limp body, bringing him back into consciousness. "This is your own fault, the consequence of failing so many times, over and over. Anyway, before you all head to the arena to prepare your eggs, we're going to sit down for a pot of tea." Indulgence held up their finger to create three stations with a small stove, a bronze teapot and cups, a bundle of tea leaves, and all the accoutrements for tea making. "Chefs, you must drink with your sponsor before you can proceed to the cooking arena."

What could this be about? Kama and I reached our station last. He still looked dazed. The tea leaves weren't anything I recognized. They were shaped like a fringed dragon's claw. The spiky texture of the leaves rubbed the tips of my fingertips raw and tingling. "Do you know what these are?"

"Oh, this is thousand dragon tea. Lyka, this was your favorite," Kama said dreamily.

Lyka. Again, he addressed me as his mortal wife. I could correct him, but that would take precious time I didn't have. Kama continued plodding forward, delving deeper and deeper into his memories, losing himself in the imagined company of his wife. I had no choice. Although I justified my deceit, guilt coated my tongue like spiced honey. His memories were not meant for my ears.

"There was something I think I'm forgetting, Lyka," he continued, ruffling his hair. "Something we had to do before you drink it. It's dangerous otherwise. Mortals shouldn't partake, no, no, no."

"Why?"

"It's addictive, my love. You won't be able to stop yourself from drinking more. It's meant for the gods. Now give me a few moments while I try to remember what it is I have to do first." He tutted while clinking the teacups. "Something about . . ."

Indulgence had been pacing between our stations to intercept any kind of collusion. I hoped Pubu knew about the crucial drawback of the tea.

Kama fussed with the teacups until I heard a loud "Aha!" that almost knocked me sideways. "It's in the preparation! You must char the leaves first—so much so that you have ash. This is what you'll use to make the tea. Let me see if there is a sieve somewhere."

There was a whirlwind of banging and rummaging before he declared that he had found it.

"What do you accomplish by burning it?"

"You rid the tea of its mystical properties. This is meant to be irresistible to the senses." He poured the boiling water into the teapot with the sieve. "For you, my love, you will get the great taste without the addiction."

A league of dragons emerged from the steam, all in a white, cloudy vapor. They flew upward to the sky. The fragrance of the tea reminded me of the high altitudes of the mountain, the blooming peonies from the rooftop garden, and the brininess of the Singing Sea. The intoxicating taste introduced an umami flavor I'd never experienced in any drink. The punch from its intensity matched my first taste of flame song whiskey and its richness, that of the most pungent king oyster mushrooms.

"This is delicious." I sighed and cradled the tea to my chest. "I can understand why it's addictive."

"It makes for a wonderful soup base." He took a sip from his tea cup. "You can't forget the egg drop soup I made the first night we had that terrible storm that lasted four days. Oh, it was a very frightful one. It was when you . . . No, no, no, no!" His cries increased in pitch. "You're dead. I carried you in my arms after you were struck by lightning."

I reached out, trying to grasp his tattered tunic.

"Kama, everything is all right. You're at the Celestial Banquet. I'm Cai, your candidate." I fumbled for his hand so I could grasp it. "Once I get you the peach, everything will right itself. You'll get your strength back."

His sobbing tore my heart in two. It wasn't melodramatic or artificial. This was visceral anguish. It was the sound I once made for Baba. I knew how it felt: sadness squeezed every piece of you until no liquid was left, and when the air hit every crevice, the dryness made you raw.

I couldn't stop him, nor did I want to. Luckily, everyone else was too busy with their tea to pay us much attention.

"We were on the beach during a storm. My affinity to lightning drew a powerful bolt to me, and thus her next to me. And it was too strong to undo. I *killed* her. The major gods shouldn't have been given immortality in the first place. It's a curse. I'm a monster."

"You are the father of the Peninsula. You care about your people." I squeezed his hands. "You are not a monster."

Over my shoulder, Guolin and Zi Rui were arguing.

"Hurry up and drink the tea so you can move on to the arena! The Jian egg will hatch otherwise." Guolin muttered a few curses under his breath. "Those birds will murder you if the shell cracks."

I smacked my forehead. I'd better heed this warning too. Of course there would be a time limit on the eggs.

I looked over at Songwon. I had wanted to warn my ally earlier, but I would be risking punishment from Indulgence. And before I could devise a surreptitious way to do it, Songwon took a drink and left us behind.

"I don't want to drink it! Zi Rui whined. "The texts at the Blade and Palate libraries state that no mortal should drink this tea."

Guolin smacked him again. "Then why has Pubu's team already passed by us? If it were so dangerous, would her candidate be able to walk out on his own will? Drink, or I will smite you myself, you little worm. I'll relish beating you to a sticky smear."

There was a pause in the conversation.

I was lucky to have the minor god that I did. Yes, he was technically weaker, less prestigious than a god like Guolin, but all of that power came at a cost. He didn't care about his team, he only cared about winning.

Tala and Seon helped me with Kama as we rushed toward the cooking arena.

There was nothing more I wanted to do than to humble Indulgence through my cooking. Yes, we were grateful they exiled Death and his demons but these major gods needed to remember whom they had saved in the first place. We were more than servants who worshipped them through the acts of cooking and feeding—we thrived in their long absences, taking care of our own, discovering new knowledge, and writing our own stories and histories.

If it weren't for those precious peaches, I wouldn't be here. The major gods needed this bait to coerce mortals and minor gods alike to dance at their command. Otherwise, what power did they actually wield?

The arrows are ready.
Three oxen drive the cart at harvest.
Sing the song of widows and orphans
and the Peninsula stands strong.

—A LETTER BY RED RIBBONS IN XIANLING
TO THE REBELS IN LUPONG

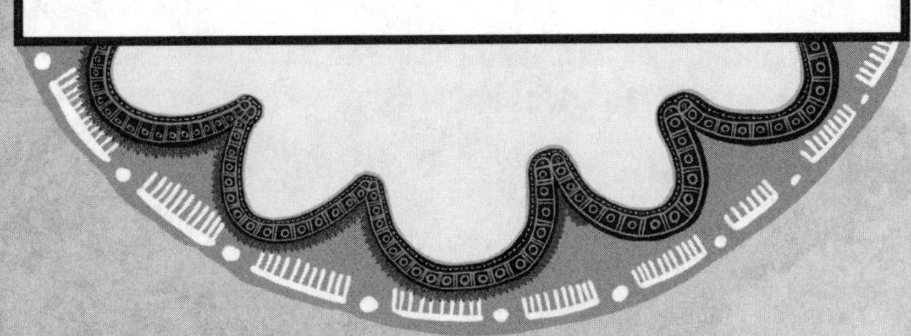

TWENTY-NINE

The corridor leading into the arena was much bigger and wider than Temperance's version. As was the case the first day, our teams headed to the audience seating, while Songwon, Zi Rui, and I waited in the tunnel to the sounds of a crowd's roar. A buzz traveled under my skin, electrifying me. I loved to perform for my regulars at the noodle stall. This should be similar.

"What has Guolin done for your addiction?" Songwon asked Zi Rui. "Pubu is providing me with water lily juniper berries to help manage it."

"Guolin gave me a temporary cure until I win the peaches." Zi Rui crossed his arms over his chest. "My sponsor wants me to be more motivated to win."

Donkey dung. This was another bullying tactic by his poor excuse of a minor god. "The bear god is a selfish jerk. He should have helped you so you have no addiction! You're doing most of the work. Giapxiao!" I fumed. "We're the ones cooking. They wouldn't have any peaches without us!"

I expected Zi Rui to defend his abusive sponsor, maybe even brawl with me in his honor. My hands were already clenched at my sides in anticipation. I'd been in scraps where I was the runt of the pack before; I could hold my own.

But Zi Rui lowered his shoulders, his barrel chest deflating. “Guolin holds my family hostage. I haven’t seen my son and my wife in five months.” He jutted out his chin. “I will not lose to you two.”

I should have been surprised by his revelation, but I wasn’t. The competition taught me that these immortals would do anything that pleased them regardless of the consequences.

“I expected nothing less.” I rubbed my hands together. “May the best cook win.”

The echoing sound of the gong signaled our entrance into the cooking ring.

The round monstrosity was an open-air theatre that could seat thousands. Other than our teams, seated on the lowest row, the spectators were specters—shadows of what a crowd would be. Seon had mentioned that live audiences were banned to keep the banquet’s secrecy.

I waved to Seon and Tala, who sat by a sleeping Kama then to Bo, who ignored the gesture. Part of me, my rebellious streak, wasn’t ready to give up. I *would* fix all this after this final feast. But the peaches came first.

Indulgence descended from the sky on their magnificent great dragon. The phantom crowd roared at their entrance.

“Is everyone ready to cook the best meal of their lives?” Indulgence raised their arms in the air. “My appetite will not be denied. Cooks, attend to your kitchens.”

Songwon, Zi Rui, and I chose our stations. My ally and I chose to flank Zi Rui on both sides. Unlike the banquet hall, here there were no markets that we could see.

"You three had an easy time with the last two feasts. Luck and Temperance were far more magnanimous than I. They provided you with every sort of luxury and tool to cook the most thrilling of dishes. However, to deny you the best ingredients would only serve to diminish my own meal." Indulgence raised their arms over their head.

A mountain of rare ingredients materialized to the right of the kitchens, as if Indulgence themself had shaken the markets and emptied them into a pile. The ground trembled, shaking to reveal rising mounds of dirt. Each mound swirled until it took the form of a human—a fierce soldier wielding a longsword. There were nine in total, and they encircled the treasured ingredients.

I had to navigate that to get my supply? I swallowed and blinked. They might be made of mud, but I had no doubt they could cut me in two. As if to confirm their destructive power, one sliced a watermelon in half with their dirt sword.

A bead of sweat traveled from my neck down the back of my tunic.

We were here to cook, not to battle monsters before we even had a chance.

I glanced around at my competitors. Songwon covered his eyes and was already whispering his prayers. I wasn't sure which god he was appealing to—hopefully to the other two we fed and not the one before us. Zi Rui pressed his fingers against his temples while muttering under his breath. Curses, not prayers. My opinion of him raised slightly.

They were resigned to their fate, but I wasn't.

"Indulgence!" I addressed the major god. There was a high chance I'd be struck down for my insolence, but it was unavoidable. "We'll all be too busy to cook. Shouldn't we have help? Perhaps a team member? It'd be far more exciting for you to watch two sets of battles. One for ingredients and one in the kitchen."

I resisted the urge to shut my eyes while the major god decided whether to turn me into a greasy human stain where I stood. Instead, I faced my potential death with a stoicism that would make Baba and Tondo the Tall proud.

"Hmm . . ." Indulgence stroked their trimmed beard.

The half-giggle and squeal that came out of my mouth was the sound of my soul reentering my body, confirming that I was still alive. The exhaustion brought on by the grueling competition frayed my sanity at the edges. Somehow, the days of the Celestial Banquet carried the weight of a lifetime.

"I agree to your proposal, you little upstart, but you three must scramble for your first ingredient. After that, your teammates can take over. The Jian egg must be the theme of your dish." Indulgence gestured for the rest of our teams to stand.

Tala propped up the limp, dozing Kama as if he were a human-shaped slab of tofu. Seon helped pull him up from the other side. Zolzaya; Jeong-ho, Guolin's noble representative; Yoshihiro; and Bo all rose to their feet.

"Choose your assistant." Indulgence pointed at me, and I blurted out, "Seon!"

I could have chosen Tala, but he was better suited to deal with those magical swordsmen, and I selfishly wanted him by my side at this last feast.

"Zolzaya!" Zi Rui shouted with confidence.

Songwon declared his choice. "Bo!"

It wasn't a surprise that Songwon would choose him. Bo was the most physically fit for this challenge. He'd never fought before. Of course, I worried about him. I wanted to ask Seon if he could look out for Bo, just in case . . .

"Assistants, enter the ring." Indulgence then made a small gesture with their left hand. Songwon, Zi Rui, and I were pulled in the direction of the swordsmen with their pointy weapons. "Get the first ingredient, candidates. The faster you are, the better off you'll be."

All three of us chefs approached the bounty. I ducked down to dodge a swing from the nearest warrior. Another popped up from behind me, sending me into a protective roll away. Songwon was also busy evading and keeping his attackers occupied rather than advancing to get any ingredient. Zi Rui ran toward me until we stood back-to-back.

"We'll work together," he said, panting. "Just this one time. Truce?"

"We also have to protect Songwon, then you'll have your alliance." I counted the three approaching attackers. I called over Songwon, who dodged and weaved his way to reach us. "We're forming a temporary partnership. Do you agree, Songwon?"

He nodded. "We need all the help we can get."

One drew close enough to me that I punched it in the nose, where my fist's indentation remained. We took turns kicking, punching, moving as a three-bodied unit. Our efforts were rewarded with a narrow corridor leading to the treasure trove of ingredients. Zi Rui's eyes sparkled when he noticed the opportunity. A swordsman waited at the side for his chance to slice the oblivious seeker.

Guolin's candidate ran for the ingredients, leaving Songwon and me behind. "No, Zi Rui! It's a trap." I yelled. But he didn't seem to hear me. I could have let Destiny deal with his selfish act—it'd be one fewer competitor to cook against and an instant showdown between me and Songwon—but I couldn't.

"Giapxiao!" I cursed myself as I pulled Songwon with me as I ran to intercept Zi Rui.

The selfish cheat didn't even see the sword coming down toward his neck. I pushed him away to safety and brought my forearm up to shield my body.

As a cook, I'd cut myself before. Various little scars decorated my arms and hands—a road map of my culinary education. Sometimes, I didn't even notice the harm until droplets of scarlet dotted my apron or sleeve. This was different. The kiss of the air against my gaping flesh carried the sting of lemon and vinegar. Blood splattered across my gray tunic and pants. Kama's mark and its beautiful raven were split in two by a line of red.

The pain almost overwhelmed me, yet I pushed the encroaching darkness out of my vision. I used my right hand to clamp the wound closed as I stumbled toward the ingredients. I grabbed the first greens I could find while Songwon picked up his choice and helped me return to my station, passing me off to Seon with a meaningful look.

"Cai! Are you okay? Give me a minute." Seon ran to pour some water over my wound, then ripped the sleeves off his tunic. With quick work, he made a tight bandage.

"Thank you," I whispered with a wince. "This is my fault. All because of my sense of nobility. Now I must cook."

I'd almost forgotten what I had grabbed. "Thousand dragon leaves." I shook my head and let out a dry laugh. I might as well have stolen some from the previous task.

The tea would make a splendid broth for cooking the rice. Omurice. The Jian eggs would make a lovely omelet for the dish. Baba and I used to share a special bowl every Lunar New Year. I'd need more spices and components for the topping sauce. Of anything I'd ever made, this one was the most special to me—I would be cooking for myself instead of trying to please the whims of a major god.

"Try and take it easy with this arm, Cai. Hopefully we'll get a chance to stitch it up. I want to be mad at you for endangering yourself, but how could I? That big heart is one of the reasons why I love you." Seon adjusted and tightened the bandage on my arm. "Now, what do you need me to get?"

Again, he said he *loved* me. It was uttered with such ease that I'd almost forgotten he'd confessed it earlier—and that he was still a chronic truth teller. It took a second for me to answer his question with a short list. "Wait, before you go, please watch out for Bo. He doesn't have any sword skills, and he doesn't really know how to fight."

"I think he's doing fine on his own." Seon tilted his head in the direction of the melee.

Bo was wrestling one of Indulgence's warriors and overpowering him. He'd never shown this kind of strength or prowess before. When did my innocent friend become this man? It was almost as if I didn't know him anymore. There were only traces remaining of the boy who left Lupong.

Seon took off with his sword in hand. He wielded it well—parrying, attacking when he saw his chance, and leaving his slower opponents behind. He'd invited me to a swordsmanship competition a few times in the past, but I'd been far too busy working to take any time off to attend.

Knowing that he and Bo were holding their own, I focused on my sole duty—cooking.

I turned to the golden egg sitting on the counter under a cradle of fabric. I picked it up, fingers moving along the smooth surface while I scanned for any hint of cracks.

Nothing so far.

I cracked the egg open into a large bowl. While the yolk was the same golden shade as its husk, the whites were a liquid silver.

The visually stunning pair would cement my decision to separate the yolk from the whites—one for the omurice and the other for the sauce.

Those who viewed these dishes as plain or too simple didn't know good food. Fancier ingredients didn't equate to better taste—that I had learned from my first day here. It was bad enough that society was divided into classes. Flavor and taste weren't defined by coin but by skill and practice. The best food in Xianling wasn't found in the most expensive restaurant. True connoisseurs knew the night market was where the true jewels were.

This feast was my final chance to show who I was as a chef. To make Baba proud. I needed to make a dish that would blow Indulgence away.

The way of the sword is a noble pursuit, especially in Xianling. The training required for this discipline continues until the death of the swordsman. Each one has the option of enlisting in the Empress's elite army—a lucrative and honorable choice. This is how the Empire managed to expand to its size. Not enlisting meant a darker life as a hired assassin.

—***THE SWORDSMAN***, **THIRD SCROLL,**
GREAT LIBRARY OF XIANLING

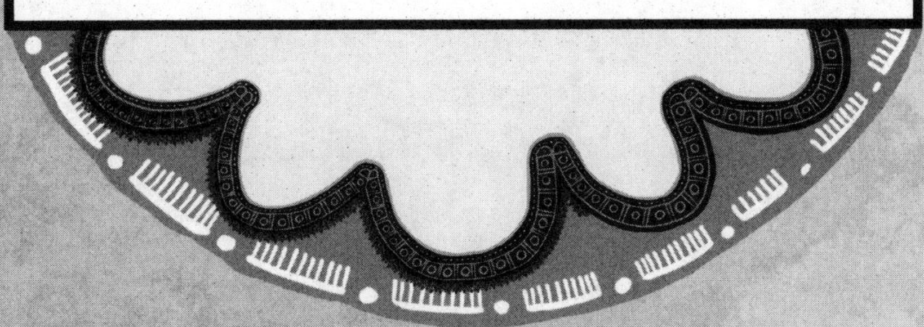

THIRTY

Songwon had already started his dishes for god and dragon both. He glanced up and waved. I raised my hand and then bowed to him. He mirrored the gesture. Even in the heat of this moment, it was good to feel seen by someone else who was experiencing it. I hoped our friendship continued when this final task was complete, no matter the outcome.

The aromas coming from Guolin's kitchen were heavenly. As much as I resented Zi Rui and his selfishness, he was an excellent cook. Towers of bamboo steamers crowded his stove. He must be creating steamed egg dishes. I stopped when I caught myself leaning to the side to get a better look.

Enough distractions. It was time to finish cooking.

After charring the thousand dragon's tea to ash, I steeped it with a silkie chicken, dried cloud's ear mushrooms, scallions, and cured, salted fish. Making a few adjustments, I added in some pungent star anise, purple scallions, scorpion chilis, and black garlic. As if I were a witch, I concocted the most powerful brew—a potent broth to steam the rice, a punch to the tongue and teeth.

Now, I had to prepare the fried rice underneath. The recipe was from my favorite stall at Lupong's night market. Auntie Chiu's rice had a line stretching out to the main road. I'd spent six months breaking down every component and re-creating the dish at night. Once I'd succeeded in replicating it, I'd taken another three months to make it my own.

This was my education. I'd experimented and observed those who were far better than I was. Every cook from the stalls to the restaurants of Lupong were my inspiration, rivals, and mentors. I yearned to be better at my craft. My curiosity was as hungry as my ambition. To stop learning was a form of death.

My left arm went limp right after I transferred the fried rice into separate bowls. My blood soaked the makeshift bandage. Seon quickly rushed over and fussed over the wound. He washed it out, added a poultice from his pack, and began sewing the wound shut. "I'm going to say it even though you won't listen. You need to slow down. Otherwise, you'll bleed out."

His stitches were even and very neat. Before I even had a chance to ask, he explained, "My mother's hobby is embroidery. She taught me a few stitches."

I twitched and tapped my feet, not from the pain, which was minimal, but from the anxiety of losing precious time. Zi Rui had already taken up his dish for Indulgence. The rice on the counter could cool off for a bit, but not too much. The sauce wasn't done and the omelet still needed to be made . . .

"Do you ever slow down? It's not an insult. I'm just curious." Seon finished his stitches and tied the ends, then looked up at me expectingly.

Kama's mark and the raven would be scarred in twain on my forearm. I took a deep breath and then answered his question. "I never have a chance to. There's always so much to do: making enough coin to feed and house myself, learning as many techniques as I can, trying out all the new ingredients I haven't tasted yet. Time has never been on my side."

"And that's why you should join me in Xianling. I meant what I said. I could give you an amazing life. I'll wait as long as you need." He released my arm and nudged me toward the kitchen. "Go do what you do best."

I poured the silvery whites over my broth and used my chopsticks to make a mass of shimmering ribbons until the sauce transformed into a galaxy of miniature birds. I split the pot into three tureens—one for Indulgence, his dragon, and one for the Empress.

The garnishing sauce was done.

As for the omurice, it'd be far more elaborate. I piled the fried rice into two separate mountains, ready for their canopy of gold. The trick was to cook the omelet evenly and then twirl it onto the rice, making a beautiful swirled blanket on top. I made a spicy gravy to dribble over it to give it a shine, and the final garnish was minced spring onions. The emerald green contrasted against the golden omelet.

With Kama out of commission, I followed my instincts and served the dragon the same meal as its master. After all, the dragon was the emperor of all creatures. My efforts were rewarded with a slight bow.

After serving the great beast, I carried the heavy tray with the ceramic tureen and platter of omurice before the heavy doors of Indulgence's chamber. I walked by Songwon's kitchen, and he was still busy making the final preparations for his dish. Zi Rui, the accomplished cook, had already emerged from the chambers.

Luck and Temperance's chambers were unique, so I was prepared to see something completely different from the last major god.

Indulgence didn't disappoint.

His chamber was at least three times the size of the others. A long path awaited me inside the doors with the god and the Empress seated at a table at the end. I had to walk through squared arches with familiar carvings painted in gold leaf. I'd been here before. This was a re-creation of a temple I'd visited many times in Lupong. Even the heavy scent of joss sticks perfuming the air was familiar.

My throat tightened as I continued onward.

Lupong's memorial temple housed all the dead, and we visited to burn incense and offerings to our ancestors. I went twice a year to honor Baba's memory and burn paper money for him to spend in his afterlife. I hadn't done so for my mother because I reasoned that Baba would share whatever he had with her.

"Don't dawdle, girl. Come on, bring the food. I'm starving!" Indulgence smacked their palm on the table.

I picked up the pace and set the dishes before the major god.

The Empress narrowed her painted brows and scowled. "This offering is still too simple. You've come this far to offer this? It will not impress me or a god. This is nothing. Good food is tantalizing to the eyes, but you've given me something equivalent to a beginner taking culinary lessons. You better remember who you are serving."

"The point of cooking is to make food sing on the tongue. That's it," I retorted. "It takes skill to make food taste good. It's a labor born out of passion and love. To create a perfect omelet, those eggs had to be whipped at a certain speed. You talk about skill, but you know nothing about it."

The tip of my tongue was loaded with curses and expletives, ready to set that old crone's face on fire. I should have let loose, but I wouldn't give her the satisfaction.

Indulgence's eyes darted between us. Their lips curled in amusement as they ate the omurice. "You mortals are always so consumed with separating yourselves. It's futile because you would be nothing without your major gods. This world isn't yours."

Their lasting gaze was directed at the Empress, who possessed enough good sense to acknowledge when she was put in her place.

I lowered my gaze and also kept my silence.

To the right of the table was a massive urn full of ash and a hundred lit joss sticks. A slat of wood stuck out like a headstone with writing on it. Since I couldn't read, I had no idea if it meant anything significant.

Indulgence must have seen me squinting at it, as they made a waving gesture with their left hand. "Perhaps you'll recognize this instead."

The name marker transformed into a painted picture of Baba.

It was how he looked before he fell ill. Vitality sparkled in his eyes and his skin, a ruddy glow. His unruly hair was brushed back, exposing the mole near his left eye and the narrow shape of his face. Baba.

"Omurice." The major god's perfect dark brows arched. "Why choose this?"

I stood my ground and crossed my arms. "It's a dish that's important to me. It's what my father cooked for us every Lunar New Year. We saved all year to buy the ingredients. It was our way to celebrate family." Try as I might, I couldn't stop glancing over at my father's portrait. They brought Baba here to taunt me, but seeing him again gave me strength.

Indulgence ladled themself more of the soup. "Your cooking has nerve. I'll give you that, girl." They licked the last grains of fried rice from the bowl. "Why do you cook?"

"Because it's how I live. We mortals have to worry about paying to keep a roof over our heads and food in our bellies. We don't have the luxury of not eating." The bite in my voice was as caustic as fermented coconut vinegar.

"If you hate this competition so much, then why enter it?"

Of course they'd point out my hypocrisy. "I had no choice. Those peaches will save Kama and give the rest of us a way to control our own fates. We don't have access to infinite power, after all."

The sarcasm in my voice was thicker than tapioca. Yes, I could be more congenial and kiss every god's feet and backside. But what good would it do? Currying favor or politicking wasn't who I was. I defied the Empress and every major god with good reason.

If I were to win, I wanted to do it on my own terms and without compromise. Indulgence would have to accept me as I was—piss, vinegar, and sugar only when I deemed the person worthy of it.

"I'm surprised that temper of yours hasn't killed you yet. Am I supposed to be impressed?"

"By my food, yes. Everything else is subjective and not important."

"Is it?" Indulgence set aside the empty bowl. "I have an offer for you. Consider it a chance to walk away from all this if you wish."

Baba's portrait went up in flames as a sob escaped my lips. As the paper turned into ashes, a soft breeze at the base of the urn stirred. The lit end of the joss sticks pulsed in an alternating pattern. A spectral form materialized from the disturbed specks.

I gasped.

"Cai, oh, how much you've grown!" Baba's rusty voice was clear. It was the sweetest sound I'd ever heard. "And you're at the Celestial Banquet!"

He hadn't aged a day. He possessed the translucence of a spirit—as if he were made of damp rice paper. His gnarled work-worn hands reached out to touch my cheek.

"Baba," I whispered, my voice breaking, "you're here?"

"Yes," Indulgence interrupted. "And if you like, he can stay with you as the world's happiest ghost. He can watch you conquer, succeed, and eventually get married. Grandchildren will know their laolao." Indulgence leaned forward over the table. "All you have to do is walk away right now from this competition. I want to know what the Celestial Banquet means to you."

When a person dies, they begin their journey to the Underworld. Surviving family members or descendants can still communicate with the departed by visiting the Temples of Death, which have been converted from places of worship to hubs that connect the living with their ghostly loved ones.

Anyone with enough coin can make the yearly donation required to commune with the spirits.

—*THE AFTERLIFE*, FOURTH SCROLL, LIBRARY OF LUPONG

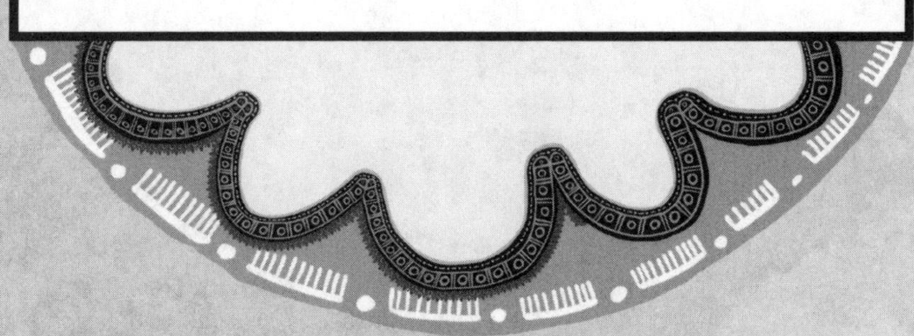

THIRTY-ONE

Temptation for me usually came in the form of sweets—sakura mochi and iced mango boba. I succumbed every time I was in a dark state of mind. These were my forms of medication when too many worries tightened my throat or the burden of reality became too heavy.

Indulgence's offer was a way of fixing what had been broken inside me. I'd spent all this time trying to keep together the pieces of the life that was shattered by Baba's absence. I wanted nothing more than to take up his offer and walk away. There were years of words I still yearned to say.

"Remember that he is in the afterlife. There's no other way to see him or hear him. All of your prayers may be heard, but this is the rare opportunity to converse with his spirit for as long as you wish. Your father will be restored in every sense except corporeal."

"Cai, what's going on?" Baba asked. "Do I have to leave?"

I held out my hand toward my father's spirit. When his fingertips touched mine, a sharp coldness seeped into my hands. He was here, yet not here. Tears sprang at the corners of my eyes as my chest constricted with a ragged sob. Death had stolen my father from me. I never thought I could recover from that robbery.

"Yes, Cai." Indulgence then echoed my father's question, "Does he have to leave?"

I closed my eyes and hugged myself. My entire being wanted nothing more than to have him stay. He'd be able to meet Seon, Bo, and Tala, to reunite with his best friend, Tondo the Tall. There were so many reasons why I *wanted* to have my father back in life. Yet, all of them were selfish.

Ultimately, this wasn't an impossible choice, because I wasn't as greedy as this major god thought I was. Even when I started this journey, I wouldn't take the offer and now, I still wouldn't. Kama and the others were relying on me. The Peninsula was relying on me. Tala. Seon. Bo. To choose my father would be a betrayal to myself, and he would be ashamed of my choice.

"I love you, Baba. I'm so sorry, but you can't stay." I addressed my father with tears streaming down my cheeks. I gulped in lungfuls of air and sobbed. "I'll see you again, I promise."

This was cruel, pure and simple. This major god wanted nothing more than to rob Kama and the rest of us of our peaches. I couldn't think anything else but pettiness could fuel this major god's motive.

"As you wish." Indulgence made a slashing motion, and the specter of my father vanished with the extinguishing of the joss sticks.

I flattened my hands against my sides, trying to stay upright when all I wanted to do was crumple onto the floor. The confused look on Baba's face when he vanished haunted me. Though this was all the major god's doing, I felt responsible—as if I'd been the one who'd killed him for the second time.

"You do realize that turning down my offer doesn't mean you'll win." Indulgence crossed their arms. "You lost the only guaranteed reward. Pubu's or Guolin's candidate could win it all, and you'll go back with nothing. Such a shame."

They were right. Songwon could win the peaches. Though my defeat would be a kick to the teeth, I wouldn't resent him for his victory because we were both on the same journey to get here. Even Zi Rui's winning was palatable now that I knew he was here for his family. With Tala, Seon, and Bo at my side, we'd figure out how to help Kama.

"You have served the unexpected. Go now, girl, and wait for my verdict. I have another dish to eat. And remember, the peaches of immortality are the most valuable treasures in the world, but they come at a price. Nothing in this world is free."

I gathered all the empty vessels and cutlery and transferred them onto the tray.

A strong wind carried me from the table out the heavy doors, which slammed shut. My team was waiting for me, save for Kama.

Seon took the platter from me. "What happened in there?"

I shook my head. "Nothing. They tried to get me to play their game, and I refused to. How's Kama?"

"He ate a bit of what you cooked," Tala replied. "Ulan is watching over him right now."

"A cormorant nursemaid. I bet he loves that."

"The final verdict is supposed to be declared at the courtyard," Seon advised us. "We should wait there in the meantime."

Songwon carried his dish past us toward the doors with a courteous nod in our direction.

I placed my arm around both Tala's and Seon's shoulders. "Then let's go and await our fate."

Songwon returned, and his team joined ours and Guolin's in the courtyard within the hour. No one knew how long we had to wait. I sat on the ground, leaning against Seon, too weak and exhausted to move.

Indulgence, Temperance, and Luck all appeared with their usual fanfare. The novelty of their grand entrances had worn away, and I could sense the impatience among the competitors. We all just wanted this to be over.

"You are all gathered here to hear my verdict of who won the Celestial Banquet," Indulgence announced.

Beside them, two versions of Luck and Temperance stood in solidarity behind their eldest sibling. My fingers flew up to my lips to make sure that Temperance's smile didn't appear.

"We are now at the final judgment." Indulgence wriggled their fingers. "Who will come out as the victor?"

Songwon, Zi Rui, and I exchanged glances. Zi Rui's eyes wandered down to the bandage on my left arm, and a slight flush crept into his cheeks. Even though I never received an apology, I was pleased. The almighty cook could feel guilt after all. He carried a flask around his hip and kept taking sips from it. It must be thousand dragon tea.

"I chose the cook with the skills, passion, and most potential to be the greatest of the decade." Indulgence narrowed their eyes and pointed at each of us. "All three of you have displayed skills worthy of the Celestial Banquet, though there can only be one winner."

I nodded at my competition. These were two of the best cooks I had ever met.

"Look!" Yoshihiro pointed at a spot to the right of the wall.

The ground trembled again, cracking until a perfect circle formed where the earth smashed the paving stones aside. The rumble continued, centralized in the spot of exposed soil. A seedling emerged, growing rapidly into a plant and then a tree. The sweet perfume of the prized fruit filled the air—ripened peaches. The small tree, with its bending branches, burst into white blossoms. There was no sign of the fruit just yet.

Adrenaline and worry gave me the strength to jump to my feet. I didn't want to disappoint my team. Despite the possibility of defeat, I was proud of what I had served. How else could I make this god understand mortality but through food?

I rubbed my palms together to keep my fingers from shaking. I was certain those beautiful pink fruits would pop out once the winner was announced and not a second before.

"The winner served me food that made me realize something I hadn't thought about before. You mortals are far more complicated than I imagined. I assumed your lives were short and meaningless. It seems as if you all appreciate food as much as we do. So, in third place . . ."

The great dragon breathed fire, bathing the wall and banners in a veil of flames. The ensuing heat reddened my cheeks as none other than Guolin's banner unfurled. I covered my mouth in shock. Tala patted my right arm while Seon reached for my left hand. Could it be us?

Zi Rui lowered his head and gave both Songwon and me a curt nod of respect, though I could see the pain in his eyes. His poor family.

"I object to this!!!" The minor bear god squared off against Indulgence, who increased their height and size so that Guolin appeared like a child.

Guolin was about to have his arse handed to him on a ceramic platter if he kept flapping his mouth. The insolence I'd displayed was nothing against a raging immortal.

Indulgence boomed, "Are you questioning my judgment?"

"Why not?" Guolin puffed out his chest. "My candidate is a rare gem. He is the only living member of two culinary guilds."

Indulgence raised their arms, gathering thick dark clouds under their feet. Lightning shot from their fingertips and their eyes—much like what Kama had been capable of in his prime. With the clouds multiplying, the major god levitated until he loomed over Guolin.

I never expected to see a barbecued minor god.

At first, Guolin stood firm, unflinching like a toddler defying its parents. The godling twitched his whiskers when the tips of his beard began to burn from a well-timed zap. He reached up to put out the bushfire, but as soon as he did, Indulgence fired off two more jolts. When his weak chin became visible, he backed down, flopping to the ground to grovel at the major god's feet. Luck and Temperance tittered in the background.

"Get out of here!" Indulgence waved them off, then returned her gaze to Guolin. "My curse will be placed on you instead of your candidate. You will be stricken with an insatiable hunger for the rest of your immortal existence. Be grateful that I spared your life."

Guolin squirmed on his belly out of the courtyard. Zolzaya covered her eyes and shook her head. She saluted Tala before marching off on her own. Her magnificent Zhenniao flapped its wings and flew ahead of her. The Nomad warrior woman's contract was completed, and she had no obligation to stay around. Zi Rui lingered for a moment, speaking in hushed tones to Indulgence. I assumed he was using Guolin's disfavor to his advantage. When he turned to take his leave with Zolzaya, there was a hint of a smile on his face. Whatever hold the bear god had over those two was broken.

For a moment, Indulgence looked surprisingly harried, but they quickly regained their composure. "Anyway, with no further ado, we'll reveal second and then finally first place." Indulgence's dragon roared, breathing another incinerating blast to reveal the last two banners. Seafoam, then gray. Kama's raven flew higher than Pubu's goldfish.

I blinked, shuddered, and sank down to my knees.

It was ours. I had won the Celestial Banquet!

Seon cupped my face and kissed me. All the air was drawn from my lungs. I melted against him, drowning in the longing from his soft lips. When he pulled away, he cradled my cheeks, stroking my jaw with his thumbs. “You did it, my love.”

Tala waited until Seon let go before enveloping me into a surprisingly warm hug, followed by Kama, who picked me up off my feet, mustering his last remaining strength, soon to be replenished.

Songwon came over and gave me a deep bow. “Well done, Cai.”

Thank you, I mouthed before returning the gesture of respect. I saw Bo cautiously approaching. “Congratulations, Cai. You did it just like I knew you would.”

“Ah, such congenial competitors. This is unexpected. So many surprises and still one left for us all.” Indulgence raised their arms. “Where oh where are the peaches, you ask?”

I glanced around, focusing on the branches to see if I could spot where the prized fruit was.

“I don’t see where . . .”

The minor goddess Pubu’s high-pitched scream snapped my gaze downward. What was she . . .

Songwon, Yoshihiro, and Bo, were grasping at their throats. An invisible force was choking them, yet it was far more devastating than it even appeared. Once while cooking, I’d squeezed an orange against a pointed stone tool and watched its sticky, sweet juice dribble down into the bowl. This was the mortal equivalent. Songwon and Yoshihiro were being pressed from the inside out—all the moisture drawn out of them until they were desiccated mummies with contorted frozen faces. Their powdery husks then obliterated into nothingness with a gentle breeze.

Bo alone stood unscathed, but still grasping his throat. Perhaps he was saved from Kama's early intervention. Our sponsor god's protection might still be working.

The scattered particles coalesced around the flowering tree, glowing pink until they formed the most perfect of peaches.

Indulgence turned to me and announced with a smirk, "I told you everything had a price."

Death's Chasm is the mark left by the great battle between the major gods. It is said to be so deep that no one knows where it ends. The great explorer Huang climbed down with a pack of pigeons that he would send up with messages detailing how far he had descended. The last known note from him contained the message, "I hear demons."

—*WONDERS OF THE WORLD*, SECOND SCROLL, LIBRARY OF LUPONG

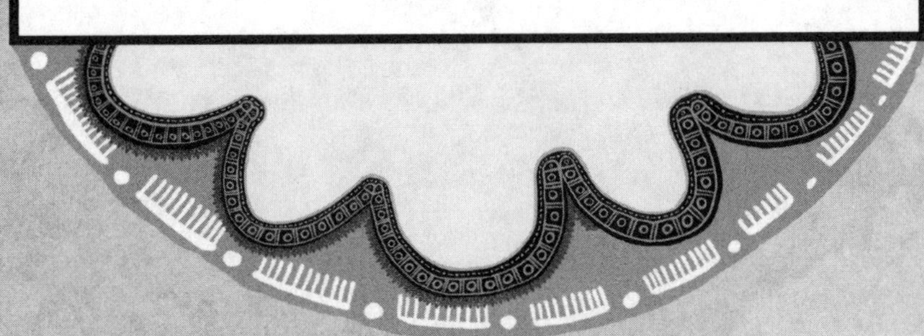

THIRTY-TWO

Everything had a price.

If I had known the true nature of the peaches of immortality, I wouldn't have competed. Gentle and talented Songwon and the quiet, wise Yoshihiro—both gone, and it could have been us, having our vitality sucked away from us. Murdered. Obliterated.

Somehow, Bo was spared. For that I was unspeakably thankful. He seemed to be in shock as he looked at the remains of his comrades.

I couldn't scream as Pubu had. It wasn't for a lack of trying.

The world spun around me at a dizzying pace. The disorientation and sheer chaos wobbled my stomach, and I vomited, dry heaving until the nausea passed. I reached up to brush my hair from my eyes as the gods came into focus.

The major god approached the weeping Pubu. They touched her forehead, and she fell into an instant, almost eerie calm.

Seon held my arm to steady me. "I think Indulgence erased her memories."

"Will our memories also be swept away?" I asked him.

"I think so, Cai."

Indulgence whispered something in the minor goddess's ear before she took her leave.

I didn't want my memories violated. Songwon and his team deserved to be remembered, as did the other lost competitors, whom I'm sure were used as well. The world needed to know how these peaches were created. The Celestial Banquet shouldn't be glorified. The grandeur of it seduced Baba and me—it was easy to get caught up in the magic, the myth, and the glory. If my father could have witnessed what I had, he would have walked away as I itched to do now. This price was far too heavy for me to accept.

The major god positioned themself near the peach tree. "Well, well. Shouldn't you be collecting your precious prize?"

I tipped up my chin. "I don't want my peach. If the others want it, I won't judge them for what they've earned. For me, I can't excuse the blood price."

Tala propped up Kama, and he turned to me, his brows drawn in agony. Though I hadn't blamed him, he wore remorse on his face like sesame seeds on jiandui. He'd never been one to hide his emotions. "Then, I don't want it either."

I turned to Tala. "If you need it to reclaim your birthright, I won't judge you."

She shook her head.

"These were people. Our friends." Seon stepped forward. "I can't in good conscience take them."

"You foolish mortals. The deed has been done. Do you want to waste their sacrifice? What would be the point of all this? And declining the peaches won't help your sorry godling." Indulgence tipped his head in the direction of Kama in Tala's arms. "If he refuses, he will waste away into nothingness. Will you change your mind, candidate? He won't be able to make a decision for himself."

Seon helped lower Kama's body to the ground and cradled his dozing head. "We can't let him die," he said to me. "He's done so much for us. We wouldn't even be here if it weren't for him."

I winced and gritted my teeth. My shoulders slumped from the weight of this decision. Kama deserved to live as much as all of us. He'd risked a comfortable life in Lupong to join this competition. He'd waited for centuries to return to the Continent, and for what? To die here in a half-fevered state when all he wanted was to protect the Peninsula?

I whispered in his ear, "Kama, you have to live. The Peninsula needs you. We need you."

Saving Kama meant going against my own principles—a measured right against a litany of wrongs. I did what I had to do. I walked up to the tree to pluck two peaches—mine and Kama's—tucking them safely in a makeshift pouch of my tunic, and motioned for the others to follow my example. The soft fuzziness of its soft skin tickled my palms. These specimens were far more perfect than any I'd seen, even at the fruit market in Xianling.

Using a small paring knife, I peeled off the skin of a peach and carved slices small enough for Kama to eat. Seon fed him each piece as if our sponsor god were a child. Tala sat with us, speaking to Kama with quiet encouragement. When I was about to discard the pit, Seon stopped me and offered to keep it for study.

Kama began perking up after the first bite. The second had him sitting up on his own accord, the third restored his strength, and the fourth returned the lightning back into his eyes and limbs. He jumped up, rubbing the sparks from his snow-white hair.

Aside from the hair, he appeared younger now, a decade at least. There were no signs of the wrinkles or worry lines that previously etched the corners of his mouth, eyes, and forehead. The most dramatic difference was in his eyes, which were now pitch-black. He levitated off the ground, commanding fire and brimstone. The terrifying transformation unsettled me.

The two incarnations of Luck and Temperance approached their eldest sibling. The panicked expressions on all their faces confirmed Indulgence's alarm. The immortals conversed in an unknown language we couldn't understand. They must have been taken aback at seeing Kama at his full power.

The future was now brighter with our victory.

Bo and Seon stood apart and their differences couldn't be more stark.

Bo was my childhood—Lupong, green grasses, and the serenity of his family farm. He was ever-present in my life for we were each other's shadow. I was content with forever staying in the city I was born in until I discovered a different path of my life.

Yet I wanted *more.*

This competition made me hungry for *more.*

In contrast, Seon was the exciting unknown—carrying the allure of Xianling and the guilds, inspiring me to achieve new culinary heights. Once he was an elusive dream, and now, he was real and desired to be with me.

I'd changed, and Seon was who I wanted in what lay ahead.

I was about to break the heart of my dearest friend and as much as I didn't want to do it, it'd be far more cruel to lead him on. With heavy steps and tears spilling down my cheeks, I walked toward Bo and took his hands in mine.

His emotions were painted on his skin—a pink flush spread across his cheeks while his dark brows tilted upward in confusion. I considered him family, and it was mutual. He sacrificed his life for me.

To choose him would be a lie to both of us. He wouldn't be happy if he knew my heart belonged to someone else, if I only remained at his side out of gratitude or obligation. He deserved more than that.

"I'm sorry I can't give you what you want." The salt of my tears ran into the corner of my lips as I spoke. "The last thing I wanted to do was to hurt you. Bo, I—"

He pressed his index finger against my lips. His dark eyes were glassy, mirroring mine. In his gaze, he begged me to change my mind, but I couldn't. I pressed my forehead against his, my tears falling on his cheeks. With one final embrace, I walked away.

Looking back would make me fall apart.

I then sought out the boy who held my heart. Before I could say a word, Seon rushed to my side and wrapped me in an exuberant hug. He kissed my temple. "You've made me so happy. I can't wait to see what new culinary heights you'll reach. How did I get so lucky?"

In his arms, I drowned in the scent of sandalwood soap and his sweet scent. He was my future. We would go hand in hand together to face the coming days.

"I feel like I'm the lucky one."

He cradled my cheeks in his palms before covering my lips with his. My body thrummed with heat and excitement. We were both breathless when he pulled away.

We all looked back toward the gods, who seemed mildly entertained by our display. It was time for their final word. Then it hit me, if I wouldn't be able to remember the competition, would I be able to remember all of this? I cycled through the events of the last few days, as if I could cement them to memory by sheer force of will. And just then, Indulgence opened their mouth to speak.

"Typically, we would not allow you to remember this feast, as it is important to maintain the competition's secrecy. How else can we keep our meals fresh?" Luck waggled their eyebrows behind them, while Temperance smiled softly. "However, this time, we think a little fear would do you Peninsula dwellers good. The Celestial Banquet is a reminder of how fragile life is—how important it is to know who you're serving. Let that be known throughout your region."

This reeked of the Empress, but I'd take it.

With that, Kama, revitalized and stronger than ever, announced, "Come, children. The Celestial Banquet is over. It's time to go home."

Home. We would actually be returning to Lupong to fulfill the promises I had made to enter this competition. I felt grief, relief, and a sense of purpose. A new chapter was about to begin.

Together, we all left the carnage behind and headed toward the Peninsula.

EPILOGUE

Our return to Lupong was a whirlwind. Everyone was poised to celebrate us, yet there was no time to dwell on our victory. The Empress now saw us as more of a threat than ever, and war was coming. Kama, Seon, and I spent all our time meeting with the city council to explain the situation, to offer the wealth from our peaches and plan our next steps, how we would save the Peninsula.

Everything around me—the sights, smells, and sounds—were the same as when I left, making me realize how different I'd become. It felt so strange to see my noodle stall again for the first time. I ran my fingertips along the scars of the butcher block. Every nick marked a moment I'd spent cooking here. I'd been so triumphant when I purchased my stall, but now, having won the Celestial Banquet, it felt like a relic of the past.

I hadn't seen Bo in the few weeks since we returned to Lupong. He was avoiding me, and I couldn't blame him. Not only had I betrayed him, but he had gone through something traumatic. He should have died not once, but twice, yet he'd lived. Still, those facts didn't change the fact that I missed him or lessen the sting that our friendship was broken. I resisted the urge to visit the farmer's market or our old haunts to give him as much space as he needed.

Now, we were preparing again to leave the city.

I was back at my old lodgings, tucking the worn-out coin box into my rucksack with one last heave.

A familiar deep voice called out over my shoulder, "You ready?"

"Yes." I greeted Seon with a warm smile. "We can get moving."

We headed outside to find Tala waiting with Ulan in her arms. She had stuck with us after the banquet. Better to stay together to accomplish our shared goals.

Nearby, the sound of whistles was accompanied by steady stomping feet. Thankfully, our eldermen chose to believe us, to back us. Seon's father may not have been an honorable man, but he gave us the support and clout we needed to be taken seriously. He was a good politician, if nothing else. When the citywide edict was announced, army recruitment increased tenfold, and construction efforts began to fortify the city gates.

The Peninsula and Lupong were strong, as was I. And I was ready to take our enemy down from the inside.

"Xianling and the Empress await." Seon held out his hand to me. "We can do this together."

His confidence calmed my nerves and made me feel safe. His fingertips traced the fading pinkness from the scar on my forearm. The hope in his beautiful eyes mirrored mine: we would prevail against the Empress's forces.

Seon lifted my hand to his lips and kissed it.

"You two can do that on the road." Tala beckoned, walking five paces ahead.

I blushed and strapped on my rucksack. "Let's change the fate of the Peninsula."

ACKNOWLEDGMENTS

JENNY BENT

You always believed in me and supported me when I wanted to write YA fantasy. Thank you for being my partner in this wacky world of publishing. Also, a shoutout to Victoria Cappello at TBA.

TIFFANY LIAO

You are such a creative force. I am so grateful to have worked with you for three-quarters of this journey. Thank you for believing in me and your wonderful guidance from the start.

LEXY CASSOLA

I love your eagle eyes and your sharp edits. I had one great editor and am so fortunate to have another. Thank you for embracing this foodie fantasy of mine with open arms.

TJ OHLER

TJ, thank you for being there throughout this book's journey and providing support and great notes. You always understood the heart of Cai and the crew.

SIJA HONG AND KARINA GRANDA

Sija made the most gorgeous cover under Karina's direction. I'm so grateful for the phenomenal outcome. I never imagined it would be this beautiful.

TEAM AT ZANDO

Julia McGarry, Nathalie Ramirez, Anna Hall, Natalie Ullman, and Emily Morris

Thank you for taking such great care of me and this book of my heart.

AYESHA CURRY

I'm honored that you've selected my book. I can't deny the Toronto connection.

RACHEL KOWAL

Thank you for thorough copy edits!

FIRST READERS

Jamie Pacton, Bethany Robison, Susan Crispell, Tom Torre

Thank you reading so many drafts of this ever-evolving story. I'm grateful for your set of eyes.

ME ABUSING MY TEXTING PRIVILEGES WITH:

Helen Hoang, Suzanne Park, Farah Heron, R. M. Romero, Sam Tschida, Andria Bancheri-Lewis, Annette Christie, Sonia Hartl, Kellye Garrett, Judy Lin, Nafiza Azad, Mike Lasagna, Sophie Schmidt

I have spammed memes, the dregs of Reddit, and animated GIFs into these little windows. I consider you all blessed with so much patience for putting up with me.

FOR MY LOCAL FAVES

Catherine at Firefly & Fox Books
Joy from Joy Bakery

You both are the best and are local gems. I'm so happy to be living in the same county.

FAMILY

Robert, Nat

Thank you for supporting me and my career of imagination and magic, and my milestone visits to Popeyes Kitchen.

ABOUT THE AUTHOR

ROSELLE LIM is the critically acclaimed author of adult novels *Natalie Tan's Book of Luck and Fortune*, *Vanessa Yu's Magical Paris Tea Shop*, *Sophie Go's Lonely Hearts Club*, and *Night for Day*, and her YA debut, *Celestial Banquet*. She lives on the north shore of Lake Erie and always has an artistic project on the go.